One of America's most critically acclaimed storytellers, David Baldacci has enthralled millions with his blockbuster novels. Showcasing his remarkable versatility, Baldacci gift-wraps a beloved holiday classic...

THE CHRISTMAS TRAIN

Disillusioned journalist Tom Langdon must get from Washington, D.C., to L.A. in time for Christmas. Forced to travel by train, he begins a journey of rude awakenings, thrilling adventures, and holiday magic. He has no idea that the locomotives pulling him across America will actually take him into the rugged terrain of his own heart, as he rediscovers people's essential goodness and someone very special he believed he had lost.

David Baldacci's THE CHRISTMAS TRAIN is filled with memorable characters who have packed their bags with as much wisdom as mischief... and shows how we *do* get second chances to fulfill our deepest hopes and dreams, especially during this season of miracles.

Praise for
THE CHRISTMAS TRAIN

"Wonderful characters...all touched by the miracle of the Christmas season."   —*Houston Home Journal*

"The makings of a classic...Don't miss this delightful book."
                                                    —*Southern Pines Pilot*

"An enjoyable journey...'All aboard!'"   —*Orlando Sentinel*

"Heartwarming...a sweet holiday tale."   —*Booklist*

"Engaging...a fun tale filled with solid characters."
                                                    —*Midwest Book Review*

"Heartwarming...a touching, morally uplifting tale."
                                                —*Fort Worth Star-Telegram*

"An entertaining mystery filled with the mystique of train travel and the wonder and charm of Christmas."
                                                —*Roanoke Times* (VA)

"A plot that's fun to follow and characters to care about...Baldacci knows how to spin a good yarn."
                                                —*Winston-Salem Journal*

"An enjoyable journey."   —*Milwaukee Journal Sentinel*

"A fun story...whistles romance and intrigue."
                                            —*Daytona Beach News-Journal*

the christmas train

the
christmas train

David Baldacci

GRAND CENTRAL
PUBLISHING

NEW YORK   BOSTON

Grand Central Publishing
Hachette Book Group
1290 Avenue of the Americas
New York, NY 10104

www.HachetteBookGroup.com

Printed in the United States of America

LSC-C

Originally published in hardcover by Hachette Book Group.

First trade edition: November 2013
Reissued: October 2014

10 9 8 7 6 5

Grand Central Publishing is a division of Hachette Book Group, Inc. The Grand Central Publishing name and logo are trademarks of Hachette Book Group, Inc.

The Hachette Speakers Bureau provides a wide range of authors for speaking events. To find out more, go to www.hachettespeakersbureau.com or call (866) 376-6591.

The publisher is not responsible for websites (or their content) that are not owned by the publisher.

ISBN 978-1-4555-3294-0 (reissued pbk.)

*This novel is dedicated to everyone
who loves trains and holidays.*

the christmas train

chapter one

~~

Tom Langdon was a journalist, a globetrotting one, because it was in his blood to roam widely. Where others saw only instability and fear in life, Tom felt graced by an embracing independence. He'd spent the bulk of his career in foreign lands covering wars, insurrections, famines, pestilence, virtually every earthly despair. His goal had been relatively simple: He had wanted to change the world by calling attention to its wrongs. And he did love adventure.

However, after chronicling all these horrific events and still seeing the conditions of humanity steadily worsen, he'd returned to America filled with disappointment. Seeking an antidote to his melancholy he'd started writing drearily light stories for ladies' magazines, home-decorating journals, garden digests, and the like. However, after memorializing the wonders of compost and the miracle that was do-it-yourself wood flooring, he wasn't exactly fulfilled.

It was nearing Christmas, and Tom's most pressing dilemma was getting from the East Coast to Los Angeles for the holidays.

He had an age-old motivation for the journey; in LA was his girl-friend, Lelia Gibson. She'd started out as a movie actress, but after years of appearing in third-rate horror films she'd begun doing voiceover work. Now, instead of being cinematically butchered for her daily bread, she supplied the character voices for a variety of enormously popular Saturday-morning cartoons. In the children's television industry it was accepted that no one belted out the voices of goofy woodland creatures with greater flair and versatility than golden-piped Lelia Gibson. As proof, she had a shelf full of awards, an outrageously large income, and a healthy share of syndication rights.

Tom and Lelia had hit it off on an overnight flight from Southeast Asia to the States. At first he thought it might have been all the liquor they drank, but when that buzz burned off a couple hours out of LA, she was still beautiful and interesting— if a little ditzy and eccentric—and she still seemed attracted to him. He stayed over in California and they got to know each other even better. She visited him on the East Coast, and they'd been a comfortable if informal bi-coastal item ever since.

It might seem strange that a successful Hollywood lady would go for a nomadic gent who ran through passports like water, could spout off funny if lewd phrases in thirty languages, and never would be financially secure. Yet Lelia had tired of the men in her circle. As she diplomatically explained it once, they were complete and total lying scum and unreliable to boot. Tom was a newsman, she said, so at least he occasionally dealt with the truth. She also loved his rugged good looks. He took that to mean the deep lines etched on his face from reporting in wind-swept desert climates with bullets flying. In fact his face was more often than not down *in* the sand in observance of local safety regulations.

She listened with rapt attention to Tom's tales of covering

major stories around the globe. For his part, he observed with admiration the professional way Lelia went about her loony-voice career. And they didn't have to live together year-round—a decided advantage, Tom believed, over the complex hurdles facing couples who actually cohabitated.

He'd been briefly married but had never had kids. Today his exwife wouldn't accept a collect call from him if he were hemorrhaging to death on the street. He was forty-one and had just lost his mother to a stroke; his father had been dead for several years. Being an only child, he was truly alone now, and that had made him introspective. Half his time on earth was gone, and all he had to show for it was a failed marriage, no offspring, an informal alliance with a California voiceover queen, a truck-load of newsprint, and some awards. By any reasonable measure, it was a miserable excuse for an existence.

He'd had an opportunity for a wonderful life with another woman but the relationship had, inexplicably, fallen apart. He now fully understood that not marrying Eleanor Carter would forever stand as the major mistake of his life. Yet, ever the man of action, and wanderlust upon him once more, Tom was taking the train to LA for Christmas.

Why the train, one might ask, when there were perfectly good flights that would get him there in a fraction of the time? Well, a guy can only take so many of those airport security search wands venturing into sacrosanct places, or requests to drop trousers in front of strangers, or ransacking of carry-on bags, before blowing a big one. The fact was, he'd blown a big one at La Guardia Airport. Not merely a nuclear meltdown, his detonation resembled something closer to the utter destruction of Pompeii.

He'd just flown in from Italy after researching yet another bit of fluff, this time on wine-making, and imbibing more of the subject matter than he probably should have to get through the ordeal of crash-learning soil diversification and vine rot. As a result, he was tired, cranky, and hung over. He'd slept for three hours at a friend's apartment in New York before heading to the airport to catch a flight to Texas. He'd been given an assignment to write about teen beauty pageants there, which he'd accepted because he enjoyed blood sports as much as the next person.

At the security gate at La Guardia, the search wand had smacked delicate things of Tom's person that it really had no business engaging, socially or otherwise. Meanwhile, another security person managed to dump every single thing from Tom's bag onto the conveyor belt. He watched helplessly as very personal possessions rolled by in front of suddenly interested strangers.

To put a fine finish on this very special moment, he was then informed that a major warning flag had been raised regarding his ID, his hair color, his clothing choice, or the size of his nose. (They were never really clear on that actually.) Thus, instead of flying to Dallas he'd be enjoying the company of a host of FBI, DEA, CIA, and NYPD personnel for an unspecified period of time. The phrase "five-to-ten" was even bandied about. Well, that, coupled with his exploited physical parts, was his absolute limit. So, the lava poured forth.

Langdon was six-feet-two and carried about 220 pounds of fairly hard muscle, and real honest-to-God steam was coming out his ears. His eruption involved language he ordinarily wouldn't use within four miles of any church as he launched himself at the security team, grabbed their infamous search wand, and snapped it right in half. He wasn't proud of his violent act that day, although the rousing cheers from some of the other passengers who had heard and seen what had happened to him did manage to lift his spirits a bit.

Thankfully, the magistrate Tom appeared before had recently endured airport security of an extremely overzealous nature, and when he gave his testimony, she and Tom shared a knowing look. Also, the red flag raised at the security gate had been, *shockingly,* a mistake. Thus Tom only received a stern warning, with instructions to enroll in anger-management classes, which he planned to do as soon as his uncontrollable urge to maim the fellow with the search wand subsided. However, the other consequence of the blowup was that he'd been banned from placing his miserable person on any air carrier that flew within the continental United States for the next two years. He hadn't thought they could do that, but then he was shown the appropriate statutory power in the microscopic print of the airline's legal manifesto under the equally tiny section titled "Lost Luggage Liability Limit—Five Dollars."

And that's when he had his epiphany. Being unable to fly, his usual and necessary way of traveling, was an omen; it had to be a sign of something divine, something important. Thus he was going to take the train to LA. He was going to write a story about it, traveling by rail from sea to shining sea during the Christmas season. He had a grand motivation, beyond spending the holiday with Lelia. Tom Langdon was one of the Elmira, New York, Langdons. To those with a keen knowledge of literary history, the Elmira Langdons brought to mind Olivia Langdon. Olivia, besides having been a lovely, resilient, if ultimately tragic person in her own right, gained lasting fame by marrying the loquacious orator, irascible personality, and prolific scribe known to his friends as Samuel Clemens, but otherwise known to the world and to history as Mark Twain.

Tom had known of this familial connection since he was old enough to block-letter his name. It had always inspired him to earn his living with words. For Twain had also been a journalist, starting at the *Territorial Enterprise* in Virginia City, Nevada, before going on to fame, fortune, bankruptcy, and then fame and fortune again.

Tom, for his part, had been imprisoned twice by terrorist groups and very nearly killed half a dozen times covering a variety of wars, skirmishes, coups, and revolutions that "civilized" societies used to settle their differences. He'd seen hope replaced with terror, terror replaced with anger, anger replaced with—well, nothing, for the anger always seemed to stick around and make trouble for everybody.

Though he'd won major awards, he believed he wasn't a writer with the ability to create memorable prose that would stand tall and strong over the eons. Not like Mark Twain. Yet to have even a marginal connection to the creator of *Huckleberry Finn, Life on the Mississippi,* and *The Man Who Corrupted Hadleyburg,* a man whose work *was* timeless, made Tom feel wonderfully, if vicariously, special.

Shortly before he died, Tom's father had asked his son to finish something that, according to legend, Twain never had. As his father told it, Mark Twain, who probably traveled more than any man of his time, had taken a transcontinental railroad trip over the Christmas season during the latter part of his life, his so-called dark years. Apparently he'd wanted to see some good in the world amid all the tragedy he and his family had suffered. He'd supposedly taken extensive notes about the trip but for some reason had never distilled them into a story. That's what Tom's father had asked him to do: take the train ride, write the story, finish what Twain never had, and do the Langdon side of the family proud.

At the time Tom had just finished a frantic twenty-hour plane odyssey from overseas to see his dad before he passed. When Tom heard his mumbled request, he was struck dumb.

Travel across the country on a train during Christmas, to finish something Mark Twain *allegedly* hadn't? He had thought his father delirious with his final suffering, and so his dad's wish went unfulfilled. Yet now, because he could no longer fly in the Lower Forty-eight unless he was fingerprinted and shackled, he was finally going to take that trip for his old man, and maybe for himself too.

Over almost three thousand miles of America, he was going to see if he could find himself. He was doing it during the Christmas season because that was supposed to be a time of renewal and, for him perhaps, a last chance to clean up whatever mess he'd made of himself. At least he was going to try.

However, had he known what life-altering event would happen to him barely two hours after he boarded the train, he might have opted to walk to California instead.

the capitol limited

Washington, D.C., to Chicago

chapter two

As he got out of the cab in front of Union Station in Washington, D.C., where his train trip would begin, Tom reflected on the few rail journeys he'd taken in the United States. They'd all been along the Northeast Corridor—the routes between D.C., New York, and Boston—on the newest Amtrak equipment, the Acela high-speed trains. Fast, beautiful, and spacious, these trains were easily in the class of their European cousins. They had cool glass doors between train cars that slid open when one approached, reminding Tom of the portal on the bridge of the Starship *Enterprise*. Indeed, the first time Tom was on the Acela and those doors slid open he started looking around for a Vulcan in a Starfleet dress uniform.

Tom had reservations in a sleeping-car compartment on the Capitol Limited train that would carry him from D.C. to Chicago. He actually had to take two trains to get to the West Coast. The Capitol Limited constituted the first leg, and the venerable Southwest Chief would handle the second and much longer jaunt. The Capitol Limited had a storied history, being part of the fabled Baltimore and Ohio line. The B&O was the first common-carrier train company in the United States, and it also held the distinction of being the first to actually haul people.

The "Cap," as the Limited was affectionately known, was always considered the most stylish and sophisticated long-distance train in the country. It had once boasted lobster Newburg on the menu and china and real glass in the dining room, and fancy domed train cars out of which to see the countryside roll by. It also had Pullman cars with legendary Pullman car attendants who made, it was said, tips of enormous proportion. In its long history the Cap had carried kings and princes and presidents and movie stars and titans of industry from Chicago to D.C. and back again, and the stories that poured forth from these trips constituted a legendary part of railroad lore. Tom could have had a lucrative career as a society reporter simply covering the ribald antics of train passengers on that route.

In his youth, because of the family connection and his father's great interest in the man, Tom had immersed himself in Mark Twain's life, work, and wit. In preparation for his transcontinental trip, he'd reread *The Innocents Abroad*, Twain's account of a five-month journey on the steamship *Quaker City* to Europe and the Holy Land. He thought it one of the funniest, most irreverent travel books ever written. If one could imagine Sam Clemens—then a rawboned man fresh from the Wild West, very removed from the world-famous, sophisticated man of letters he'd become—in the company of a boatload of pious Midwesterners on their first sojourn to the Old World, the outrageous possibilities became readily apparent. Tom wasn't going abroad, but in many ways he felt like a pilgrim traveler in his own country, because, ironically, he'd seen far more of the rest of the world than he had of America.

The Capitol Limited left D.C. at precisely 4:05 P.M., made

twelve stops between Washington, D.C., and Chicago, and arrived the following morning in the Windy City punctually at 9:19 A.M. Tom had a layover in Chicago until that afternoon where he'd board the Southwest Chief and sail on to LA. It was a good plan and it got his juices going in a way that articles detailing the best times to prune one's holly trees or pump out one's septic tank never had.

He picked up his tickets, checked his ski equipment with the baggage agent—Lelia and he were going to the elegantly chic slopes of Tahoe for Christmas—and observed the grandeur of Union Station, which, before it was revitalized, came very close to falling victim to the wrecking ball. In the late 1960s and '70s it had become the National Visitors Center—basically a broken slide show in a big hole that no one ever visited. After that $30 million misfire, the National Visitors Center with no visitors was quietly closed except for one tiny and leaky part of the building where one could, of all things, actually board a train.

Tom's father, returning from the Second World War in 1945, had come through this Romanesque-style train terminal on his way home. As Tom walked through the lavishly sculpted and adorned marble halls, he imagined himself retracing his father's optimistic steps back to the safety of civilian life after helping to save the world from tyranny with nothing more than a gun and a young man's courage. It seemed fitting that Tom should start his journey here since his father had ended one life and begun another through this portal. The son could only hope to do as much.

Tom took a few minutes to look at the enormous model Christmas train set up in the main hall's West End. The area was packed with children and adults doubtless intrigued by the miniature metal creations racing through elaborately built town and country sets. Trains had a nostalgic magnetism that was undeniable, even for the many Americans who'd never even been on one. In this spirit, Tom found himself smiling broadly as the little cars whizzed by on the tiny tracks.

The train would be boarding shortly, so he headed to the departure area. Even though some train stations had recently implemented baggage screening, a person could still literally arrive at the last minute and make their ride. There were no security checkpoints, no nosy wands, no inane questions about whether you'd let a complete stranger load a small thermonuclear device in your carry-on bag while you were in the men's room, as though you wouldn't have volunteered such information on your own. You just jumped on and went. In the modern world of endless rules, the simplicity of it all was actually very refreshing.

Tom sat down in the Cap waiting area and began studying his fellow passengers. When he had ridden the Acela to New York, virtually all the waiting passengers had been businesspeople, dressed sharply and outfitted with all sorts of corporate weapons: cell phones, BlackBerries, Palm Pilots, laptops, ear receivers, laser-guided power pointers, plutonium-charged thingamajigs and hard-drive ready-to-wear. These were people with a mission, raring to go, and when that door opened to let the masses board, they boarded with a vengeance. Tom nearly had all his clothes stripped off because he didn't step fast enough. One tiny but determined CEO bore down on him like he was holding a little red cape, her sole purpose in life being to expose his entrails to the open air.

The group waiting for the Cap was more varied. There were whites and African Americans and Native Americans, Muslims dressed in traditional garb, Asian Americans—a nice sampling of ethnicity and origins, pretty equally split between men and women.

An attractive young couple sitting next to Tom were sipping

Diet Cokes and holding hands, looking very nervous. Perhaps this was their first time away from home. Tom had traveled so much at such a young age that he could relate to the anxiety they might be feeling. Next to them was an elderly man of the cloth taking a little siesta, his feet up on his duffel.

Sitting across from the priest was a slender woman with very angular features, a geometric project honed from skin and bone. Tom couldn't really tell her age because she was wearing a long, multicolored scarf around her head, almost like a turban. She also wore wooden shoes the size of thirty-pound dumbbells. Spread on the chair next to her were Tarot cards, which she was studiously poring over. When anyone passed she'd glance up with a look that seemed to say "I know all about you." It was a little unnerving, actually. Tom had had his palm read by an old fellow in the Virgin Islands once. He'd promised Tom a long life filled with a passel of kids, a loving wife, and nothing but good times. Tom had often thought about hunting the liar down and getting his money back.

He watched one elderly lady maneuvering around on a walker. She reminded him of his mother. After her stroke she couldn't speak, so he'd concocted a little system. He'd lay a photo of her and himself when he was a boy on his mother's chest and she'd pick it up with her good hand. That meant things were okay, that she was still there. He'd never forget the time he laid the photo down and waited eight hours for her to pick it up. She never did. She died the next day.

A few minutes later Tom and the other passengers all grabbed their bags and headed out. The mighty Capitol Limited was calling his name.

chapter three

～

Outside, the air was very cold, the fat clouds holding the promise of snow or at least sleet. In such weather airplane passengers worried about flight delays and icy wings, but such inclemency meant nothing to the stalwart Cap; it was bound for Chicago. Tom's spirits started to soar; the beginning of any journey always drove his adrenaline level high. His last published article, for a health magazine, had explored the tremendous potential of a six-week diet relying solely on plump prunes and the close proximity of a bathroom. Tom was desperately ready for an adventure.

He walked to the front of the train and saw the twin diesel electric engines that would be pulling the Cap. He'd read about these monsters. They were General Electric P-42s, each weighing a staggering 268,000 pounds, cranking sixteen cylinders and packing 4,250 horsepower. As his gaze lingered over these hulking machines, he imagined how wonderfully they might perform on the congested Washington Beltway. What a P-42 couldn't outrun, it would simply run over.

Walking back on a track siding that ran under the station, he saw an old, hunter-green railroad car that looked interesting. An Amtrak employee was nearby, so Tom asked what it was. The fellow answered, "That's Franklin D. Roosevelt's old train car, the Marco Polo, Train Number Seven. It's owned by Norfolk and Southern now. They wine and dine VIPs there, right on the spot."

As they stood watching, a stretch limo pulled under the tunnel near the former Roosevelt train car.

Tom said, "Are they having an early dinner on the Marco Polo? Perhaps with Churchill and Stalin?" he added with a smile.

The man didn't get the joke. "Nope, some big shot getting on the Cap Limited. They bring 'em in that way, then there's a ramp underneath the station the limo can go out. We do it for privacy, like sneaking movie stars through airports."

"So who's the big shot getting on my train? Probably some political type, right?"

The fellow looked at Tom. He appeared to be a veteran railroader with probably lots of terrific stories to tell, if only Tom had the time. "Well, if I let you in on that, it wouldn't be a secret, now would it?"

Tom waited a bit to see who'd get out of the limo, but no one ever did. The odds of an eventual sighting were high, though, since once on the train it would be difficult for the VIP to stay concealed. Give Tom Langdon a train flying down the tracks, pen, paper, trusty binoculars, and full indemnity, and he'd bag a VIP every day of the week.

Today the Cap's configuration of cars, called the "consist" in train-speak, was two engines, one baggage car, three coaches, one dining car, two sleeper cars, and one dormitory transition car. The transition car was where most of the service crew was quartered. It had high and low doors that allowed the double-decker cars to have access to the single-level cars, hence the term "transition" car. Tom kept walking until he reached a sleeping-car attendant and showed him his ticket.

"Next sleeper car down, sir. Regina will take care of you," the fellow told him.

Tom went to see Regina. She was standing in front of an impressively large sixteen-foot-tall double-decker train car that was called, in Amtrak parlance, a Superliner, the heaviest passenger-train car in the world. Trains, although some considered them an outmoded form of travel, held an undeniable mystery for Tom. He'd read most of the classic suspense yarns that had taken place on rolling stock, and the elements for edge-of-your-seat story-telling were all there. You had the romance of sophisticated yet unhurried travel in a confined space, with a set number of suspects from all walks of life. In what he thought were the best of such stories, passengers held their breath in the darkness, blankets pulled to their chins because they could just sense something terrible was about to happen. Soon, with the tension at its peak, there'd come a slash of light, a scream, and a dull thud as a body fell. In the wee hours of the morning, the corpse, peepers wide open and skin pale as chalk, would be discovered by an incredibly dense traveling maid who'd scream her head off for about ten minutes while a pair of brooding eyes watched from a shadowy corner. Anyone unmoved by such a scenario should check his pulse, Tom strongly felt.

Regina possessed flawless, dark brown skin and seemed to be too young to be working on a train or anywhere else; in fact, to Tom, she looked like a high-school junior gearing up for her inaugural prom and first serious kiss. Tall and slender, she was personable and obviously enjoyed her work. She was wearing a red and white Christmas hat, the sort donned by Santa's helpers at the mall, and she was assisting the nervous young couple Tom had seen holding hands in the waiting area. The priest had already checked in and was hauling his big duffel inside the train. After Regina had finished with the couple, Tom stepped forward and showed her his ticket.

She looked at the name and marked it off her list.

"Okay, Mr. Langdon, you're on the upper level. Compartment D. Stairs are to your right and then left down the hall."

Tom thanked her and gingerly placed a foot on the august Capitol Limited. His experience with sleeper cars was limited solely to viewing the movie *North by Northwest*, directed by Alfred Hitchcock and starring the impeccably elegant Cary Grant, a nubile Eva Marie Saint, and a very sinister James Mason. Most fans of the movie remember the famous cropduster plane scene where Cary, dressed in his superbly tailored gray suit, is standing alone in the middle of vast, lonely farmland waiting for a meeting with the mysterious George Kaplan, who of course doesn't exist. Some wily minds at the CIA had concocted Kaplan's identity for their own nefarious purposes. Those folks at the Agency were always lying about something to make the world safe for democracy. Yet, to be fair, it was all in good fun and solely at taxpayer expense.

Now, the movie scene that Tom remembered most was the one that featured a lot of kissing inside Eva Marie Saint's spacious sleeper compartment. Cary and Eva went at it pretty hot and heavy even by today's standards. Watching it as a young man, hormones afire, Tom remembered thinking impure thoughts about all women everywhere, or at least those who looked like Eva Marie Saint.

Having seen that film, he knew that his sleeper compartment would be elegantly appointed and spacious, have room for a couple of beds, and feature a nice study area, a small foyer in which to formally receive visitors, a full bathroom with whirlpool tub, optional servant quarters, and perhaps an out-door patio/balcony combo. There was a reason that at the end of the movie Cary and Eva had honeymooned in that very same sleeper compartment: It was bigger than any apartment Tom had ever had.

He started to climb the stairs as instructed by Regina. With luggage the going was a little tough, the stairs turning at tight ninety-degree angles. He assumed all the extra space had been devoted to the mammoth sleeper compartments. Then he looked up and realized he faced a considerable obstacle.

She was old, dressed in what looked to be a sleeping gown although it was not yet four o'clock, and was teetering on the top step coming down. Tom was on the second to the top step. He only had one more step to go, one narrow little riser to navigate, before he was off to fantasize about Eva Marie in his rolling penthouse.

"Excuse me," he said politely.

"Coming through," the woman announced in a thunderous baritone that actually made the rough, tough former war corre-spondent feel dangerously effeminate.

"If you'll just let me squeeze past," he replied. But that was out of the question. She wasn't nearly so tall as Tom, but she was, to put it delicately, considerably wider in frame.

"Hi there, Regina," the woman called down.

"Hi there, Agnes Joe," said Regina.

Neither of them backing down, Tom and Agnes Joe en-gaged in an awkward tango, one foot forward, one foot back. Performed vertically on the stairs, it actually made Tom a little queasy.

Finally he said, "Agnes Joe, I'm Tom Langdon. I'm in Com-partment D. If you can just step back for a sec—"

He never finished the sentence, because instead of stepping back, she gave him a little nudge. Actually it was a meaty forearm launched to the right side of his head, which sent him, already off-balance, stumbling back down the stairs, where he hit bottom and fell flat on his back.

Agnes Joe followed his plummet and was polite enough to gingerly step over his prostrate carcass. Tom very seriously doubted this was how Mark Twain had begun his cross-country railroad journey. Agnes Joe walked over to Regina, who was busy helping some other people on board and luckily hadn't seen what had happened, for which Tom was grateful. After all, an elderly woman had just pulverized him at King of the Hill.

"Here you go, honeypie. Thanks for taking my bags." Agnes Joe handed Regina some cash.

Tom picked himself up and headed over to Regina after glaring at the old woman as he passed her.

"I'll get your bags, Mr. Langdon, just put them over there while I get everybody checked in."

"Thank you. And it's Tom," he said, handing Regina a handful of dollars. She graced him with a cute little look. He glanced at Agnes Joe, who was slowly making her way back up the stairs.

"So have you been working on this train long?" he asked Regina.

"Four years."

"That's a long time."

"Shoot, we have people been on this train twenty years."

Tom looked back at Agnes Joe, who was still on the same step. Her legs were moving, but she didn't seem to be ascending. It was actually fascinating to watch, sort of like witnessing pokey lava.

"So you know Agnes Joe?"

"Oh, sure, she's been riding this train for 'bout, oh, ten years, or so I hear."

"Ten years! She must really like the ride."

Regina laughed. "I think she has family she goes to see. She's nice."

Tom rubbed his head where "nice" Agnes Joe had walloped him. "Is she on this sleeper car?"

"Yep, right next to you."

Oh, joy, joy, he thought.

He went back to the stairway where Agnes Joe was, inexplicably, still on the exact same step.

"Agnes Joe, do you need some help?"

"I'm fine, honeypie. Just give me a little time."

"Maybe if I get in front of you and pull?"

Tom's plan was to get in front of her, run like hell, and lock himself in his magnificent suite with Eva Marie while Cary Grant kept guard outside.

"Just give me some space, sonny!"

She finished this last retort with a heavy elbow that somehow found Tom's left kidney. By the time the pain had ceased and he was able to straighten his torso, Agnes Joe was gone. He slowly made his way to Compartment D. Damn if he didn't feel like a war correspondent again.

chapter four

As Tom stood in the doorway of Compartment D, it occurred to him that if Cary and Eva Marie had shot the kissing scene here, *North by Northwest* would have been rated triple X. He wasn't sure of the exact dimensions of this deluxe accommodation, but two normal strides later he'd bumped into the opposite wall. There was no foyer, no study, no desk, no double beds that he could see, and he was reasonably certain that the balcony/patio combo, whirlpool, and optional servant quarters were myths too.

There was a sink and a mirror and an outlet for an electric razor. The cabinet below was well stocked. He saw toilet paper, so there must be a bathroom hidden in here somewhere. There was a tiny closet in which to hang his coat, a large mirror on the far wall across from what he assumed was the bed, and what looked like an upper bunk as well. There was a chair and a fold-down table with a checkerboard engraved on it, which he could use as a desk. And the picture window was huge and gave an inviting view of the outdoors, where a few trickles of snow were starting to fall, getting him more into the Christmas spirit. The door to the compartment locked and had a heavy privacy curtain. Okay, it wasn't bad, he decided. In truth, space-wise, it easily beat out even first class on an airplane.

This impression lasted until he opened the door and saw his private bathroom. Actually, according to the sign posted inside, this was the bathroom *and* the shower. He was expected to pee and shampoo in the same space? In his overseas reporting days, he'd actually endured showers consisting solely of camel spit, and that definitely wasn't by choice.

His real dilemma here was one of capacity. He looked at his girth and then eyed the bathroom/shower. He edged closer and studied the situation some more. He was reasonably certain that he could wedge himself inside this chamber. Of course, once in, it would take three or four strong men with heavy machinery to free him. And no doubt Agnes Joe would be standing there waiting to take a shot at the one good kidney he had left.

He'd read about the unfortunate woman on a transatlantic flight who'd committed the unpardonable sin of flushing the toilet in the plane lavatory while she was still sitting on it. This seemingly innocent action somehow created a mighty suction vacuum that trapped her on the toilet seat. (He'd wanted to write a note to the plane engineers inquiring why they hadn't tested for this unfortunate possibility.) She endured the entire flight in the fully upright position until the plane landed and an elite crew armed with giant spatulas and baby oil stormed the lavatory and freed the poor hostage. If it had been Tom, he believed he would have gnawed off his legs and broken the seal himself.

Unwilling to think about it anymore, he turned back and was about to sit down, when he saw something flash by against the wall opposite the bed. At first it didn't register, it was so fast. But then it happened again. It was Agnes Joe. How could that be? This was a very peculiar definition of *private* accommodations. Then he saw the problem. The walls between compartments must open, perhaps for maintenance or reconfiguration or something, but the result was that he could see into the woman's room. He'd bivouacked with the aforesaid dirty, spitting camels, and desert nomads whose last bathing experience had been at birth, and various other unwashed persons, with mortar fire as his alarm clock. Yet he'd never slept with an Agnes Joe, and he didn't really want to start now.

As he went over to the wall to push it back into place, he peered through the crevice between their rooms and found himself cornea to cornea with the woman.

"You best not be peeping at me, sonny boy," she said. "Besides, you don't want to look at my old stuff, honeypie. Find yourself some girl closer to your own age."

Okay, Tom thought, the lady is the town eccentric, only on rails. He decided to play along.

"Your stuff looks pretty good to me."

"Now, don't make me call Regina."

"You don't want to do that. Why mess up a nice twosome with a third wheel?"

"Don't you try to sweet-talk me—it won't work because I'm not that sort of girl. But we could have a drink together in the lounge car after supper and get to know each other." She actually batted her eyelashes.

"Now that's an offer I'd be a fool to refuse."

She gave him a playful smile. "I'm sorry about knocking you down the stairs, Tom. My hand must have slipped."

"If it had to happen, I'm glad it was you."

He turned and saw Regina standing there, his bags in her hand. She glanced over at the wall and shook her head. "Did that wall pop out again? I told maintenance to check it."

"Hi, Regina," said Agnes Joe through the opening. She pointed to Tom. "You watch that fellow, he's slick."

"Okay."

Tom pushed the wall back into place.

Regina said, "Sorry about that."

"That's okay. She seems pretty harmless."

Regina gave him a sly look. "I wouldn't be too sure about that." She brought his bags in and then sat down on the edge of the couch that apparently transformed into a bed at midnight and pulled out a notepad.

"I'll take your dinner reservation now. Dining car opens at five-thirty. Or if you don't want to eat in the dining car, you can get some food from the café. It's in the lounge car; the one past the dining car, lower level. You'll see the staircase about halfway through on the right. Just show your ticket to Tyrone—he's the lounge-car attendant—and tell him you didn't eat in the dining car. It's all free for sleeping-car passengers."

"I'll eat in the dining car. How about seven?"

She wrote this down.

"While you're eating, I'll come in and get your bed made up. And we have soda and bottled water and coffee and fruit at the top of the stairs where you came up. I check it all the time, so everything's fresh. Help yourself."

"Is there a dress code or anything in the dining car?"

Regina looked amused. "Well, I've seen people wear just about anything a person can wear on this train." Was it Tom's imagination, or did her gaze flick in Agnes Joe's direction? "But most people are pretty casual. Lot of families on this train, with little kids. What you're wearing is fine."

"That's what I needed to know."

He questioned her about the small size of his shower/bath, and she told him that larger facilities complete with changing room were available on the lower level on a first-come, first-serve basis. "Most of the physically enhanced people opt for that," she added diplomatically.

As she rose to leave, Tom said, "I'm a journalist. I'm writing a story about my train trip across the country."

She looked very interested. "Are you taking the Empire Builder to Seattle, the California Zephyr to San Fran, or the Southwest Chief to LA?"

"Southwest Chief to LA."

"That's a great train. The Chief has a cool history. And they're wonderful people on board; you'll have fun. Most people who work the Chief never want to leave."

Tom pulled out his notepad and started jotting things down. "The way you describe it, the train almost seems like a person."

"Well, they sort of are. I mean, you spend so much time on them, you learn their quirks, their strengths and weaknesses. Some are more temperamental than others, some more forgiving. It's sort of like having a relationship. I know that sounds strange, but that's just the way it is."

"Hmmm, with some of the relationships I've had, dating a hundred-ton diesel might be a welcome change."

Regina laughed. "My mother, Roxanne, works on the Southwest Chief, as the chief of on-board services. That's the big boss. I'm going to see her when we get into Chicago. I'll let her know you'll be on. Now *she* can tell you some stories."

"Is that common? I mean, do lots of family members work for Amtrak?"

"Well, I've got my mom, and I don't know how many uncles and aunts and cousins and such spread all over. That's how

I found out about working on the trains. And my son works for Amtrak too. He's a coach cleaner."

Tom stared at her. "Your son? You look like you just got out of high school."

"Agnes Joe was right: You *are* slick." She smiled shyly. "But thanks for the compliment. And you get some really famous people as passengers. Singers, athletes, movie stars—and they're all nice, for the most part." Her expression grew more serious. "Where I come from, working on the train, that's something special. People look up to you. It's cool, you know?"

Tom nodded. This element really intrigued him. He'd have to work it into his story. "You think some of the other people on the train will talk to me?"

"Oh, sure, I'll spread the word. Everybody who works on a train has stories to tell."

"I bet they do."

As she left, Tom felt the train start to move. Diesel electric trains have no need of a transmission, so there were no obstinate gears to shift. The resulting acceleration was smoother than the finest automobile on the road. Tom checked his watch. It was 4:05 P.M. exactly. The legendary Capitol Limited, carrying Tom Langdon on a mission, was on its way.

chapter five

⟨⸦⸧⟩

Cleared for takeoff by rail traffic control, the Capitol Limited soared down the metal- and wood-ribbed runway, lifting off cleanly. It dipped its stainless-steel sheathed wings in salute to a passing band of birds, flushed out a nest of lobbyists plotting near the Capitol, and headed west, as Mark Twain had in his relative puberty. The young Sam Clemens had made the trek from Missouri to the Nevada Territory on a bouncy overland stagecoach, sleeping on mailbags at night and riding on top of the stage in his underwear by day. While he encountered much that was beautiful and rare, he also fought alkali deserts, desperadoes, ornery Mexican plugs, bad food, and boredom, while Tom Langdon was pulled along by a thousand tons of raging horsepower and enjoyed a comfy bed, toilet, and Agnes Joe in the next room. Tom wasn't yet certain whether he or Mark Twain had gotten the better travel deal.

He called Lelia on his cell phone. He hadn't told her about the train trip because he wanted to surprise her. She was certainly surprised, but not exactly the way he intended. Her reaction made him thrilled that there were currently about three thousand miles separating them.

She yelled into the phone, "You're taking a train all the way across the United States of America? Are you insane?"

The way she said it, Tom was beginning to think he was.

"Folks used to do this all the time, Lelia."

"Right, during the Stone Age."

"It's for a story, about Christmas." He didn't want to share with her the other reason he was doing it, because he wasn't really sure how she figured into his future—at least the one he hoped to discover on this trip.

"I've chartered a private jet that leaves at six P.M. sharp on Christmas Eve."

"I've got my skis, I'll be there. The train gets into LA that morning."

"What if it's late?"

"Come on, it's a train. We make our station stops, we pick up passengers, we let out passengers, we roll along, and we get into LA in plenty of time."

He heard her let out a long sigh. Actually, lately she'd been letting out many long sighs. They had that seemingly ideal relationship where they didn't have to live with each other every day. Where issues of cooking, cleaning, which end of the toothpaste gets squeezed or who gets what side of the bathroom weren't present to produce a destructive force on the otherwise happy couple. They ate out a lot, took romantic walks along the beach in Santa Monica or shopped on Fifth Avenue, slept until noon, and then didn't see each other for a couple of months. If more marriages were put together like that, Tom firmly believed, the divorce rate would plummet. So, he wondered, why all the sighing of late.

"Just get here. I don't want to mess up everybody's plans."

"Everybody? Who's everybody?"

"The people going with us to Tahoe."

This was news to him. "What people?"

"Friends from the industry—my agent, my manager, and some others. We talked about this."

"No, we didn't talk about this. I thought this was just going to be you and me. We've done this the last two years."

"That's right, and I thought a change would be nice."

"Meaning what? That you're getting bored being with just me?"

"I didn't say that!"

"You didn't have to. The army of people you invited into our Christmas said it loud and clear."

"I don't want to argue about this. I just thought that a nice group of people together for Christmas at Tahoe would be fun. You know most of them—it's not like they're strangers—and it's not like we won't be spending time alone, we will. I only booked us one bedroom, honey. And I bought a new teddy, just for you. It has a Christmas theme, a naughty one," she added in her best breathless tone. Tom's skin started tingling. It was no wonder the lady made such a good living with her pipes.

It had always bothered Tom that women thought they could win an argument with a man simply by appealing to his baser instincts, by holding out the mere possibility of award-winning carnal knowledge. It was the gender-battle equivalent of a preemptive nuclear strike. He thought it unfair and, quite frankly, disrespectful of the entire male population.

And yet he heard himself saying, "Look, baby doll, I don't want to argue either. I'll be there on time, I swear."

He clicked off and for a few moments had visions of naughty teddies dancing in his head. *Sometimes I'm such a guy*, he thought ruefully.

While he was chiding himself there was a bustle of movement in the train corridor. By the time Tom opened his compartment door and drew his bead, all he could see of the passing group was a trailing arm and leg. Though he'd only gotten a glimpse, there was something familiar about that arm, and that leg. He assumed they were heading to another section of sleeping compartments. VIPs, of course, would have first-class accommodations. He thought about following them, to see if it was actually the folks from the limousine, but concluded he'd catch up to them later.

He sat back down and watched the scenery go by. The ride had been very smooth so far, and the sound of the revolving train wheels was soothing. It really wasn't a clickety-clack sound, he decided. It was more of an extended hum, and then hush, hum and then hush, and then a big old siss-boom-bah. It was good to know that he had that weighty issue worked out.

The first stop was Rockville, Maryland, barely twenty-five minutes after leaving Washington. Near Rockville was St. Mary's, a modest white church located on a small hill. It was here that F. Scott Fitzgerald was buried, for no other apparent reason than in fulfillment of his request to be planted for eternity in the country. Tom made a mental note to write out very specific instructions concerning his own future interment, then pulled out his laptop and entered some observations for his story, though he hadn't really seen all that much. Besides being mauled by Agnes Joe and humbled by Lelia, the trip thus far had been fairly sedate.

He got up to see whom he could find to talk to. The train started up again, and he placed one hand against the wall in the corridor to steady himself. Somebody had strung holiday garlands up along the passageway, and there was even a Christmas wreath on the wall next to the door connecting the train cars.

As he passed Compartment A, the elderly priest he'd seen in the waiting area earlier came out and bumped into him as the train rocked along.

"Hello, Father," Tom said, cutting a handshake short to help steady the older man. Eleanor Carter was Catholic, and wherever in the world she and Tom had happened to be they'd gone to Mass. She'd always joked that she'd just keep hammering away and at some point Tom would either be saved or spiritually lobotomized. Actually, he'd briefly wanted to be a priest when he was in high school. As a teen, he was skinny and awkward, growing far too quickly for his tendons and coordination to keep up. That and his startling and persistent acne made him incredibly unpopular. As a result, he contemplated a career of solitude, introspection, and prayer. Only two things stopped him: He wasn't Catholic, and then there was that annoying vow of celibacy. After he had learned about that requirement, Tom wanted to be a rock star instead.

"Retired now," the holy man said amiably. "Though I still dress like a priest because I own no other clothes besides a chocolate-brown polyester leisure suit from the 1970s that I still ask forgiveness for."

"Once a priest always a priest."

"I'm Father Paul Kelly, late of Saint Thomas Aquinas."

"Tom Langdon. You spending Christmas in Chicago?"

"No, I'm going on to Los Angeles. My sister and her offspring live there. I'm spending the holidays with them."

"Me too. Taking the Southwest Chief, I guess."

"The very one. From what I hear of the countryside we'll be seeing, that's truly God's work."

"Maybe I'll catch you in the lounge car after dinner. We can whittle down some cigars I brought." Tom had noticed the stem of a pipe sticking out of the priest's coat pocket.

Father Kelly graced Tom with an impish smile, and he placed a gentle hand on Tom's sleeve. "Bless you, my son, trains indeed are the civilized way to travel, are they not? And perhaps we'll see those film people around too," he added.

"What film people?"

Father Kelly drew closer and checked the corridor, apparently for eavesdroppers. Tom instantly imagined himself to be an undercover spy for the Baptists or Methodists, on assignment in Rome, discovering closely guarded ecclesiastical secrets from a gossipy priest and later writing about it with profitable hilarity while scorching memorandums flew furiously around the Vatican.

"They came in a grand car, pulled up almost to the train. I discreetly inquired as to who they might be, being a curious person by nature—and of course people feel at ease confessing all sorts of things to a priest. Trust me, Tom, if people can imagine it, they'll confess it, whether they've actually done it or not, and thank the Lord, they usually haven't. There are two individuals, so I heard. From what I could gather, one is a famous film director or producer or some such, though I didn't get his name. The other is a star or maybe a writer. They're taking the train across the country in preparation for a film they're doing about such a trip."

Film people, thought Tom, a star. Maybe that was why something about one of them looked familiar. "That's pretty coincidental," he said.

"Why is that?" Father Kelly asked.

Tom explained to him that he was writing a story about the train trip, and the elderly priest seemed pleased to hear it. "Well, you picked the right subject to write about. I've taken many a train in my time, and they're always full of surprises."

"I'm beginning to see that," said Tom.

chapter six

After he left Father Kelly, Tom passed through the next section of sleeping accommodations. These were the standard compartments, without bath or shower facilities. Communal baths were on both levels, and, as Regina had informed him, there were also larger showers on the lower level, which he'd probably be using since he wasn't going to risk getting stuck in the one in his compartment. In the deluxe car section, because of their larger size, the compartments were situated on one side and the aisle on the other. In the standard section, the smaller compartments ran down both sides of the car, with the aisle in the middle. Tom noticed that across this corridor were stretched a pair of hands, holding one to the other.

As he drew closer, he saw that it was the young nervous couple. They had compartments right across from one another, with the guy on the right and the girl on the left.

"Okay, do I have to pay a toll to pass through?" he said jokingly.

They both looked at him and returned the smile.

"Sorry," the guy said, while the girl looked away shyly. They were about twenty and looked like brother and sister, with their blond hair and fair skin.

"So, on your way to Chicago for the holidays?"

"Actually," began the young man a little sheepishly.

"Steve," interrupted the woman, "we don't even know him."

"Well," Tom said, "it's different on a train. We're all on this long journey together. It opens people up. I'll go first. I'm a writer, doing a piece about a trip across the country. There's my story, so what's yours?"

The two looked at each other, and Steve said, "Well actually, we're getting married."

Tom knelt down and extended his hand to them both. "Congratulations. That's great. I'm Tom, by the way."

"Steve. My fiancée is Julie."

"So are you tying the knot in Chicago?"

"Uh, no, we're getting married on the train," Steve said.

"The train? This train?"

"No," said Julie. "On the Southwest Chief, on the way to LA. It leaves tomorrow afternoon." Her accent sounded Southern to Tom, while Steve's speech cadence suggested New England origins.

".That's great. I'm going to be on that train too."

Tom had actually planned to propose to Eleanor on a train heading back to Frankfurt after their visit to the great cathedral in Cologne, Germany. They were riding in third class on the train even though they had purchased first-class tickets but hadn't realized it, because their German wasn't very good. Back then the train route paralleled the Rhine, and Tom had been wondering when would be the best time to pop the question. His original plan had been to ask her in the cathedral, but there'd been lots of tourists with cameras and screaming kids around, and it just didn't seem right. He only planned to do this once in his life, and he wanted to get it absolutely perfect.

The smooth ride of the train, the busy day behind them, a couple of glasses of Pilsners and thick German bread and juicy sausages inside them, coupled with the moonlight reflecting off the legendary and romantic Rhine, all combined to make it seem like the ideal time.

Tom envisioned himself getting down on one knee in the aisle, pulling out his ring, pouring out his love for her, and proposing right there. He imagined her crying and then him too. The entire third-class section of economy-minded Germans would stand up and give them an ovation, because obviously the marriage proposal ritual would transcend all language and culture barriers. When they arrived in Frankfurt perfect strangers would wish the newly engaged couple the best in both German and pretty good English, and some of them would even press crumpled Marks in their hands.

And yet none of that had happened because he hadn't proposed that night to Eleanor, or any other night. He just sat in his seat, the ring in his pocket feeling like a cannonball; he couldn't begin to lift the thing and place it on her finger.

He refocused on the couple. "So, is the wedding party and your family already on board, or are they meeting you in Chicago?"

Now Julie looked away, and Steve licked his lips. Tom had obviously touched a nerve here.

"Well, actually, our families don't, you know . . ."

"Don't know you're getting married?"

"Don't know and don't *approve* of us getting married," said Julie as she dabbed at her eyes with the back of her hand.

"Come on, Jule, Tom doesn't need to hear about this."

"Well, he asked," she shot back.

Steve looked at Tom and tried to affect a carefree attitude. "So we're doing it on our own. Because we love each other."

But Julie said, "His family doesn't approve of me. They think because I'm from some little podunk Virginia town in the Appalachian Mountains that I'm some sort of white trash. Well, my father might have worked in the mines since he was sixteen, and my mother never finished high school either, and"—she looked at Steve—"your parents are high society in Connecticut, but my family is not trash. They're every bit as good as yours, and in lots of ways better," she added with fervent Southern spirit.

Tom noted that he'd been right about their origins: the Virginia gal and the Connecticut boy. "So, does *your* family approve of the marriage?" he asked Julie, trying to defuse the tension a little.

"They like Steve a lot, but they think I'm too young. I'm in college. We both are, at George Washington University in Washington. That's where we met. They want me to finish school before I get married."

"Well, that's understandable, especially if they never had a chance to go to college. I'm sure they just want the best for you."

"The best thing for me is Steve." She smiled at him, and Tom could tell the young man's heart was melting at what she was going through. These two might be young, but they were old enough to be absolutely head-over-heels in love.

Julie continued, "And I'm going to finish college, and then I'm going on to law school, at the University of Virginia. I'm going to do my parents proud. But I'm going to do all of that as Steve's wife."

"Well," Tom said, "it's your life, and I think you should follow your heart."

"Thanks, Tom," Julie said, and she gave his hand a pat.

If only he'd followed that advice with Eleanor, things might have been different. Ironically, they too had met in college. Eleanor had been one of those incredibly smart people who graduated high school at sixteen and college at nineteen. After college, they'd done some investigative reporting in the States, and scored a couple of big stories, before taking the leap and signing on as the entire overseas bureau for a fledgling news service. They had collected the experiences of a lifetime—several lifetimes, in fact. They'd fallen in love, like Steve and Julie. They should have been engaged and then married, too, yet it had ended so abruptly that Tom still found it intensely painful to think about their last moments together.

"So, is the minister on board?" For a second Tom thought Father Kelly might be officiating, but he'd said he was retired and surely he would have mentioned a wedding.

Steve said, "He gets on in Chicago. The ceremony takes place the next day. Our maid of honor and best man are getting on in Chicago too."

"Well, good luck to both of you. I take it everybody on the train is invited," he added.

"We sure hope *somebody* will come," said Steve.

"Right," added Julie nervously, "otherwise it will be a pretty lonely wedding."

"No bride should have to settle for that. I'll be there, Julie, and I'll bring all my train friends with me." Tom didn't yet have any train friends, but how hard could it be to make friends on the Cap? He sort of already had Agnes Joe in his back pocket.

"Lounge car at nine in the morning," said Steve. "The station stop is La Junta."

"That means 'junction' in Spanish," said Julie. "Seemed appropriate for a marriage."

"I'm curious: Why the train in the first place?"

Julie laughed. "I guess it'll sound silly, but after my grandfather came back from World War Two, my grandmother met him in New York City. They'd been engaged before the war started but postponed their wedding because Gramps volunteered."

"You'd think they'd want to tie the knot before he left," Tom said.

Julie shook her head. "No, that's exactly why they didn't. Gramps refused to leave her a widow. He said that if he made it through the war, then it was God's way of telling them they were meant to be together."

"That's really nice."

"Well, he made it back of course, and Grandma, she'd been waiting four long years, so she went up to New York City with plans to get married up there, but so many other soldiers were doing the same thing that it would have taken them weeks. So they paid a preacher to get on the train with them, and once they crossed into Virginia, they were married."

"And I assume things worked out?"

"Fifty-five years of marriage together. They died within a week of each other two years ago."

"Well, I wish you both the same," Tom offered.

"Do you really think complete strangers will come to our wedding?" asked the girl.

Tom was just a guy—with a guy's dubious perspective on weddings—but still he understood how important it was for the bride. By comparison, the groom had it easy. He simply had to show up reasonably sober, say "I do," kiss the bride while the old ladies in the crowd tittered, and not pass out until *after* the wedding night official duties were completed and the gift money counted.

Tom said, "Not to worry. There's something about a train that opens people up. And besides, you do have a captive audience."

He wished them well again and headed for Tyrone in the lounge-car café, but his mind was straying once more toward Eleanor. After she walked out on him in Tel Aviv, he was hurt, angry, and confused, all those things that made one completely incapable of doing anything rationally. By the time he'd gotten his head screwed on right, so much time had passed that he'd ended up not doing anything to contact her. Then the years really got away, and he felt any attempt to get in touch would be swiftly and painfully rebuked. For all he knew, she'd already married someone else.

He went through the dining-room car and nodded to the attendants there. All of them wore some holiday article of clothing. They seemed to be working hard to get dinner together, so he decided not to hit them up with a lot of questions. He ventured on to the lounge car. There a few people were sitting around watching the TV; others were idly gazing outside at the passing countryside. He made his way down the spiral staircase and found Tyrone, the lounge-car attendant.

The space he worked in was small, but neatly organized with refrigerated cabinets against the walls loaded with cold sandwiches, ice cream, and assorted cold goodies. There were also bins with other foods, chips and stuff, and hot and cold drinks. There were also cafeteria-tray rails to slide your purchases down. At the end of the hall was a door marked as the entrance to the smoking lounge.

Tyrone was about thirty, Tom's height, and looked like Elvis, only he was black. At first Tom thought the man might be wearing a hairpiece but, upon closer inspection, confirmed it was all his own. The man was truly the King, in splendid ebony. Tom liked the effect a lot.

"I'll be open in about twenty minutes, sir," said Tyrone. "My delivery was in late. I'm usually up and running by now. I'll make an announcement on the PA."

"No problem, Tyrone. Regina told me to come down here if I needed anything."

Tyrone looked Tom over with interest as he methodically laid out his wares. "Hey, you the writer guy Regina told me about?"

"I'm the writer guy, yes."

"Cool. What do you want to know?"

"For starters, whether you're an Elvis fan."

He laughed. "It was the hair, right, man? It's always the hair."

"Okay, it *was* the hair."

"Thankyou, thankyouverymuch." Tyrone did a little bump and grind.

"I'm impressed."

"I know all the songs, all the hip moves. The man could cut it pretty good for a white dude."

"You been on this train long?"

"I've been with Amtrak since '93. Been on this train about seven years."

"I bet you've seen a lot."

"Oh, let me tell you, I've seen some stuff. People come on a train, man, it's like they lose some inhibition gene or something. Now, I know all the crazy stuff that goes on in airplanes, when people get drunk and stuff, but those folks got nothing on crazy train people. Hey, you want a soda or something?"

"Unless you got something stronger, and I'm really hoping you do."

Tyrone opened a beer for him and Tom settled against the wall to listen.

Tyrone said, "My first trip on this train heading north, we're pulling out of Pittsburgh at about midnight, okay, when I hear this yelling coming from one of the sleeper cars. Lounge car is all closed up, okay, and I'm off duty, but I go up there because there's only one attendant per sleeper car, and I'm the new guy and wanted to make sure things were cool. Well, I get up there and you got one guy, naked as a jaybird, standing in the hallway with a nice-looking babe who's got a little towel wrapped around her, see. And then we got one ticked-off lady in pajamas going for the guy's throat, while Monique, the sleeping-car attendant, is trying to hold her back."

"What had happened, a little mixup in the sleepers?"

"Oh, I bet Hubby wished that. See, thing was, the naked dude was caught in the act with his little mistress whom he'd paid to travel in her very own sleeper compartment two doors down from where he and the missus were staying. I guess he was into thrills or something. Hubby thought he slipped the little woman a sleeping pill so that he could go have himself some joy time with little miss whoopee, but the wife, she knew something was up, didn't actually swallow the pill, followed her man and nailed them both."

"What happened?"

"The mistress got off at the next stop. And the last I saw of lover boy, he and his chewed-up butt got off at Chicago."

As Tyrone was talking and working, a chain necklace slipped out of his shirt. Tom noted the object attached to it.

"Where'd you get the Purple Heart?" he asked.

"Persian Gulf," Tyrone said, tucking the chain back in his shirt. "Army. Caught a leg full of shrapnel when a round hit our Bradley."

"I covered that war. The fighting was more intense than the reports showed back home."

"Well, it was intense enough for me."

"So I take it you like working here?"

"Hey, it's a job, but it's fun too. I got me my little entertainment routine that I'm always working on, adding, subtracting. I have fun with the passengers, and the kids, especially. Man, there's something about trains and kids, they just go together, you know what I mean?" He kept talking as he worked. "I'm on three days and then get four off. That's how it works for the service crew on the long-distance trains. On the really long-route trains, like the Chief and the Zephyr, you work six and then get eight days off. Sounds like a lot of downtime, and it is, but six days going up and back, up and back, it gets to you after a while. You need time just to recover. Because when you're on this train, you're basically on call the whole time. Goes with the territory, but I like it. The crew is a team, we all pitch in, cover each other's back, like a family."

"Think you'll stay on the Cap?"

"Don't know. What I'm really thinking about is moving up the ladder to where the real money is."

"Where's that? In management?"

Tyrone laughed. "Management? Get serious. The cash is in being a redcap. Them dudes make tip money like they're printing it."

"I want a drink and I want it now!"

They both turned and stared at the speaker. It was a man dressed in a three-piece pinstripe suit who didn't look happy about one thing in his life right now.

Tyrone rolled his eyes. "How you doing, Mr. Merryweather?"

"I'm not doing good at all, and I want that drink. Scotch and soda on the rocks. Right now."

"I'm not open yet, sir, if you could come back—"

Merryweather stepped forward. "This gentleman has a beer that I'm assuming came from you. Now, if you refuse to open the bar for me, a paying customer, then"—he glanced at Tyrone's nametag—"then *Tyrone*, I suggest you start looking for other work because once I get off this train you'll be unemployed." Merryweather checked his fancy watch. "I'm waiting, Tyrone."

"Sure, coming right up, no problem."

Tyrone mixed the drink and handed it to the man. Merryweather sipped it. "More scotch—you people never put enough of the liquor in. What, are you stealing it for yourself?"

"Hey," said Tom, "why don't you lighten up?"

Merryweather turned toward him. "Do you happen to know who I am?"

"Yeah, you're a jerk and obviously very proud of it."

Merryweather smiled so tightly it looked as though his cheek balls might pop through his skin.

"Tell him who I am, Tyrone. You know, don't you?"

"Look, I'm putting a bunch of scotch in your drink. Why don't we just call it a truce?"

"I'm Gordon Merryweather. And I'm the king of the class-action lawsuit. Piss me off, and I'll see you in court, and I'll walk away with everything you have—although, from the looks of you, you clearly don't have much."

Tom stepped forward, his fists balled.

"Oh, I hope you do," said Merryweather. "Then I get to put you in jail too."

Tyrone stepped between them.

"Hey," said Tyrone, "everything is so cool, it's like it's snowing right inside the train. Let's all walk away now. Hey, it's Christmas, right. You going home for Christmas, right Mr. Merryweather, to see the wife and kids? Bet you're bringing them lots of presents."

"I'm divorced. My children are spoiled brats unworthy of either my affection or my largesse."

With that, Gordon Merryweather walked off, sipping his scotch. About halfway down the corridor they heard him laughing.

Tom looked at Tyrone. "I'm surprised he didn't say 'Bah, humbug.' "

Tyrone shook his head. "You don't want to mess with that man. He'll tie you up in court for years. His picture is right in the dictionary, beside the word *nightmare*."

"No offense, but why is the 'king of the class-action lawsuit' taking the train? He probably can afford his own jet."

"From what I've heard, the oh-so-tough Mr. Merryweather is afraid to fly. I wish he'd just buy his own train and stay off mine."

"Well, thanks for stopping me from knocking that scotch down his throat. I actually have plans for my life that don't include prison."

Tyrone smiled. "No problem. Any time."

Tom could tell Tyrone was really hustling to get things ready, so he decided to wrap things up. "And thanks for the info and the beer."

"Come on back after dinner. I serve some hard stuff."

"Hard stuff, now that's always been my kind of drink."

chapter seven

━━━◦━━━

Tom went back to his compartment and looked out the window; it was already dark at five-fifteen. They'd just cleared Harper's Ferry, West Virginia, a place immortalized when John Brown made his famous raid on the federal armory there prior to the Civil War's commencing, and went to the gallows as his price for being in the history books.

At Cumberland, Maryland, the Cap would be going through the Graham Tunnel, which ran about a third of a mile in length. According to Tom's train brochure, both the entrance and exit to the tunnel were in West Virginia. Yet due to the mysteries of geography and the happenstance of surveyors etching state lines, Tom supposed, the tunnel itself was actually in Maryland. The Cap would also be navigating the famous Cumberland Gap, the same natural breach frontiersmen had used to get through the wall of the Appalachian Mountains on their way to the Plains and the Pacific. But for that hole in the rock, America might still be a motley strip of thirteen very oppressed English colonies.

After Cumberland, the train would next encounter Lover's Leap. Here, legend had it, an Indian princess forbidden by her father to marry the American soldier she loved threw herself off in despair. The anguished chief then supposedly threw himself over too. Tom didn't think he'd be sharing that tale with Steve and Julie. They were nervous enough.

Deciding it was finally time to hunt down the film people, Tom passed between cars in the opposite direction of the dining room and found himself in the other sleeping-room section. By now he'd adjusted his balance to the gentle rocking and swaying of the train, and he was proud to note that he took a tumble only once out of three clear opportunities to do so. He slowed his pace. Deluxe units were marked with letters, while the economy compartments were numbered. He was sure that Hollywood types would only travel first class, especially famous or infamous ones. He drifted toward this section, hoping one of the movie folks would come out of hiding and he could strike up a conversation, perhaps get a part in a blockbuster for a million bucks and become merrily infamous himself.

He moved to the first compartment. There the curtain was pulled tightly across the opening and he could see nothing, although he heard someone moving around inside. As he went to the next compartment he could see that the curtain was pulled back a bit. He stopped, checked the corridor, and then took a quick peek. The room had been outfitted as an office. There was a laptop computer set up, what looked to be a printer, a power strip complete with surge protector, and a tall young man, with a flattop haircut and wearing a dark turtleneck, pacing in the small space. As he turned, Tom could see that he was wearing a phone headset with his cell phone riding in a belt clip.

This couldn't be the famous director, could it? This guy didn't seem like the director type—not that Tom knew what that type was, exactly. Then he had to be either a star or a writer. Tom's money was on his being a writer. He had a computer and a printer, after all. And he seemed like the young, hip scriveners probably much in demand out there. As everyone knew, people over thirty were ceremoniously stripped of their cool gene and given a bad haircut and a pair of sensible shoes in return.

Tom went to the next compartment. He was about to take a look when a man slid the door open and almost collided with him.

"Sorry," he said. Tom glanced at the unlighted cigarette in the man's hand. "I was just told I can't smoke in my compartment," he explained.

Tom quickly ran his gaze over the fellow, a longtime reporter's habit. He was medium height, early sixties and slim, but with the beginnings of a small paunch. He had thick silver hair, a healthy California Christmas tan, and was dressed very expensively in black slacks, white silk shirt, tweed jacket, and, on his feet, Bruno Maglis. To Tom he just reeked of casual, frolicking millions.

"They have a smoking lounge on the lower level," Tom advised.

"Well, I guess that's where I'm headed then. Tried a hundred times to kick this habit. Did the patch, even hypnosis. Nothing."

"I was a two-packer a day, but now I limit myself to the occasional cigar."

He looked interested. "How'd you manage it?"

"Well, my life sort of depended on it."

"I hear you. Who wants to die of lung cancer?"

"No, that's not what I mean. I used to be a news correspondent overseas. I was in a convoy of journalists that was attacked by guerrillas. One of the cars in front of us was hit. Our guards told us to remain calm. Then a truck in front of us exploded. The guards told us to keep calm, stay put. Then a mortar round hit right next to us, and the guards told us one more time to keep calm. Right before they jumped out and ran."

"My God, what happened?"

"Well, they obviously had us in range, and we weren't waiting for the next shot to find us. We all jumped out and ran for the mountains. A guy from Reuters, about fifty and a heavy smoker, didn't make it. He dropped to the ground, probably due to a heart attack."

"Did you stop and help?"

"I would have, but I was carrying somebody at the time—twisted ankle, the person couldn't run. I was hauling up that mountain, my heart and lungs near to bursting; it seemed like every smoke I'd ever had was coming back to haunt me. But we made it to a friendly camp, barely."

"And the other guy?"

"I hope the heart attack killed him before the guerrillas reached him; they weren't known for their compassion. I haven't touched a cigarette since." Tom added, "I wouldn't recommend that method for everyone, of course. It could have some serious side effects."

"I guess so. Wow, what a story. War correspondent, huh?"

"Not anymore. The most dangerous things I report on these days are how to construct his and her closets in a way that allows the husband actually to live, and the harrowing pitfalls of home barbecuing."

The man laughed and put out his hand. "That's good. That's funny. I'm Max Powers, by the way."

Tom thought he had recognized him, and when the man

said his name it all clicked. He *was* a very famous director, regularly in the top ten of the most powerful people in Hollywood. Though he was known more for his enormous box-office successes, he'd also done some work that had pleased the critics, been nominated several times for Academy awards, and had taken home the grand prize a few years ago.

"Tom Langdon. I've seen a lot of your movies, Mr. Powers. You really know how to tell a story. And I'll take that over the highbrow stuff the critics always tout."

"Thanks. That's all I try to do, tell a story. And it's Max." He slipped the unlighted cigarette into his shirt pocket and looked around. "Well, we're trying to cobble a story together about this mode of transportation."

"Because there's something about a train?"

"You got that right. Cars? Forget it! Crazy drivers, jammed interstate highways, eating fast food till you drop? No thanks. Planes are impersonal and nerve-racking. Now, I don't like to fly, but in my business you have to. I was coming back on a flight once from Cannes, and we hit some really bad turbulence and I went into the lavatory and lighted up, because I was so nervous. Well, the smoke alarm went off, and when we landed they took me to jail. Jail! All for smoking one unfiltered menthol. Cost me thirty grand in legal fees, and I still had to do community service."

He calmed. "But trains, that's something else. I'm a native Californian, and my old man was a conductor on the Santa Fe passenger line back in the days when trains were really the classy way to travel. He'd arrange it so I could ride up with the engineer. Let me tell you, there's no greater feeling in the world. Ever since, I've known there's a story to be told about riding the rails, and not like the stuff that's already been done. And now I'm finally doing something about it."

Tom told him about the story he was writing and some of his impressions of train travel. "It's not getting from A to B. It's not the beginning or the destination that counts. It's the ride in between. That's the whole show," he said. "If you only take the time to see it. This train is alive with things that should be seen and heard. It's a living, breathing something—you just have to want to learn its rhythm." Tom wondered where this was all coming from, but there it was. Maybe the Cap was growing on him.

Max gripped Tom's arm excitedly. "You understand exactly what I'm trying to get at here." He suddenly smacked his forehead. "I just had an unbelievable brainwave. This is always happening to me, Tom, all the time. Look, you're a writer, seen stuff all over the world, and you're on this train trying to take the pulse of America over the holidays."

"Right, so?" Tom said cautiously. He had no idea where this was going, but Max Powers seemed to be floating in the clutches of his brainwave.

"So, you and my writer should team up—I mean, for this trip, for the research part. Swap notes, stories you've heard, brainstorming, stuff like that. And I'm not talking for free. I'll pay you, believe me."

"But I'm already working on a story."

"That's the sheer beauty of it. You write your story, fine. But the same stuff you're doing for your story can help my writer put the film plot together. It's perfect. Two bangs for one. Get it?"

Tom nodded. However, he wasn't really looking forward to working with the ten-year-old with the headset. Tom was neither very young nor very hip, and if the guy called him "dude" just once or perhaps blurted out "Ciao!" instead of simply "goodbye," it might get ugly.

To Tom's surprise, Max led him right past the compartment with the headset-wearing hipster and went to the first compartment and rapped on the glass.

"You decent? It's Max."

The door slid open, and in that instant Tom felt every bit of breath leave his body. He could no longer even hear the hum, hush, siss-boom-bah of the mighty Cap as Eleanor Carter stared back at him.

chapter eight

~

Max said, "Eleanor Carter, Tom Langdon. Tom, Eleanor."

Neither Tom nor Eleanor uttered a word. They just stared at each other for so long that Max finally said, "Um, do you two know each other?"

"It was years ago," Eleanor said quickly.

She was even more lovely now than the last time Tom had seen her, and that bar had been set pretty high. She was tall and still slender, and hadn't cut her auburn hair short as so many women closing in on forty do. It was still shoulder-length and sexy. Her face, well, there were a few more lines there, yet they possessed an attractiveness—a statement that the owner had actually *lived*—that smooth, unblemished skin could never match. And the big green eyes still packed a wallop and made Tom want to find a chair to sit in before he fell over. She was wearing gray wool slacks, stylish black, low-heeled shoes, and a white sweater with the collar of a blue shirt sticking out.

Tom remembered vividly the first time he ever saw Eleanor on campus. She wore short shorts, showcasing those long legs, a red sleeveless sweater, flip-flops, and a yellow bandanna in her hair. He couldn't take his eyes off her. For the next fifteen years he rarely had.

Both journalism majors, they'd decided to be a team after graduation. Their first investigative assignment for a little newspaper in Georgia had been following the legendary Reverend Little Bob Humphries around the Deep South, from Anniston, Alabama, to Tupelo, Mississippi, and every backwater in between. Reverend Bob, dressed in his white suit, white shoes, and wide, wide white belt, could heal the sick, calm the angry, cheer the bereaved, and save the wicked, all in a night's work, and for a very reasonable amount of money (namely, all that you'd brought). You could hide your last penny as well as you could, and Reverend Bob would find it and take it with a charm and manner that made you feel ashamed for holding out on him.

The holy man drove a custom-built Impala, the biggest Tom had ever seen. It was mostly for the prodigious trunk space, he discovered, for the good minister unabashedly accepted everything from legal tender to salt-cured hams to the occasional spare relative to serve as an assistant. Tom had always thought that the Reverend must be related in some way to the Duke and the Dauphin, the shysters of *Huckleberry Finn* infamy. As far as Tom knew, unlike the genteel highway robbers in Twain's masterpiece, Little Bob had never been ridden out of town on a rail tarred and feathered. Yet the defrauded citizens could have indeed done such a thing and God probably wouldn't have even blinked. In fact, He might have sent a miracle or two their way as compensation for such a good deed.

Yet Tom had to admire the man's tenacity. During their investigation, Tom had even ended up giving Little Bob his last twenty bucks and he wasn't even Baptist. It was a moment of insane weakness that Tom still felt shame for. However, to

Eleanor's credit, she'd gotten Tom's twenty back, the only person living or dead ever known to have retrieved money from Reverend Bob without recourse to the courts. Their resulting exposé of the charlatan hit the national newswire, made their reputations, and also stopped the Reverend's little con game.

"How have you been?" Eleanor asked coolly.

"I've been working. Mostly here in the States the last year," Tom managed to say.

"I know. I read the piece on Duncan Phyfe furniture you did for *Architectural Journal*. It's the first article on antique furniture that made me laugh. It was good."

Vastly encouraged by that, Tom said, "Well, between you and me, I didn't know Duncan Phyfe from Duncan Hines when I pitched that story, but I crammed like hell, got the gig, and blew the money on something. You know me."

"Yes, I *know* you." She didn't even crack a smile, although Max chuckled. Tom's gut tightened, and his throat dried up as those big emerald eyes bored into him with nothing whatsoever inviting in them. Tom felt cement shoes forming around his ankles. The sensation of imminent doom was somehow of solace to him, as though the end would be quick and relatively painless.

He found his voice. "So you're a screenwriter?"

Max said, "She's one of Hollywood's best-kept secrets. She specializes in script doctoring. You know, where a script has real problems and you need a miracle on a short fuse? Eleanor comes in and whips it into shape, like magic. She's pulled my butt out of the fire on a bunch of occasions when the A-list writer I paid millions to fumbled the ball. My last five films she basically rewrote all the scripts. I finally talked her into doing her own original screenplay."

"I'm not surprised—she was always a terrific writer."

Again, there was no response to this compliment. The cement was now inching up Tom's calves.

"So what's up, Max?" Eleanor said with a slight nod of her head in Tom's direction. She obviously didn't want a trip down memory lane; she wanted to bring this all—meaning him—to a hasty close.

"I had this brilliant idea." Max explained his "brilliant idea" to Eleanor, while Tom stood there wondering whether he should throw himself through one of the windows and under the wheels of the Cap. It couldn't be clearer that Eleanor wasn't at all pleased with the percolations of the director's genius.

Yet she said, "Let me think about it, Max."

"Absolutely. Hey, I tell you what, later, we can have a drink. Somebody told me they drink on this train."

"They do," Tom said. Then he added jokingly, "In fact, the whole train is a bar." He looked at Eleanor, but she was simply staring off. Tom's arms were now immobile.

"Done, then. Drinks around, what, eight?" said Max.

"They serve dinner here too. I have reservations at seven?" Tom looked at Eleanor again, as though trying to will her to say she'd join him.

"I had a late lunch in D.C.," she said. "I'm skipping dinner."

Max said, "Yeah, dinner's not good for me either, Tom. I've got a few calls to make."

"Well, don't starve yourself." Ironically, it was at this point that the cement seemed to arrive at his mouth.

"Not to worry: Kristobal brought some of my favorite stuff on board. I'm more of a snacker, really."

"Kristobal?"

"My assistant. He's in the compartment right there." Max pointed to the compartment where Tom had seen the headset kid.

As if the mention of his name by his boss had reached his ears through the closed door, Kristobal emerged from his room.

"Do you need anything, Mr. Powers?"

"No, I'm fine. This is Tom Langdon. Tom might be helping us on our project."

Kristobal was as tall as Tom, and young and handsome and well built. He was very stylishly dressed, and probably made more in a week than Tom made in a year. He also seemed efficient and intelligent, and Tom instantly disliked him for all those reasons.

"Excellent, sir," said Kristobal.

Tom reached out and they shook hands. "Good to know you," Tom said, ignoring the imagined crunch of gravel between his teeth.

Max said, "Okay, that's settled. Eleanor will think about it and we'll have drinks at eight, and now I have got to go smoke before I start hyperventilating." He looked around, puzzled.

Tom pointed, "That way, two cars down, through the dining room, into the lounge car, down the stairs, to the right and you'll see the door marked 'smoking lounge.'"

"Thanks, Tom, you're a gem. I know this is going to work out; it's an omen. My palmist said something good was going to happen. 'A chance meeting,' she said. And look what happened. Yep, a good day." He stuck the cigarette in his mouth and hustled off in his Bruno Maglis.

Kristobal called after him: "Your lighter is in your right-hand jacket pocket, sir."

Max gave a little wave; Kristobal retreated to his office hovel. And then it was just Eleanor and Tom.

For a few moments they stood there, each refusing to make eye contact.

"I cannot believe this is actually happening," Eleanor finally said. "Of all the people to see on this train." She closed her eyes and slowly shook her head.

"Well, it kind of took me by surprise too." He added, "You look great, Ellie." As far as he knew, Tom was the only one who ever called her that. She'd never objected, and he loved the way it sounded.

Eleanor's eyes opened and focused on him. "I'm not going to beat around the bush: Max is a wonderfully gifted filmmaker, but sometimes he comes up with these off-the-wall ideas that just won't work. I really believe this is one of them."

"Hey, I just walked smack into his enthusiasm. I don't want you to do something you don't want to, and frankly, I haven't even really thought about it either."

"So I can tell Max you're not interested?"

"If that's what you want, Ellie, that's fine."

She studied him closely now, and he felt himself shrink from the scrutiny.

"That's exactly what I want." She went back inside her room and slid the door closed.

Standing there, he was now a fully kilned statue of stone, ready for primer and paint. Not even the hum-hush, siss-boom-bahs and cunning whipsaws of the mighty Cap could budge the man in his rigid, unyielding despair. He wondered if it was too late to get a refund on his train ticket based on the recent occurrence of his living death.

chapter nine

Tom staggered back to his compartment and collapsed on the foldout bed. Eleanor was on this train? It couldn't be possible. He'd never envisioned sharing his journey of self-discovery with the one person on earth whose absence in his life may well have led him to take the damn trip in the first place! And yet whose fault was her absence? He'd never asked her to stay, had he?

As he sat up and stared out the window into the blackness, he suddenly wasn't on a train heading to Chicago; he was in Tel Aviv. They'd chosen that coastal city because of its proximity to Ben-Gurion Airport; one was never really more than two hours' flight time from the sort of stories Eleanor and Tom were there to cover. The Middle East was nothing if not unpredictable in its predictableness. You knew something would happen; you just didn't know exactly where or what form it would take.

Mark Twain had visited the Holy Land and wrote extensively about it in *The Innocents Abroad*. The book was published in 1869, a year before Zion was resettled by the Jews and almost ninety years before Israel was established as a sovereign state.

Twain had found Palestine to be very tiny, writing that he "could not conceive of a small country having so large a history." Tom understood exactly what he meant. The place that loomed so enormous to folks all over the world could be traversed from end to end in hours by car. The walled city of Jerusalem seemed but a handsome miniature the first time Tom saw it. Yet the intensity there, and the people who called it home, lived up to its reputation as one of the most magnetic places on earth.

They'd traveled the country in search of stories, although Eleanor had also sought out more personal experiences, once even being baptized in the Jordan River. Twain, too, had swum in the Jordan River after a long, dusty ride from Damascus, though more for hygienic than spiritual purposes. Tom and Eleanor had bought Jordanian water in clear bottles molded to look like Jesus and sent them back home, together with holy air in a can, collected in churches of antiquity in Israel. Tom had always understood that both items were immensely popular with American tourists, who'd rush home with the air and water and bestow it on their own places of worship. He supposed they did so in the hopes of raising them a few pegs in the eyes of God— hedging their bets, so to speak.

During the years they had lived in Israel, the pair had also ventured to Bethlehem one Christmas with a tour group because Eleanor had wanted to see the place where the son of God had been delivered into a sinful world. Though he was not a particularly religious person, it was still a humbling event for Tom to be in close proximity to where an event of that magnitude reportedly took place.

In his trip to Bethlehem Mark Twain had reported that all sects of Christians, except Protestants, had chapels under the roof of the Church of the Holy Sepulchre. However, he also observed that one group dared not trespass on the other's territory, proving beyond doubt, he noted, that even the grave of the Savior couldn't inspire peaceful worship among different beliefs. Some things clearly hadn't changed since Mark Twain was a pilgrim in the Holy Land all those years ago.

The American journalists had been two of the very few in Israel who celebrated the holiest of Christian holidays. Tom and Eleanor had put up a small Christmas tree in their apartment and cooked their holiday meal and opened presents. Then they looked out on the darkness of the Mediterranean and took in the sights and smells of the desert climate while celebrating an event most Americans associated with snow, a jolly fat man, and crackling fires. Then they fell asleep in each other's arms. Those Christmases in Tel Aviv were some of the most wonderful of Tom's life. Except for the last one.

Eleanor left the apartment to do some last-minute grocery shopping. About forty minutes later she came back and said that she wanted to go home, that she was tired of covering the perils of this strange world, that it was just time to go home. At first Tom thought she was joking. Then it became apparent she wasn't. In fact, while he was standing there, she started packing. Then she called El Al to get a flight home. She tried to book Tom one too, but he said no, he wasn't leaving. Everything had seemed wonderful barely an hour before. Now he was standing in the middle of their tiny apartment in his skivvies and his whole life had just collapsed.

He questioned her as to what had happened in the last forty minutes to cause her to make this major, life-altering decision for both of them, without bothering to consult him first. The only answer she gave was that it was time to go home. They talked, and then the talk snowballed into an argument, and then it cascaded downhill from there. By the time she had her bags packed they were screaming at each other, and Tom had become so confused and distraught that to this day he had no idea half of what he'd said.

She took a cab to the airport, and Tom followed her, where they continued their argument. Finally, it was time to go up the escalator to get on the shuttle bus. That was when Eleanor, her voice now calm, asked him once more to come with her. If he really loved her, he'd come with her. He remembered standing there, tears in his eyes, feeling only a deep stubbornness fueled by anger. He told her no, he wasn't coming.

He watched her ride up the escalator. She turned back once. Her expression was so sad, so miserable, that he almost called out to her, to tell her to wait, that he was coming, but the words never came. It was like the night on the train from Cologne, when he was supposed to propose to the woman he loved but hadn't. Instead, he turned and walked out, leaving her, as she was leaving him.

That was the last time he'd seen Eleanor. Until five minutes ago, on a swaying train headed to Chicago by way of Toledo and Pittsburgh. He still had no idea what had happened to make her leave. And he still had no rational explanation as to why he hadn't gone with her.

With a jolt, Tom was transported back to West Virginia on steely Amtrak rails. He lay down on the couch, and the warm compartment, the hum-hush, siss-boom-bah of the wheels, his overwrought mind, and the darkness outside combined to push him into a troubled doze.

Whatever it was must have hit Tom's sleeper car directly. The sound was very loud, like a cannonball clanging off the side. He almost fell off the couch. He checked his watch. Six-thirty, and they were slowing down fast. Then the mighty Capitol Limited came to a complete stop, and looking out his window, Tom saw that they were not anywhere close to civilization. He smelled something burning, and although he wasn't an experienced railroad man, that didn't seem like something you'd want your train to be doing.

In the darkness outside he saw lights here and there, as presumably train personnel checked where the broadside had come from and what damage it had done. He went out into the hallway and saw Father Kelly.

"Did you hear that?" the priest said. "It sounded like a shot."

"I think we hit something," Tom replied. "Maybe there was something on the track and we ran over it."

"It sounded like it hit our car, and we're in the middle of the train."

Well, that was true, thought Tom. "I don't know, I just hope we start moving again soon."

Regina walked by with a worried look. She was carrying a huge cluster of newspapers all balled up.

Tom said, "Hey, Regina, what's up? We're not moving. Did Amtrak's credit card bounce or something?"

"We hit something, that's for sure. They're checking it out. We should be heading on shortly."

He looked at what she was carrying. "I take it you're really into newspapers."

"Somebody stuffed them in the trash can. I don't even know where they came from. Only newspaper on this train is the *Toledo Blade*, and we don't pick that up until early tomorrow morning."

She walked off. Tom was starting to feel very smart for building extra time into his travel schedule. It looked like he was going to need it. In Twain's day, the trip from St. Joseph, Missouri, to California measured nineteen hundred miles and by overland stagecoach took about twenty days. While Tom had to go over a thousand miles farther than Twain had, he was being pulled by something a little more potent than equine power. And yet it was beginning to look like Twain's travel time might not be in any real jeopardy. Tom started thinking of small islands where he could hide out from Lelia when he didn't show for Christmas. The list was short and not very promising.

Agnes Joe joined them. She was still wearing the nightgown, but she had a robe on over it.

"We hit something," she said.

"Appears that way," Tom replied, as he tried to get past her. However, he found that when Agnes Joe faced him head-on, the woman's body actually spanned the entire width of the hall. Amtrak really needed to build its trains larger to accommodate the widening of Americans.

She pulled an apple from her pocket, rubbed it on her robe, and started chomping. "I remember once three—no, four years ago—we were heading up right about here in fact, when, bam, we stopped dead."

"Really, what happened?" asked Tom.

"Why don't you come in my compartment, set yourself down, get comfortable, and I'll tell you."

Father Kelly and Tom exchanged glances, and then the priest scooted into the safety of his rabbit hole, leaving the journalist all alone. So much for the support of the Church in times of crisis, thought Tom.

"Well, I'd like to but I have to get ready for dinner. My reservation is at seven."

"Mine too."

With the look she gave him, Tom began to think she really had a thing for him. All he could do was give her a weak smile as he finally managed to squeeze past and into the safety of his compartment. He locked his door, drew his curtain, and would have slid the bed against the door had it not been bolted to the wall.

He dressed for dinner, which meant he splashed water on his face, ran a comb through his hair, and changed his shirt. He peeked out the door, checking for roaming Agnes Joes, saw the coast was clear, and still ran for the safety of the mess car. Unfortunately, though not a world-class sprinter, he was still moving faster than the Cap.

chapter ten

⟳

As Tom surveyed the dining room, his mind once again drifted to his rail-travel touchstone, *North by Northwest*. In the film Cary Grant, on the run from the police and the train conductor—as a poor fugitive from justice, Cary had no ticket—comes into the elegant dining car. The splendidly attired maitre d' escorts him past fashionably dressed diners, to the table of the ravishingly sexy Eva Marie. Turns out she'd tipped the waiter to seat Cary with her. Beautiful women were always doing that to poor Cary Grant. They order, they drink, they laugh; they conduct a sort of sophisticated verbal foreplay right there at the table, one of the more subtly erotic movie scenes ever Tom felt. Right now, in the role of Eva Marie, he could only see Eleanor. And wasn't that pathetic, he told himself—pathetic that there was no possibility of it coming true.

On Amtrak, diners were seated to encourage conversation and the forming of friendships, however fleeting. In this tradition, Tom was seated across from two people, a middle-aged man and a woman who, unfortunately, looked nothing like

Eleanor, or Eva Marie for that matter. The guy was dressed in a suit and tie. Across the aisle from them at another table were Steve and Julie. They were drinking glasses of red wine, holding hands, talking in low voices, and still looked very nervous. Young love: There was nothing better or worse, Tom decided. Except perhaps old love, unrequited. Actually, after seeing Eleanor, he was sure of it.

By what he could overhear from the other diners, the subject of the stalled train was dominating the conversation. At least the longer the train was stopped the longer he'd be on it with Eleanor. And how exactly did that help, Tom asked himself, since it was so clearly obvious how she felt. He'd held out some hope that she still loved him despite how it had ended. He'd kept that thought safely in his pocket all these years and it had carried him through some troubling times. Now that pocket was empty; actually, it had been ripped right off his pants.

"This is the second train I've been on this week where something has happened," said the woman across from Tom. She introduced herself as Sue Bunt from Wisconsin. She was dressed professionally, was about fifty or so, tall and on the heavy side, and her hair was cut very short. The guy in the suit was next to her. Tom knew they weren't together, because the man had been seated right ahead of him. Sue had already been at the table alone.

"How about that," the man said. He didn't offer up his name.

"I usually don't take the train, but the flights aren't as convenient in my circuit anymore," she explained.

"What do you do?" Tom asked, deciding to get into the spirit of conversation.

"I'm a sales rep for a health-food company," she said as she slathered her roll in butter.

"Happy holidays," said the waitress as she came over and presented them with complimentary glasses of eggnog, a Cap holiday tradition, they were told.

"Happy holidays," they all replied, and then Sue asked the waitress about the condition of the train.

"Conductor said we'll be up and running in no time. We just ran over something on the track." She wore a Christmas hat, and Tom noted that the windows and tables were strung with holiday lights.

They placed their orders. The menu was very good, and Tom could actually smell the meals being cooked in the downstairs kitchen, which would then be sent up to the dining car via dumbwaiters. He ordered the prime rib and, instead of the salad, asked for a screwdriver as his appetizer. He was just putting it to his lips when he felt himself being propelled to the side of the dining car. He turned and there was Agnes Joe wedging next to him, leaving him about six inches in which to eat his dinner.

"Hi, Agnes Joe," the man and Sue said in unison.

Tom looked bewildered. *Did everybody on this train know the woman?*

"Hi there, honeypies."

When Tom looked her over he was stunned. Agnes Joe was wearing nice dress slacks—stretched to the fabric's absolute breaking point, no doubt, but still nice slacks—a tasteful sweater, and her hair was done. She had on some makeup, and she didn't look nearly as old as before. It was such a stark transformation that he could only stare.

"Hi," he said dumbly.

"Hello, Agnes Joe," said the waitress as she came up. "You want the usual?"

"That'll be fine, with extra onions."

"I take it you ride the train a lot," Tom said as the waitress walked off.

"Oh, I love the train and the people on it. Good folks. I tried flying for a while. I'm a licensed pilot in fact, general aviation, but I prefer the trains."

For Tom the vision of Agnes Joe crammed inside the cockpit of a two-seater Cessna, her hammy fingers curled around the yoke, her enormous feet on the rudder pedals, wavered right on hallucinatory.

The man turned to Sue. "You say you're in health care?"

"Health *foods*, as a sales rep. I used to be a legal secretary, but I couldn't take working for lawyers anymore."

Well, Tom had also had his fill of the species *americanus legalis cannibalis* during his divorce, and more recently with Gordon Merryweather. He held up his glass to her in a sign of empathy.

"What do you know about ginseng?" asked the man.

The guy was in his fifties and seemed like a normal business type, yet he had exhibited some fairly strange physical tics that set him apart from his fellows. For example, his mouth kept opening really wide, at which point he sucked in air like he couldn't get his fair share. Then his eyes would bulge out, causing Tom to think he was going to pitch headfirst into his salad any second. He'd also lick his lips, so furiously you thought his tongue would cramp up or simply fall off. Finally, he had the incredibly annoying habit of looking like he was going to say something, his lips puckering, his fleshy neck quivering, his eyes blinking rapidly, his hands rising to the sky, all building to some titanic outburst of wisdom or at least scandalous gossip, and then it all would just collapse; he'd simply pick at the olive in his drink. After the fourth time he performed this maddening feat it was all Tom could do to keep from going over the table at the man.

"Ginseng?" Sue said. "You mean the herb?"

"Yes. Let me tell you why I'm asking." He gave each a conspiratorial look and lowered his voice. "I met this woman. An Asian woman, or Oriental, or whatever the PC term is these days, I can never remember. I guess it's not 'slanty-eyes,' is it?" he said, trying for humor and failing badly.

"No, it's not," said Agnes Joe. "And please don't go there. Tolerance and understanding of other cultures make for a peaceful world. On top of that, I have ancestors of Japanese descent."

Tom looked at the massive woman and wondered if she were actually carrying some of these ancestors on her person. And he noted that her vocabulary and diction had kicked up a notch too. What was that about?

The fellow continued. "Right. Sorry, bad joke. Well, this woman, she seemed, you know, to be attracted to me. And I was definitely attracted to her. We went out for dinner one evening, and she brought up this ginseng thing. To make a long story short, she actually sent me some ginseng. I guess it was from China."

"Actually, ginseng is grown in Wisconsin," said Sue, as she put even more butter on her roll, such that there was no longer any bread actually visible. "The soil is perfect for it."

Tom stared at her. The state of Wisconsin had perfect ginseng soil? This sounded crazy to him, but what did he know about it? Maybe the Green Bay Packers were all ginseng groupies.

"Okay, Wisconsin," the man said, "but the point is, she sent me this stuff, and I'm not sure what to do with it. I mean, do I cook it or drink it or what?"

Tom said, "Just because she gave it to you doesn't mean you have to use it."

"Well," said the man, eyeing the ladies a little nervously, "I assume she gave it to me, you know, because it's supposed to possess certain performance-enhancing attributes. At least that's what she intimated. I should add that she's much younger than me."

Tom began to realize where this was going when Agnes Joe said, "You mean so you can romp like a young stud in the sack with a woman half your age and not let her feel she's cheating herself with some old bag of bones."

There was a long period of silence before the man finally said, "That's sort of my point, yes." And then he went back to massively sucking wind and picking at his pitted olives with renewed vigor.

"I'd mash it up," continued Agnes Joe as her gaze bored into the man, "and shoot it right into your veins with a hypodermic needle. Do it right before you get into bed, and then fly out of the bathroom, screaming and pounding your chest like Tarzan, and just jump her. I hear Asian women like that."

The man looked at Tom with wounded eyes, obviously seeking some gender support. Yet all Tom could offer was, "I heard that too . . . honeypie," and then he swallowed his screwdriver in a mighty gulp.

He ordered a glass of merlot as a chaser, then ate his meal, which was wonderful. He looked around the car and observed that at one table two Muslims and a man of Native American descent were engaged in animated conversation, a verbal sparring match. Each was smiling, so it seemed civil at least. At another table, a middle-aged and attractive African American woman was very obviously having the moves put on her by a young, handsome Korean man. She was deflecting his advances with good-natured banter, but Tom could tell that the woman was flattered. At yet another table, some businesspeople were supping with the Tarot card lady. She was examining their hands and even had her cards spread out in front of the remains of her Shenandoah Valley baked chicken. As she methodically forked the award-winning train cheesecake into her mouth, the corporate suits, their cell phones put away for now, were listening intently.

Tom could only shake his head. Ginseng, flying Agnes Joes, passengers of every race and religion, the easy coupling of formal commercial power and whimsical Tarot cards intermingled over a hearty feast: Maybe there really was something about a train. As he finished his merlot, he marveled at how incredibly quietly and smoothly the Cap rode the rails at zero miles per hour.

chapter eleven

As soon as dinner was over, Tom fled to the lounge car, which, as he soon discovered, was known under a different name by all seasoned train travelers: the *bar* car. Years before, there'd actually been a manned bar in the upper-level lounge, but that had been lost in budget cutbacks. Tom went downstairs, where Tyrone fixed him up libation-wise, then he went and sat in the lounge car's upper level. The train still wasn't moving yet. He checked his watch. The Cap should have been well on its way to Connellsville, Pennsylvania, and they hadn't even made it to Cumberland, Maryland. At least he'd stopped smelling smoke.

The TV was on in the lounge car and showing the movie *How the Grinch Stole Christmas*, the one with Jim Carrey playing the Grinch. A gaggle of kids, young and old, and their parents were gathered round watching it. In other corners of the car there were little groups of people chatting and drinking, and a few solitary types who just stared out the darkened windows at their own reflections. The lounge car too had been decorated for the holidays with wreaths, strung tinsel, and other Christmas ornamentation. Tom sipped his gin and chewed his peanuts and pretzels and focused on the group of adults sitting nearby. One was reading, one was knitting, another was listening to music through headphones. Tom kept glancing at the door to the lounge car to see if Max and Eleanor might still pop in, but so far nothing.

"Are you all heading somewhere for Christmas?" Tom asked with what he hoped was a friendly and interested expression. He found that gin always made one appear relaxed and happy, if a bit fuzzy in the head.

The knitting lady looked up and smiled. "South Bend, Indiana. My grandson is a sophomore at Notre Dame. I'm spending the holidays with him. I'll probably end up cooking and cleaning and doing his laundry for him, but that's okay. That's grandma stuff. And it's Christmas. Who wants to be alone?"

"You got my vote there," Tom said as he introduced himself.

She reached out and shook his hand. "Pauline Beacon."

"You live in the D.C. area?"

"Yes, Springfield, Virginia. You?"

"Right in D.C."

"I don't know how you take the traffic." This came from the guy who'd been reading a book. He was midforties, balding and soft in the middle. "I'm heading back to Toledo. I was in Washington on business and had to rent a car and drive around that Beltway thing you folks have. I don't know how you people do it. It's like the Wild, Wild West on wheels. Crazy." He shook his head. "I'm Rick," he said and smiled. "Just call me Toledo Rick."

"So I take it you folks like trains," Tom said.

"I don't like to fly," said Pauline. "And trains are a connection to my childhood. How about you?"

Tom said, "I fly a lot, but it got to be a little old. I thought I'd try a more civilized way of getting around."

"Well," said Rick, "we're not getting around anywhere at the moment. I normally fly too, but I got this great deal on a train ticket." He looked outside and frowned. "Only right now it doesn't seem like such a great deal. At least I'll be home for Christmas."

"You have a family?"

"A wife and six children. Four of my kids are teenagers, three of those girls. I don't even come close to understanding anything about them."

"Girls *are* different," said Pauline.

The guy with the headphones was now listening to the conversation. He introduced himself as Ted from Milwaukee. "Boys are a tough nut too," he said. "I've got four of 'em, all grown now. I had a full head of hair when I had my first, and none when I had my last."

At that moment Agnes Joe came in with a beer and settled down with them. Tom pushed his bowl of snacks her way. The woman cleaned it out with one swipe. She didn't introduce herself. Like in the dining car, everyone seemed to know her already.

"How about you, Tom?" asked Rick. "Where you heading? Family?"

Tom shook his head. "I don't really have any."

"Well, everyone has family somewhere," said Pauline.

"Not everybody," said Agnes Joe. "I'm a loner too."

"I didn't say I was a loner. I'm a reporter. Been all over the world. Probably have friends in sixty or seventy different countries."

"Friends are friends, but family is family," stated Pauline, and maybe she was right.

"Divorced or never married?" asked Agnes Joe, as she casually munched her almonds. She glanced at his naked ring finger in response to his surprised look.

"Divorced. Although my marriage was so brief I never really felt married."

"Well, you obviously didn't marry the right woman," said Pauline.

"How can you know for sure?" asked Toledo Rick.

"Lots of ways," ventured Agnes Joe. "Mostly it just feels right. Like you don't care if you eat, drink, sleep, or even breathe so long as you're with that person." She glanced at Tom. "You ever feel that way about anybody?"

They all looked at Tom awaiting his answer.

"Hey, that's getting a bit personal," he said.

"Well, there's just something about a train," quipped Pauline with a smile as she effortlessly knitted one and purled two.

Tom sat back, stared out the window for a moment.

"What was her name?" asked Agnes Joe quietly.

"Eleanor," he finally said.

"Been a long time since you've seen her?"

"Actually, not that long ago." He snapped out of his musings. "But what's past is past. I'm going out to LA. To see my girlfriend, Lelia, spend Christmas with her."

"Is she an actress?" Pauline asked excitedly.

"In a way, yes."

"Would I know any of her work?"

Tom hesitated, then said, "You ever catch Cuppy the Magic Beaver on Saturday morning TV?"

Pauline just stared at him blankly and actually dropped a stitch or two of her knitting. After several unsuccessful attempts at further explanation, Tom decided to drop the whole line of conversation.

They all watched as one of the attendants, dressed as Santa Claus, came into the lounge car. In a flash all the kids, even the older ones, deserted Jim Carrey and the Grinch and gathered around the man in red. Such was the timeless and universal appeal of old Saint Nick.

"That's nice," Tom said, as Santa handed out goodies to everyone.

"They do it every year," said Agnes Joe. "Even when the train's not broken."

Tom looked at her, suddenly interested. It had just occurred to him that Regina had said Agnes Joe rode the trains a lot, to visit her family, she thought. Yet Agnes Joe had just confessed she was a loner. So where was she going on all these trains?

"I guess you've been on these Christmas trains before?" he asked.

"Oh yes, lots of times."

"Are you going all the way to Chicago?"

"That's right."

"Spending the holidays there?" Tom asked.

"No. I'm heading on to LA. Like you."

"By train?"

"The Southwest Chief." She shot him a glance. "And you?"

Agnes Joe for about two days on the Chief. He wondered what would happen if he jumped off the train right now while it wasn't moving. Right as he was about to reply, the wonderful old Capitol Limited gave a lurch and started on its way again. A cheer went up around the lounge car. Tom just couldn't bring himself to join in.

A voice came on over the PA. "Sorry for the delay, folks, but we've got everything patched up. We have a technical team standing by at the next station stop. We'll be there a little while to make sure everything's okay, and then we'll push on. We hope to make up some of the time en route. We've called ahead and nobody will miss train connections. Thank you for understanding and thank you for choosing Amtrak. Happy holidays."

Santa came over and handed out small packages to all. Tom received a miniature of the Santa Fe's famed Super Chief locomotive. Ted went back to his headphones, while Toledo Rick and Pauline excused themselves and left.

Agnes Joe leaned close and took a gander at Tom's model. "The Southern Pacific's Super Chief Santa Fe was the precursor to the Southwest Chief, the one I'm going to be on to LA. It's a great train with views of the mountains and the plains. Goes through eight states on its way to the coast."

"That's interesting, thanks." Tom was now convinced that she'd searched his compartment and found his train ticket for the Chief. He resolved to booby-trap his room using the heaviest object he could find. They had two engines on this train; maybe they wouldn't miss one of them. He could probably cram it into his bath/shower and set it on a spring load.

"Yep, it's a nice trip. Good way to get to LA."

"I bet it is." Tom put down his drink. "So, what are you heading to LA for?"

"I have friends out there. We switch off each year for Christmas. This year it's my turn to go west."

"Sounds like a nice tradition. Regina said you travel by train a lot. And it seems like people know you."

"Oh, I'm just a friendly sort. Always have been. Just because a gal's petite and naturally shy doesn't mean she has to be a meek little wallflower all the time."

At first Tom thought she was serious, but then she smiled at her own joke, and he reluctantly concluded that Agnes Joe wasn't so bad. If she'd just stay away from his kidneys and personal belongings everything would be fine.

"So this gal you're seeing, you serious about her?"

"Depends on what you call serious," Tom said. "We've been seeing each other off and on for about three years."

"Off and on? What, is that a California thing?"

"It's *our* thing."

"Well, I wouldn't advise you to get married. I've tried it twice and neither worked out."

"Do you have any kids?"

"A girl, all grown now, of course. That was from my first marriage. I met husband number one when we worked together at Ringling Brothers."

"You worked for the circus? What, in administration?"

"Oh no, I was one of the performers. Horsewoman, gymnast, even did the highwire in my younger days."

"The trapeze!"

She stared at him. "I was a little lighter then. My daughter still works for the circus."

"Do you see her often?"

"No." With that, she picked up her beer and left. He should have been relieved, but he wasn't. The woman seemed to be growing on him, like a wart maybe, but still growing. It wasn't just idle curiosity either. There were inconsistencies in her background that intrigued the investigative-reporter gene in him.

As he sat there, the train flashed through the Graham Tunnel and soon after slowed as it approached Cumberland, Maryland, once known as the Queen of the Alleghenies. The Cap jauntily made its way right down the middle of the town's main street. Tom saw brick and wood buildings, a Holiday Inn, a McDonald's, and a place called Discount Liquors that was probably very popular, for the town just had that thirsty look to it.

They would be crossing into Pennsylvania soon. The state lines were all oddly configured here. Indeed, at certain times the engine and the tail of the train could be in Maryland while the middle of the Cap labored in West Virginia. This was explained by the Pennsylvania border riding a straight line with its sister Maryland, while the points where West Virginia and Maryland hugged followed the lay of the land. By the time they had quit the Gap and passed safely into Pennsylvania, Tom was altogether done with the conundrums of official state boundaries.

As he sat there staring at the snow falling, Eleanor and Max walked in, trailed by the faithful Kristobal. Tom took a deep breath, finished his drink, and contemplated ordering up cocktails in bulk from his friend Tyrone. He figured he'd need every ounce of alcohol possible to survive this.

chapter twelve

Max and Kristobal were dressed in the same chic clothes, and the latter still wore his headset and cell-phone pack, swaggering in like some futuristic gunfighter looking for trouble. Eleanor, though, had changed into a long turquoise skirt and white denim shirt with a chain belt around her slim waist. Her hair was tucked up. Perhaps, Tom thought, she'd showered in her little water closet, the steamy, soapy liquid pouring down over her long, curvy . . . No, he absolutely could not go there and expect to retain his sanity. Yet the fact that she had freshened up and was here ostensibly to see him was wonderfully reassuring, until he noted her expression. It was not, to put it mildly, one of unadulterated bliss. *Homicidal* was actually the word that drifted through his ginned-up mind.

"Tom!" boomed out Max, in that enthusiastic voice that said "I'm both filthy rich and fun to be around." They all found a private corner.

"Sorry we're late," said Max. "Eleanor and I had a few things to clear up. Boy, what a ride so far, huh?"

Kristobal stared out into the darkness, his pretty-boy looks woeful. "Well, at least the thing's moving."

"Your first train ride, Kristobal?" Tom asked.

"And hopefully my last."

He was, Tom was sure, very much into private planes, free-flowing bottles of champagne, and no one to bother him as he fully reclined in his seat-bed and dreamed of becoming a film mogul.

"He's from another generation," said Max, as he playfully slapped his assistant's arm. "He's not train folk; not like you and me."

"Well, Ellie and I took quite a few trains when we were overseas. We were on an old clunker once from Amsterdam to Paris. Got on at five in the morning with the notion we'd eat on board. We weren't told there was no food on the train because the stewards were on strike. Then, while we're slowly starving to death, we notice that in the fields the train is passing through, all these people are standing there, taking pictures of the train. I thought that maybe the train had been hijacked—you know, by the striking stewards—and we were hurtling to our doom at the station in Paris."

"What happened?" asked Max.

"When we got to Paris, there was a marching band. And then a sleek red bullet train came sliding up to the old one we'd been on. It was the last train ride on that route before bullet service took over. That was all the commotion. So while the band played, we spent about a billion francs filling our bellies. Remember that, Ellie?"

"I go by Eleanor now, just Eleanor. And, no, I don't really remember that."

The gin had now warmed Tom from his toes to his mouth, which had become an 80mm howitzer. "Right. Ellie, that's clearly in the past. Out with the old, in with the new and improved." He looked at Max. "So, you said you and *Eleanor* had talked."

"Yes, we discussed things. And if you want, you two can get started right now."

Tom glanced at her in confusion. "I thought—"

"When Max gets excited about something, his enthusiasm spreads rapidly and overwhelmingly," she explained in a tight voice without meeting his gaze.

Tom said, "You sure you weren't *railroaded* into this? No pun intended, of course."

"Not at all," said Max. "Right, Eleanor?" She nodded.

"Well, how should we begin?" Tom offered pleasantly.

Max said, "What have you discovered so far?"

Tom sat back and cradled his empty glass. "Well, ginseng is grown in Wisconsin, for starters, and it makes old guys perform like Rambo in bed. There's a crazy woman named Agnes Joe on board whom everybody knows for some reason; she outweighs me and performed on the trapeze for Ringling Brothers." He pointed to Steve and Julie. "Those two are getting married on board the Southwest Chief. They're good kids, but scared. I've got a contact on board the Chief who can tell us plenty of great stories. The Tarot card lady over there has charmed mighty business moguls with her peeks into the future. Oh, and Elvis Presley has been resurrected as a black man named Tyrone who serves a concoction called a 'Boiler Room' in the lounge car, that, if it doesn't kill you, will at least make you wish you were dead in your ecstasy. And there's a priest on board, who might have to give me the Last Rites if we don't get to LA on time because my girlfriend will murder me."

Tom said this last as he stared right at Eleanor. She'd

walked out on *him*, after all. She blinked. The lady actually blinked. He had no idea if she had something in her eye or whether it was a reaction to his statement, but it sobered him up a bit.

"Wow," said Max, "you've really gotten around already."

"Once a world-class reporter, always a world-class reporter. Just like Ellie—I mean, Eleanor."

"She never really talked about that part of her life."

Eleanor said quickly, "Maybe Tom and I should get to work, Max. We don't have all that much time."

Tom shrugged. "Actually, we have the rest of the trip to Chicago and then to LA. Hell, at the rate we're going, we'll be together until the spring thaw."

"No, I meant I might have to get off in Chicago and fly to LA. It's personal business, Max. It just came up."

Tom put down his drink. *I bet it did, in the form of me.* "So, we should get going then," he said.

Max didn't look pleased at Eleanor's possible change in plan, but then he eyed Steve and Julie. "You say they're getting married on the Chief?"

Tom explained the situation with their respective families and Julie's anxiety about the few people at the ceremony. Max, looking intrigued, asked a lot of questions.

"That poor girl," said Eleanor with genuine sympathy. "That's not how weddings are supposed to be." She glanced at Tom. "You said she's from the mountains of Virginia—what town?"

"She didn't say. Why?"

"In case you forgot, I grew up in eastern Kentucky, just over the state line from there. I've probably been to her hometown."

With all the discussions of weddings Tom took a quick

peek at Eleanor's hand. There was no wedding band, and nothing that looked remotely like an engagement ring. It was hard to believe she hadn't found someone else. Yet, look at him.

"So what's the angle of your screenplay?" he asked. Tom knew nothing about moviemaking, but he now attempted to take on the air of a seasoned celluloid impresario.

"Depends on what we see on board. Max wants a romantic comedy. I'm leaning toward a mystery, with a reasonably high body count."

"Why not both? Done properly, there's nothing funnier than a pile of stiffs on rails."

Max pointed at Tom and looked at Eleanor. "See? I love this guy. He goes outside the box. You ever think about writing for movies, Tom?"

Tom's gaze went to Eleanor. "Not until about two hours ago."

"It's not as easy as it looks," she said.

"Hell, what is?" he shot back.

Max excused himself and walked over to Steve and Julie, followed by the puppy dog Kristobal. Max started talking animatedly to them, but Tom couldn't hear any of it. It must have been something exciting, however, because Steve and Julie looked truly stunned at whatever the director was saying. The guy probably had that effect on a lot of people.

"Max plotting something?"

"He usually is," replied Eleanor.

"I never would have figured you'd end up in LA."

"We all have to end up somewhere." She glanced up. "Look at you. From Beirut to Duncan Phyfe?"

"Covering wars is a young man's game. I'm not that young anymore," Tom said, then added, "Besides, how many ways can you write about people wiping each other out? I ran out of nouns, verbs, and adjectives five years ago."

"Did you ever end up changing the world?" Though the statement itself appeared sarcastic, the way she asked it was not.

"Look around," he said, "and there's your answer."

"You lasted longer than most." *Longer than you*, thought Tom. She paused before asking, "How are your parents?"

"I've lost them both. My mom just recently."

"I'm sorry, Tom. They were good people."

He thought about telling Eleanor why he was on the train but finally chose not to. The feeling of intimacy just wasn't there anymore.

They watched as Max and Kristobal rushed off, leaving the stunned couple beached in their wake.

"Where should we start?" asked Eleanor finally.

Tom rose and pointed at Julie and Steve. "That looks like a good place."

They settled down with them after Tom had introduced Eleanor. Steve and Julie took turns explaining, in awed tones, what Max Powers had proposed.

"He's going to cater the whole event, with decorations, and even have some sort of music too," said Julie.

"And he's paying for everything," added a relieved-sounding Steve. "He said he'd work it out with Amtrak. I don't know what they'll say to all that though."

"Max usually gets his way," opined Eleanor.

"Is he really the famous movie director?" asked Julie.

"He is," answered Eleanor. "And his heart is almost as big as his ego," she added.

"I feel like we just won the lottery," said Steve, as he gripped his bride-to-be's hand.

"Well, it sounds like you did," Tom commented.

"Where in Virginia are you from?" Eleanor asked Julie.

"You probably never heard of it, Dickenson County."

"My dad went to Clintwood High. Two of my aunts live in Grundy, Virginia."

"Oh my gosh!" said Julie. "I've never met anybody who even knew where it was."

"I grew up on a little farm in eastern Kentucky that would make Clintwood seem like a metropolis." Eleanor looked at them both. "I think it's very brave what you're doing."

"We don't feel very brave," said Steve, laughing nervously and glancing at Julie.

"If you really love each other, you'd be surprised what you can accomplish."

Julie gripped Eleanor's hand. "You came from where I did, and look how you turned out. It drives me crazy that his parents can't see that it doesn't matter where you're from, it's where you're going."

Eleanor said, "You're not marrying Steve's parents. And it may be that they think no one is good enough for their son. Moms tend to be that way especially. But give them time, and you may see them come around. If they don't it's their loss, and it's your life together."

"Growing up there made me so strong. I feel I can do anything," said Julie.

"Having to depend on yourself for just about all you have, it does make you strong, especially when people never bother to get to know you, just label you dumb country." Eleanor added, "But that just makes it all the sweeter when you prove them wrong."

Julie looked very determined. "You got that right. And I've got a long list of people who'll be getting that comeuppance."

Tom nudged Steve. "Have you been practicing your 'Yes, Dear' and 'No, Dear' lines? I think you're going to need bunches of them with this woman."

Father Kelly walked in and inquired as to their availability in the lounge downstairs, where a high-stakes poker game was taking place. They adjourned from further talk of nuptials and repaired to the adult section of the bar car.

chapter thirteen

Tom had walked into many poker war zones in his life; these places were usually inhabited by cagey, stone-faced, underpaid journalists looking to supplement their income as they hunkered in their paper-lined foxholes. While a beat reporter for the *Territorial Enterprise*, Sam Clemens had also engaged in many gentlemanly games of cards. He routinely carried his old Navy revolver with him during these "friendly" matches, presumably in case a participant drew the wrong conclusion from a high card placed in error in one's boot or sleeve.

On the surface, the group in the lounge car looked fairly innocent, but these were the types one had to watch out for, Tom knew. The most money he'd ever lost in a game of cards was at a dear little convent in a foreign location he absolutely refused to disclose out of sheer embarrassment. The Mother Superior had drawn to four consecutive inside straights, a record surely unmatched in poker history. Tom drew some comfort from the fact that no cardplayer, however exalted, could hope to best an opponent who had the Almighty behind her.

Since the "chips" being used in the game were actually potato chips, they bought several bags of Doritos, and on a dare from Tom, Eleanor even purchased one of Tyrone's Boiler Room concoctions. The ebony Elvis and the journalist shared a triumphant look until the woman downed it in one swig, wiped her mouth with the back of her hand, and sat down to play some cards.

"That just ain't human. You telling me you know that lady?" Tyrone whispered.

"I'm not sure," Tom replied.

They raced through poker, blackjack, hearts, spades, gin rummy, euchre, and other assorted family entertainment, and finished with about as many Doritos as they'd started with, plus lots of material for both Tom's story and Eleanor's movie. There was one gent with six fingers who won far more than he lost. Tom was guessing it had something to do with that extra digit and perhaps an ace or two secreted there somehow, though he couldn't prove it beyond a reasonable doubt, which was the prevailing legal standard on board, he was informed. There was also an obnoxious type who snorted every time he took a pot, belittled his neighbors' cardplaying errors, and generally made himself a nuisance. Eleanor leaned over at one point and whispered into Tom's ear, "That guy gets butchered in the film's first act."

As they rose to leave, Tom pulled out his Havanas and pointed at Father Kelly, who'd proved himself a nimble cardplayer as well; his explanation was: "Too much free time in the rectory during my formative years in the priesthood."

"The smoking lounge beckons, Father."

Eleanor followed them, though Tom knew she didn't smoke, at least she hadn't when he'd known her. He glanced at her with a questioning expression.

She shrugged. "Max is the boss. In for a dime, in for a dollar."

There were ventilation fans inside the lounge that were theoretically supposed to rid the atmosphere of any smoke within a short period of time. However, judging from the thickened atmosphere, the machines had given up the fight and gone home with their blades between their legs.

Most of the seats were taken, but they found three near the back. Some of the smokers had placed a piece of plywood on top of one of the ashtray stands and were playing checkers on this makeshift table. Another group was discussing the upcoming football playoffs. Although the sign on the door had said no food or drink allowed, everyone had something they were munching or sipping. One man said that it was okay unless the conductor came by, and then everyone with contraband should hide it post-haste. Tom looked at the beer bottles, superlarge ice-cream sandwiches, and big jugs of homemade concoctions that didn't quite look like Kool-Aid and wondered exactly how those items were to be effectively concealed.

They sat and attempted to soak it all in without too much damage to their lungs. Father Kelly and Tom coaxed their cigars to life while Eleanor sat back and closed her eyes.

"Tired?" Tom asked between puffs. "You must still be on West Coast time."

"Actually, I spent a week in D.C. before we started."

"What's in Washington?"

She never opened her eyes. "Somebody."

Tom lowered his Havana and let his gaze idly wander over the people in the smoking lounge. *Somebody.* Eleanor had somebody. Well, why shouldn't she have somebody? She was still young and smart and beautiful and probably rich with all her movie work. And he had somebody, sort of. What was her name again? Linda? No, Lelia. He didn't take that memory lapse as a good sign.

Tom's pursuit of Eleanor had commenced the moment he saw her. As she'd walked by that first time on campus it seemed everything slowed, and that it was just the two of them in the whole world. It wasn't just her beauty, it was all of the usual suspects: how she carried herself, how she spoke, how she looked you in the eye and really listened to what you had to say. Yet it was more than that even. As Agnes Joe had said, Tom didn't care if he ate, slept, or even breathed so long as Eleanor was around. And her temper—and she had a well-nourished one—exerted its own attraction. Her opinions were uniquely her own, and she would draw and fire them off with deadly accuracy and unwavering impunity. Almost always an eruption was followed by the gentle touch of her hand and eventually her lips against his, for he'd at last won her heart over the strenuous attacks and counterattacks of several serious rivals.

Tom's musings were suddenly interrupted by the man's appearance at the doorway. He was six-feet-four, and slender, about twenty-five or so, and appraised them all with a very smug look. He had chic beard stubble, faded jeans, and a tattered belt. Yet his silk shirt was an expensive designer production and his hair had the appearance of being professionally tousled and his jeans seemed expertly if prematurely aged. A fake slob, Tom deduced, who obviously thought way too much of himself.

Under one arm the man was carrying a chessboard and box of chesspieces. Tom watched as he methodically set up shop. Eleanor's eyes were now open, and she studied the intruder as well. Over the next hour he vanquished all comers. As Father Kelly explained it, lots of amateur chessplayers rode the rails. "There's something about a train that brings them out, particularly in the smoking car," he said. "I've even heard that chess grand masters ride the train incognito and play anyone who wants to, just to stay sharp. And they occasionally lose too."

Why would chess grand masters have to travel *incognito*? wondered Tom. Yet he kept his mouth shut and watched. The guy was good, really good. The average match time was only ten minutes. With each defeat, as his foe stalked off in disgrace, he'd laugh. Laugh! And then call out in a loud, condescending voice, "Next victim!" If Tom had had any chance of beating the guy, he'd have gone for it, but even checkers taxed him too much.

After a while Father Kelly left. Tom didn't expect to see him back because the priest had imbibed quite a bit, and the smoke chaser had apparently finished him off. "If I had to conduct Mass right now, I'm not sure I could. I'm not even sure I could tell you how many components there are to the Holy Trinity, even with a clue or two."

Tom bid him goodnight and then watched as Eleanor rose and challenged the chess king, whose name, they'd learned, was Slade. She was the only woman in the smoking car, and thus all eyes turned toward her as she sat down across from the hated one. As she made the first move, Slade's expression was so confident that Tom wanted to make him eat a couple of rooks as penance. He hadn't even known that Eleanor played chess, and then it came back to him. When they'd lived in Israel, they'd become friends with a rabbi who was an exceptional chessplayer. He'd taught Eleanor one strategy—only one—yet it was almost foolproof. You'd be able to tell in about three moves if your opponent had bitten on it. And it seemed to work best against the most talented players, particularly if they were overconfident.

Three moves later, Tom saw just the tiniest hint of a smile from Eleanor and he found himself smiling conspiratorially in return. Four moves after that the mighty Slade and his tousled hair was staring in disbelief. Eleanor had his black king in check with nowhere to flee except into the embrace of her white queen or bishop. A hoarse cheer rang through the black-lunged smokers and they even gave her a standing ovation. Spurred on by drink and a confluence of emotions, Tom clapped until his hands were blood red. Slade grabbed his chessboard and pieces and stalked out, muttering something about beginner's luck. If Eleanor hadn't had *somebody* in Washington, Tom probably would have kissed her.

As he stared at her, all sorts of possibilities raced through his mind. He was twenty-five again, and he and Eleanor were taking on the world, one cover story at a time. Nothing was beyond them.

He'd hold this wonderful feeling for about four more minutes, and then it would be gone.

chapter fourteen

The figure who entered Tom's sleeper was dressed in black, and intent on plucking an expensive-looking pen; then Father Kelly's silver cross was swiped. After that the thief flitted to the other first-class sleeper suites, pinching Max's gold-plated money clip, Eleanor's silver brush, and Kristobal's four-hundred-dollar designer sunglasses. The last target for now was Gordon Merryweather's suite, where the thief stole the lawyer's fancy watch, cash, and Palm Pilot. The crimes took all of ten minutes, for the person was much practiced in the art of felony. No one observed the thefts, and by the time Regina walked down the corridor to refill the coffeepot at the head of the stairs, the person was gone, together with the loot.

The first train robbery in the United States occurred in Indiana in 1866 along the old Ohio and Mississippi Railroad line. The two robbers, ex–Civil War soldiers cast helplessly adrift after Lee's noble surrender, were quickly caught. Numerous robberies followed by other criminals, but the rise of the well-funded Pinkerton Detective Agency—whose men, per capita, wielded their firearms far better than the men they hunted, which included Jesse and Frank James' gang—soon put an end to that lucrative line of larceny. The thief on the Capitol Limited had made a decent haul without one shot having been fired. Poor Jesse would have no doubt been envious.

Tom and Eleanor stood outside the smoker car taking deep breaths to clear their lungs.

"You nailed that guy. The look on his face, it was beautiful." He gave her a hug that she only partially returned. "Thank God for a chessplaying rabbi in Tel Aviv. What was his name?"

"I don't remember," she said quietly.

He looked at her and all his fine spirits melted away, replaced by something vastly harder. *Rabbi Somebody, Tel Aviv, the scene of the final meeting—final bloody battle was more like it.*

He shouldn't do it, he knew he shouldn't do it, but he was going to anyway; it was as though his mind and tongue were wired for bad timing opportunities. "Can you tell me now, since you've had all these years to think about it?"

"Tell you what?"

"Oh, I don't know, why don't we start with why you walked out on me all those years ago? That seems like a good enough place, and we'll work forward from there."

"You're saying you don't know why?"

"How could I? Not one thing you said made any sense."

"Because you weren't listening, as usual. That's not my problem."

"That's a crock and you know it."

"I don't have to stand here and listen to you raving."

"You're right. Sit down on the floor and I'll keep going. I've had years to prepare. In fact, I can keep raving until the good old Southwest Chief runs into the Pacific Ocean three days from now!"

"I knew this would happen—as soon as I saw you, I knew it would. You haven't changed a bit."

"What exactly did you expect, Ellie?"

"It's *Eleanor*."

"Forgive me, I was living in the past for a moment, when you were just Ellie."

"You're so incredibly maddening, so off base. Don't you ever take off those enormous blinders you wear and see the world as it actually is?"

"I've seen plenty of the world, far more than most, and I wasn't wearing rose-colored glasses during any of it!"

"That wasn't my point. You saw what you wanted to see, that was all."

"Was it another guy, was that it?"

Eleanor rolled her eyes and waved dismissively. "Why do men always think it's another guy when it's usually men who cheat?"

"I never cheated on you! Ever!"

"I never said you did. And I can say the same."

"Then why did you walk out on me?"

She shook her head wearily. "Tom, if you don't understand why by now, there's nothing I can say that would clear it up for you."

He stared at her. "I'm sorry, I'm sort of rusty on female-encrypted speech. Can you help me out here? What the hell did you just say?"

She shook her head. "Even after all these years you still haven't managed to accomplish it."

"Accomplish what?"

"Growing up!" she snapped.

Before he could answer, they heard singing. The next minute the pair watched as a group of Christmas carolers, composed of both train crew and passengers, gathered around them. Tyrone had taken a break from the bar and was leading the pack with a hearty rendition of "I'll Be Home for Christmas," though in respect for the more prim members of the caroling company, he kept his pelvic gyrations within strict statutory limits. Agnes Joe was in the back, carrying the entire bass section all by herself.

"You two want to join in?" asked Tyrone. "A lady who can slam back a Boiler Room like that is a lady I need to get to know."

Eleanor stalked off, arms folded across her chest.

Tyrone stared after her and then looked back at Tom. "Hey, man, was it something I said?"

"No, Tyrone, it was something *I* said." And then Tom walked off too.

He thought about going after Eleanor and resuming the "discussion" but couldn't find the energy, and he was afraid too, more of what he would say than she. On the way back to his compartment he heard laughter drifting up from the lower level of his sleeper car. Laughs—he could use some right now. He hurried down the stairs and headed right, following the sounds. These were less expensive sleeping accommodations, smaller than his and with no shower, but each compartment had a toilet and a drop-down sink. At the end of the corridor, he saw Regina and the Tarot card lady standing outside one compartment and talking with someone inside the space.

Regina saw him and waved him over. When he walked up he saw that there was an older woman sitting on a seat in the compartment. Then he noticed the wheelchair folded up and placed against the facing chair situated against the other wall. He turned and studied the Tarot card lady. She still wore her multi-colored headdress, but she'd taken off the dumbbell shoes and was in slippers. That made her about four inches shorter, and she turned out to be rather petite. Up close she had intensely lumi-nous blue eyes filled with both mischief and charm, and a warm smile. He noted that the compartment across the hall had a brightly colored beaded door, where the curtain had been pulled back and secured. He also thought he smelled incense, although he assumed that would be strictly against Amtrak policy.

"I'm assuming those are your digs," he said to her.

"Why, Mr. Langdon, you have psychic powers of your own," she said with a throaty laugh.

"How did you—" He stopped and looked at Regina. "Okay, no aliens need apply. You told her."

Regina said, "Meet Drusella Pardoe, Tom, and you don't have to tell Drusella anything, she already knows it."

Drusella put out a dainty hand. "My good friends call me Misty. And I already know that we're going to be good friends, so you just go ahead and call me that."

Misty had a Southern accent augmented by something a lit-tle spicier. "New Orleans?" he said.

"By way of Baltimore. Very good, Tom." She drew closer to him, and he concluded that the incense smell was actually Misty's perfume.

"Misty used to be a CPA there in Baltimore," said Regina.

"I found I had a gift for numbers, and gifts should be used for a higher purpose than the avoidance of taxes, don't you think, Tom?"

"Undoubtedly."

"You're right, he *is* cute, Regina," said the wheelchair lady. She was just finishing up her dinner, which was on a tray in front of her.

"I didn't know there was room service on this train," said Tom smiling. "I had to schlepp to the dining car."

"Oh, sure," said the lady, returning the smile. "You just need one of these things, and Regina will bring your meal right to you." She pointed to her wheelchair.

"Where are my manners," said Regina. "Lynette Monroe, Tom Langdon."

Lynette was about sixty-five, with long silver hair and elegant features, still a very attractive woman. She seemed full of good spirits despite her disability.

"I hear you're working with those film people, Tom," said Regina.

"Is that really Max Powers?" asked Lynette. "I love his pictures."

"That woman with them," said Regina, "on the passenger list it said Eleanor Carter, but I think she's really a movie star or something, traveling, you know, incognito. That lady has class. And she's drop-dead gorgeous. Is she a movie star, Tom?"

"Actually, I know her, and she's a writer, not an actress. Although I wouldn't disagree with you about the classy part or the drop-dead-gorgeous thing." Her sanity, however, was not something he could vouch for right now.

"You knew her, like before today?"

"Yes, years ago. We did some reporting together."

"I heard it was a little more than that," said Misty.

Tom stared at her. "What do you know about it?"

"Word travels faster on a train than anywhere else except maybe church. People overhear things. You know"—she drew even closer to Tom—"such tight quarters and everything."

"You mean people eavesdrop," he said.

"Well, that's a less polite way of putting it. My motto is, If you don't have anything good to say about someone, come find Misty and tell her all about it."

"I have to go now, ladies," he said, gently disengaging himself from Misty.

Regina picked up Lynette's tray. "Me too."

As they walked off, Misty called out, "Oh, Tom?"

He turned back, and she fanned out her Tarot cards. "I just have this little premonition that we are connected somehow."

"Misty, he has a girlfriend in LA he's going to visit for Christmas," said Regina. "She does the voice for Cuppy the Magic Beaver on TV."

Tom stared at her, stunned. "How do you know *that*?"

"Agnes Joe told me."

Tom looked at the women, exasperated. "With you two, what do we need the CIA for?"

"Now, Tom," drawled Misty, "a grown man needs a grown woman. Cartoons can't keep you warm at night, sweetie."

"That Misty is a piece of work," Tom said to Regina after they had climbed the stairs.

Regina smiled. "Oh, she's just Southern friendly is all. She doesn't mean any of it. Well, at least not all of it. We're good friends."

"I take it she rides the trains a lot."

"Oh yeah. She tells people their fortune, reads their palms, does the card thing, all for free. She usually takes the Crescent train out to D.C. right on to New Orleans. Has a little shop in the French Quarter just off Jackson Square. I've been there; it's cool."

"And Lynette? That was nice of you to take her food."

"Well, trains aren't easy to get around in a wheelchair. She has MS, but she never lets it get her down. We have a great time."

"You really seem to get to know your passengers."

"They mean a lot to me. Actually—"

"You little thief!"

They looked up, and there was Gordon Merryweather.

"Excuse me?" said Regina.

Merryweather stomped toward them. "I've been robbed, and I'm betting you did it. In fact, you're the only one who could have done it. I'll have your job, and you'll be spending Christmas in prison," he roared.

"Hold on," said Regina, "I don't appreciate your tone, or your accusation. If you're missing something, I'll take a report and we'll file it with the proper authorities."

"Don't read me the little speech," snapped Merryweather. "I want my things back and I want them back right now."

"Well, since I don't know what those things are, or who took them, that would be a little difficult, sir."

Tom stepped between them. "Look, Gord, I'm not a big-time lawyer like you, but I do know that people are innocent until proven guilty. Now unless you have direct evidence of who took your stuff, then you're slandering this woman in front of a witness, and that can be a costly thing, as I'm sure you know."

Merryweather eyed him. "What do you know about slander?"

"Name's Tom Langdon. I'm an investigative reporter. Won a Pulitzer, in fact. I wrote one story about an American lawyer in Russia who was doing some really bad things. He's currently writing his own appellate briefs in prison. And if I've found one thing that's even mightier than legal papers filed in court, it's a story in the newspaper that the whole world can dig their teeth into."

Merryweather took a step back and then snapped at Regina: "My Palm Pilot, two hundred in cash, and my Tag Heuer watch. I want them back before I get off this train in Chicago, or heads will roll." He stalked off.

Both Tom and Regina let out long breaths.

"That guy is a trip," said Tom. "Maybe he heard Max Powers is on board and he's auditioning to play Scrooge."

"My mother taught me to love everybody, but she never met Gordon Merryweather."

"I take it you've run into him before."

"Everybody who works on this train has." She paused. "Thanks, Tom. Thanks a lot."

"Hey, you would have done okay all by yourself."

"Did you really win a Pulitzer?"

"No. Actually I won two."

"Wow, that's impressive."

"Not really. All you have to do is spend your life running from one awful place to another, write about every horrible thing you see. The civilized world reads about it, then forgets it, but pats you on the head for doing it and gives you a reward as appreciation for changing nothing."

He walked off to his compartment to get some sleep.

chapter fifteen

Eleanor went directly to her compartment, closed and locked the door, and drew the privacy curtain. She sat down slowly on the bed, which Regina had made up during the mealtime. She flicked the light off and sat there in the dark. She could now look outside and watch the snow coming down even harder. It didn't bother the Cap much; the train seemed to be going at full tilt. They flashed by clusters of modest houses and then dense woods and the occasional creek cutting through the earth. Smoke curled from the chimneys of the homes, seeming to write secrets in the tangle of snowfall, messages Eleanor couldn't decipher. Her fingers moved across the cold glass, marking her own intricate symbols on the smooth surface. She began to softly cry, placing her head against the pillow Regina had placed in the corner, her body curling up in despair.

As she looked out the window, in her mind's eye, the landscape changed dramatically. As Tom had earlier, she was now transported to Tel Aviv over Christmas. She'd been so happy, and yet so miserable there, that the schizophrenic quality of her existence had come close to driving her insane. And maybe it had on that Christmas morning when her future with a man she loved had disappeared. She still remembered so vividly how she'd looked back at him as she was heading up the escalator at the airport, and how he'd simply turned away and left her. At that memory, the tears started to spill, and the tight control with which she'd come to lead her life eroded to nothing. She'd thought him incapable of doing this to her ever again, and yet he had, with no more than a look and a word or two. She was helpless.

There was a knock on her door and she tensed. She wasn't ready to see him again, not right now, possibly not ever.

"Eleanor? You're not sleeping, are you?"

She'd been holding her breath, and she let it out in relief. It was Max, not Tom.

"Just a minute."

She put on the lights, wiped her face with a wet towel, and reached for her brush to swipe at her hair; however, her brush wasn't where she had left it. She ran her fingers through her hair instead and opened the door.

Max quickly stepped in and closed the door behind him.

"You okay? You don't look very good."

"Probably just tired."

"Well, it's all set up, the wedding stuff. I talked with the Amtrak folks, they had no problem with it."

"That's wonderful," Eleanor said quietly.

"So how's it going with Tom? You guys getting some good stuff?"

"Great material. I'll be putting some notes together soon."

"It's that pioneer spirit. You don't take a train because you want to get somewhere fast. You take it for the journey itself. To be surprised."

"Well, I've certainly been surprised on this trip."

He looked at her tenderly. "Life is full of funny coincidences. I went to get some lunch at Paulo's once—you know, that really expensive Italian place over near Rodeo Drive? Well, I walk in and who's there? Not one, not two, but all three of my exwives."

"That's amazing. They were all there separately?"

"Oh no. Apparently they meet every Tuesday and talk about how awful I was to be married to. Sort of like a book club, only its purpose is to crucify yours truly. Of course, they never mention that the alimony I pay each of them allows them to sit on their fashionably dressed derrières in a five-star restaurant for four hours and complain about me." He looked at her. "You want to tell me about this Langdon fellow? If you ask me, it seems you two were a lot more than reporting colleagues."

Eleanor nervously played with her hands. "Do you remember when we first started working together, you asked me what made me want to write, what power drove me?"

"Sure I remember. I ask all my writers that."

"Well, Tom Langdon is the answer to that question."

"I don't understand."

"I loved him, Max. Loved him with everything I had to give. When it ended there was this void, this hole in me as large as a dead star. The only outlet I had was the written word."

"Lucky for me, not so good for you," Max said quietly. "So you loved him, he clearly still cares for you, what happened?"

She stood up and paced in the small area while he watched.

She finally said, "Two people can care for each other but not want the same things. Then it doesn't work, no matter how much you love each other."

"So what does Tom want?"

"I'm not sure he even knows. I know what he doesn't want: to be tied down anywhere, or by anyone."

"And do you know what you want?"

"Who knows, Max? Who really knows what they want?"

"Well, I guess I'm not the best person to ask—my interests keep changing. But I guess that's part of life. Maybe to be happy, maybe that's what we're all looking for. And we find it in lots of different ways."

"*If* you find it. Many people never do, and maybe I'm one of them."

"Eleanor, you're a smart, talented, successful, beautiful woman in the prime of your life."

"And maybe that woman doesn't need a man in her life to be complete," she said.

He shrugged. "Maybe not. I'm not saying everybody has to be married to be happy."

"So what *are* you saying?"

The director rose. "I'm just saying, Don't assume you *don't* need someone in your life to be happy either."

Max left and went to Kristobal's compartment, where he observed his assistant tearing his room apart.

"What are you doing?" asked Max.

"Looking for my sunglasses."

"Sunglasses! Look out the window, it's nighttime."

"I mean they're missing."

"So buy another pair."

"These cost four hundred dollars!"

Max looked at him intently. "Exactly how much do I pay you, Kristobal?"

The young man swallowed hard and eyed his boss nervously. "I saved up for a whole year to buy them."

"Uh-huh. Look, the wedding is a go."

"Terrific, sir. You're a genius."

"So you keep telling me. Now you've got your assignments. I don't want any screwups."

"When have I ever let you down, Mr. Powers?"

"I know, but see, nobody's that good, and I just don't want the first time you do fail to be this time. Okay?"

"I understand, sir."

"You're a good kid, but when we get to LA I'm cutting your pay."

"Why, sir?" asked an astonished Kristobal.

"Because even I don't spend four hundred bucks on sunglasses, that's why."

Tom lay on his bed and studied the underside of the bunk above him. He'd fallen asleep for a while but was now wide awake. He got up and took out his notebook, but couldn't find his pen. He searched everywhere, but it wasn't in his compartment. The pen had significant meaning to him. Eleanor had given it to him when they'd first gone overseas together. He finally gave up and, hearing music, stepped into the corridor. The song was coming from Agnes Joe's compartment. The door was open and the light on. He moved to the threshold and cautiously peeked in. Agnes Joe was seated fully dressed, and on the fold-down table next to her was an old phonograph she'd plugged into the outlet. He recognized the song. It was "Silent Night." Agnes Joe looked up, saw him, and seemed a little embarrassed at being discovered.

"I hope the music isn't disturbing you."

"Hey, what better than Christmas carols during Christmas week?"

"Singing with Tyrone puts me in the mood. I bring this little phonograph with me everywhere I go. It belonged to my mother. You're welcome to come on in and listen."

He hesitated for just a moment but then sat down on the couch. The woman looked like she could use some company.

She eyed him keenly. "Regina told me how you helped her out with the nasty lawyer. You did a good deed tonight, Tom. Played guardian angel."

"Well, they say there are more guardian angels during the Christmas season than at any other time."

"I've never heard that. Did you just make that up?"

"Actually, I did, I think."

"It's a nice thought, though."

They sat and listened to several more uplifting carols. The compartment smelled of lilac soap and was very neat. Tom noted a very full duffel bag wedged in between the chair and the wall, with a blanket partially covering it. When he looked up, Agnes Joe was staring intently at him, a look of sadness on her face. Just then a family of four—mom, dad, and two children—passed down the corridor. They were laughing, and the boy did a little jig and almost fell down.

"Trains are nice over Christmas. People are in good moods. It's really a great way for families to travel together," said Agnes Joe.

"So how come you're not spending Christmas with your family?"

"A girl has to be asked to the party, doesn't she?"

"So you and your daughter don't get along?"

"I get along fine with her. She seems to have a problem with me."

"I'm sorry, Agnes Joe. I really am."

"I've got lots of friends on the train though."

"Like that lady in the lounge car said, friends are friends, but family is family."

She smiled. "Pauline the knitter? What does she know about anything? And that was the ugliest sweater I've ever seen."

She paused and said, "I say that your family is where you find it. You just have to look. Like you."

"What do you mean, like me?"

"That film lady, Eleanor. She's the Eleanor from your past, isn't she? The one love of your life?"

"We're not even friends now."

"But you could be. And a lot more."

He shook his head. "No. Too late."

"You're wrong there." Ignoring his puzzled look, she said, "I've seen enough in this world to know that two people who can make each other that miserable must love each other a lot."

He thanked her for the musical interlude and went back to his compartment. However, he didn't intend to waste his time on something that clearly would never happen. He'd lost Ellie once and it had devastated him; the aftershocks still pounded him all these years later. He was never going to chance being that hurt again. The past was dead, resurrection out of the question. He had reconciled himself to this fate when Father Kelly popped his head in.

"You haven't seen a silver cross lying around, have you?"

"Why, did you lose one?"

"Well, I can't seem to find it."

"That's strange. I'm missing a pen."

The priest shrugged and walked off as Tom's cell phone rang. He checked his watch and saw it was after midnight. He clicked the phone's answer button.

"Hello?" he said.

It was Lelia calling from LA.

"I've been tracking you on the Internet. According to the schedule you're in Pittsburgh. Right?"

Tom looked out the window. The train was slowing and he was trying to see a station sign. A few moments later, he saw it:

Connellsville, PA. They were far from Pittsburgh. They must have stopped again while he'd been asleep.

"So you're in Pittsburgh, right?" she asked again.

"Yep, you can see the stadium from here. Remember those great Steeler teams of the seventies?"

"I don't follow baseball. I just know you're supposed to be in Pittsburgh."

"The Steelers are a football team. And do you realize it's after midnight my time?"

"You can't possibly be sleeping on the train—isn't it far too noisy and bumpy?"

"Actually it's a very nice ride, and I *was* sleeping," he lied.

"You can set up right over there, Erik," Lelia said to someone.

"Erik, who's Erik?" asked Tom.

"He's my FBTT."

"FBTT? Sounds like a disease."

"Full-body therapeutic technician. It's all the rage out here now."

"Oh, I'm sure it is. So what is old Erik going to do for you in the privacy of your own home?"

"My lower back, hamstrings, and he's going to give me a pedicure too."

"Lower back and hamstrings. Anything in between those points?"

"What?"

"Are you clothed during this process?"

"Don't be silly. I have a towel on."

"Oh, gee, that's a relief. Look, why do you need this guy to come to your house to do all this? I thought you belonged to that fancy spa."

"My back was hurting, and my toenails really needed some emergency work: I'm wearing open-toed high heels tomorrow."

"Yeah, I guess that does qualify as a crisis. So why not try a hot-water bottle and nail clippers? That seems to work for the rest of America."

"I'm not the rest of America."

"How do you know this Erik?"

"He's my kickboxing instructor. He's an FBTT on the side."

While there were many legitimate kickboxing enthusiasts, when Tom had gone to one of her kickboxing sessions in LA he had found it inhabited mostly by accountants, lawyers, actors, and chefs who paraded around in designer spandex, flailing at rubber bad guys with their feet and fists. Two or three modestly rowdy kindergartners could have vanquished the whole lot of them.

"The six-foot-four-inch blond-haired, blue-eyed Adonis guy from Sweden, that's Erik? That guy is in your house right now while you're in a tiny towel?"

"Jealousy: I like that, it's healthy for a relationship. And Erik is Norwegian."

"Fine, could you put Norway Erik on, please?"

"Why?"

"I'd like to make an appointment with him for when I'm out there. I think my back is going to need some work after this train ride. I'm assuming he does both women and men?"

"Yes, he does. But you have to promise you won't be mean. I know how you can get sometimes. Promise?"

"Absolutely. Hey, my back is hurting and I like a little FBTT as much as the next person." He heard her passing the phone over with some words of explanation.

"*Ja*, this is Erik, may I help you?" came the voice of the Norwegian Adonis.

"Erik? Tom Langdon. Before I make an appointment I was

just wondering if you have an infectious disease disclosure policy."

"Excuse me? This thing I do not know."

"Infectious disease disclosure policy. It's all the rage everywhere, except possibly where you are. Let me explain it in really simple terms. Since you work with people's bodies—like Lelia in the towel there—and you come in contact with human skin, you run the risk of being infected with some serious and contagious diseases, which you could then potentially pass on to other clients, like me. So I wanted to know what safety precautions you take and also what disclosure procedures you have. For example, I'm sure Lelia has informed you about her hepatitis Z condition and the serious risks associated with it. I was wondering how you disclose that to your other clients."

"Hepatitis!"

"Not to worry. Although there are, of course, no cures, the new drug therapies work wonders, and the side effects are fairly limited: nausea, loss of hair, bloating, impotency, that sort of thing. In fact, death only occurs about half the time, if it's caught early enough."

Tom heard the phone drop and then feet running away on Lelia's highly polished hardwood floors. Then he listened as Lelia frantically called out, "Erik, Erik, where are you going? Erik, come back!"

After a door had slammed, Tom heard the phone being picked up. He could almost envision smoke pouring forth from the woman who had made Cuppy the Magic Beaver and Sassy the Super Squirrel the favorites of millions.

"What exactly did you say to him? And I mean *exactly*!"

"We were just talking about my appointment and what I was expecting and then he was gone."

"I distinctly heard him say hepatitis!"

"Hepatitis? Lelia, I said *gingivitis*. I asked him if he had gingivitis, because my old masseuse did, and I have to tell you, it was really not enjoyable, you know, breathing that really bad breath for an hour. I guess Erik's English isn't that good."

"I don't believe you, not for an instant, Tom Langdon. Do you realize what you've done? My back is killing me, and what about my toenails?"

"Perhaps Tylenol and an emery board?"

"This is not funny," she yelled.

"Look, I'm beat and the cell reception is bad here. I'll call you when we get into Pittsburgh."

"What? I thought you *were* in Pittsburgh."

Tom slapped his forehead at this gaffe. Under enormous pressure, he struck on what seemed a brilliant plan. "Uh, Lelia?" He tapped the phone with his finger. "Lelia, you're breaking up. I can't hear you."

"Tom, don't you dare try to pull that—"

He spoke slowly and in a very loud voice, as though to a hearing-impaired idiot:

"IF . . . YOU . . . CAN . . . HEAR . . . ME . . . I'LL . . . CALL . . . YOU . . . WHEN . . . WE . . . GET . . . INTO . . . CHICAGO."

He clicked the off button and sat back. The phone rang again, but he didn't answer it. It went to voice mail and then it rang again. He finally just turned it off. Well, that had gone reasonably okay.

In his time, Mark Twain was probably the most often-quoted person in America, and one of his famous sayings came from a miscommunication that had led the world to believe the great man had passed away. When asked to comment on his *alleged* demise, Twain had mischievously opined that the news of his death had been greatly exaggerated. Tom had a feeling that if he were unfortunate enough to be within Lelia's grasp right that minute, there'd be no one capable of overembellishing the circumstances of his violent death.

As the Cap began to move, he settled back, turned off the light, and took up sentinel at the window. The train slowed once more, however, and as he squinted into the darkness, he could make out the tombstones of a small cemetery the train was now idling beside.

Unnerved by the proximity of so many lost souls, Tom rose and went strolling once more. He had never done so much walking as he had since stepping foot on this train.

chapter sixteen

Tom poured a cup of coffee from the snack station near the stairs and headed for the lounge car. Most compartments were dark at this late hour, and he saw no one in the corridors. It could be him alone on this ten-car train chugging on. The dining room was also quiet and dark, the service crew long since having gone to their quarters in the dormitory car, he assumed. In the lounge area the lights had also been turned down, and it was empty as far as he could tell. The train started up again and he balanced himself against one of the seat backs. He recoiled when his hand touched skin, and he almost spilled his coffee.

Eleanor looked up at him. She seemed as startled as he. She was also holding a cup of coffee.

"God," she said, "I didn't even hear you come in."

He eyed the coffee. "Still have insomnia too?" They'd both suffered from it, perhaps because of too many time zones and too much travel, and too many horror stories covered that came back to torture them in their sleep.

She rubbed her temples. "Funny, I thought I was over it. It seems to have come back very recently."

"Okay, I get the hint. I can find another place to drink my coffee and mull my truly limitless future."

"No, I can leave," she said.

"Look," said Tom, "we're both adults. I think we can coexist on something as big as a train, at least for a little while."

"That's actually very mature of you."

"I have my moments."

They were both silent as the Cap picked up speed again, beating the tracks at nearly eighty miles an hour. Darkness had never flown by with such purpose, Tom thought.

"I've been wondering why you're really on this train," Eleanor said. "You were always into getting there the fastest way possible."

"I told you, I'm doing a story about a train trip, which is a little difficult to accomplish unless you actually ride one."

"Is that all?"

"Why shouldn't it be?"

"Because I know you too well, I suppose. You don't have to tell me. It's not like you owe me an explanation."

He thought about the double meaning of that statement— as in: she didn't owe him an explanation either—but decided to let it pass. Instead he told her about his father's wish and what he was doing about it, not that his dad would know.

"I think maybe your father *will* know," she said quietly.

"Okay now, being the suspicious, paranoid, conspiracy-theorist investigative-reporter type, I have to tell you, your being on this train seems like one heck of a coincidence."

"We were supposed to be taking the Capitol Limited yesterday." She looked at her watch. "Well, since it's already tomorrow, I mean the day before yesterday. But then apparently Max's plans changed, he got into D.C. a day later, and we had to take the train you were on."

Tom shrugged. "So maybe it's a coincidence."

"Trust me, if I'd known you'd be on this train, I wouldn't have been."

"So it was really that bad, huh?"

"Look, we didn't work out, it happens to millions of people. Some folks just aren't the marrying kind."

"I was married once."

Eleanor was clearly stunned by this. "What?"

"Well, it was over so fast—the marriage, I mean—that I barely remember it."

Eleanor rose, her fury barely contained. "Well, I'm glad you loved a woman enough to actually ask her, however long it lasted."

"Ellie, it wasn't like that, it was the worst decision of my life—"

She turned and walked out.

He watched her leave as the Cap came to a stop.

He rose and leaned against the window. He said quietly, to himself, *Actually it was the second worst decision of my life.* Then he said out loud, "What the hell is going on? I could've walked to Chicago faster."

"What is going on," said a voice, "is that a freight train is on the tracks up ahead blocking the Cap's way, that's what."

Tom looked in the direction the voice had come from. In the far corner of the lounge car, in the darkness, was the silhouette of a man. As the figure rose and seemed to float toward him, Tom thought he was about to encounter the Ghost of Christmas Past, who was coming to foretell his future of doom.

When the fellow came into the small wash of ambient light from the window, Tom let out his breath. He was tall in stature and lean, salt-and-pepper-haired, about sixty or so, with hand-some, chiseled features; he clearly would have turned many a young lady's head in his prime. He was dressed in a white button-down shirt, tie, and dress slacks. He was also wearing what looked to be a conductor's cap.

"Do you work on the train?" asked Tom. He was looking at the man's hat.

"No," he said, taking off his cap and shaking Tom's hand. "Although I used to. Retired now. Name's Herrick Higgins."

Tom introduced himself and they sat down.

"You say there's a freight train up ahead? So why don't they get it to move out of the way?"

"Well," said Higgins, "the easiest explanation is that Amtrak doesn't own the track, the freight company does, so freight takes priority over people."

"Are you serious?"

"Amtrak doesn't own any of the tracks it runs on, except along the Northeast Corridor and other bits here and there. When the private train companies gave up passenger rail, they weren't about to give up their tracks. You see, rail freight is very profitable, hauling people isn't. Amtrak has arrangements with a whole hob-gob of folks. And sometimes it's a logistical headache."

"No offense, but that doesn't sound like a great way to run a railroad," commented Tom.

"Amtrak was never appropriated the funds to either buy the tracks or build new ones. Its only choice was to deal with the owners. So if a freight train gets backed up or derails, we wait. Happens all the time, and we really can't do anything about it. Sorry, I keep saying 'we'; old habits die hard."

"How long were you with Amtrak?"

"Sometimes it seems like my whole life. I was actually

around when it started up in '71. Been a railroad man since I took my first breath, just like my father was. He worked the UP, the Union Pacific."

Higgins looked at Tom's cup of coffee and smiled. "Sleep comes slowly if at all on the first night on a train, but the second night, you'll sleep through anything, trust me." He looked out the window. "This route is laid over what used to be a turnpike. George Washington owned stock in the turnpike company. I often wondered what the father of our country would say, seeing the old Cap running up and down that same path. But maybe not much longer. Future doesn't look too good for long-distance passenger trains. Government's talking about busting Amtrak up, privatizing, spinning off the Northeast Corridor."

"Well, America is such a large country, train travel just doesn't make a lot of sense."

Higgins eyed him. "You're right, train travel as presently configured in this country doesn't make a lot of sense. Amtrak folks are some of the most creative and dedicated souls there are; they have to be to get by on shoestring budgets and old equipment. They say rail travel is a financial drain. Well, I wonder what it's worth to the environment to get ten million polluting cars off the highway or a bunch of noisy jets from over the top of people's homes. Did you know that the United States spends more on cleaning roadkill off the highways than it does on passenger rail?"

"True, but passenger rail *is* subsidized, the airlines aren't."

"Did the airlines build the airports? Do they pay for air traffic control? Fact is, the airlines have been given tens of billions of dollars by Uncle Sam and they still barely make any money. The highways get over eighty cents out of every transportation dollar and the result is we keep building roads and we keep buying gas-guzzling cars to drive on those roads and we're one big traffic jam and dependent on foreign oil. With just a one-penny-per-gallon fuel-tax fund, Amtrak could build a world-class passenger-rail system, but the government won't give it to us. Ironically, this country was built by rail. Connected the east to the west and made America the center of the world."

Higgins put his hat back on and adjusted it with a practiced hand. "I hear that they're working on a commercial aircraft that will be able to fly seventeen thousand miles an hour. You could actually commute daily to Europe for work."

"Well, that has appeal."

"Oh, sure, if you're into the destination only as opposed to the trip itself. It's been my experience that most folk who ride trains could care less where they're going. For them it's the journey itself and the people they meet along the way. You see, at every stop this train makes, a little bit of America, a little bit of *your* country, gets on and says hello. That's why trains are so popular at Christmas. People get on to meet their country over the holidays. They're looking for some friendship, a warm body to talk to. People don't rush on a train, because that's not what trains are for. How do you put a dollar value on that? What accounting line does that go on?"

Higgins fell silent, rubbing his chin and looking at the floor. "I'm not saying that riding the train will change your life, or that passenger rail will be a big moneymaker one day. But no matter how fast we feel we have to go, shouldn't there be room for a train, where you can just sit back, take a breath, and be human for a little while? Just for a little while? Is that so bad?"

chapter seventeen

～

As Tom left Herrick Higgins sitting there in the dark and walked slowly back to the sleeper cars, the Cap started up again. Over the sounds of the rolling train he heard something else. Something that made him race down the hall and clamber down the stairs as he followed the source.

There, sitting against one of the bulkheads was Julie, sobbing, and Eleanor sitting next to her, her arms around the younger woman.

"What's going on?" asked Tom.

"I'm not sure," said Eleanor. "I just found her like this."

In a voice often halted by sobs, Julie explained that Steve's parents had called. They'd found out what the couple was planning and had threatened to both disown and disinherit Steve if he married Julie. Steve, apparently, hadn't been very decisive in telling them he was going ahead with it. In fact, he'd started to waffle so much that Julie and he had had a serious argument and she'd fled her fiancé to cry her heart out.

"Where is he?" asked Tom.

She told him that Steve was back at his compartment.

"Take care of Julie, I'm going to see him."

"What are you going to do?" asked Eleanor.

"Stop him from making the mistake of his life."

Tom stalked off and soon found young Steve staring forlornly out the window of his compartment. For the next ten minutes, he read the younger man the riot act, and voices and tempers flared on both sides, until Tom finally asked, "Do you love her? Do you? It's really that simple."

"Yes," Steve said without hesitation.

"Then you take her without reservation, disclaimer, parental demands, or otherwise. You take her as she is with all her faults, weaknesses, idiosyncrasies, and requirements. You take her without qualification, with no strings attached by anyone else, because that's what loving someone means. If you let that woman out of your life, you're a fool. She's given up as much as you, if not more. This may be the only shot you have at happiness. She may be the one woman in the entire world who you will love and who will make you happy. If you blow it, there's no going back, Steve, trust me."

"I love her, Tom, I really love her."

"Then that's all you need, that's *all* you need."

Steve looked past him. Tom turned, and there was Eleanor and a red-faced Julie. They'd apparently heard pretty much everything. Julie flew to Steve's embrace. Tom stepped out and closed the privacy curtain. As he and Eleanor walked back, she said, "That was a good thing you did. I'm impressed."

"Why sit around and watch someone mess up his life?"

They were going through the darkened dining car when Eleanor gasped, screamed, and then pointed. Under one of the tables, two eyes were peering out at them.

"What is that?"

At that moment a depressed-looking Kristobal came into the diner. When he saw Eleanor, he said, "God, Eleanor, I've been looking everywhere for you. Max is going to cut my salary. Can you talk to him?"

"Why is he cutting your salary?"

"Oh, because of a little misunderstanding about a pair of sunglasses I lost."

"His?"

"No, mine. They cost—"

He looked where Tom was staring and screamed louder than Eleanor had. Jumping on one of the tables, he yelled out, "What is that?"

Tom crept forward for a closer look. About the time he started to smile, Regina had come racing up in her robe.

"What's going on now?" she asked.

Tom was squatting in front of the table where the two eyes still peered out. "We have a visitor here, and I don't think it has a ticket."

When Regina saw the two eyes she drew back and clutched at her robe. "What is it?"

"A stowaway of the reptilian variety. Do you have a flashlight, a cardboard box or a Styrofoam ice chest, and a spare blanket?" asked Tom.

She ran off and was back shortly with an ice chest, blanket, and flashlight. Tom poked a couple of air holes in the chest, then shone the light under the table; that caused the creature to draw back in fear. Tom smiled.

"Okay, Kristobal," he said, "position yourself so that if it takes off, it won't get past you."

Kristobal remained on the table. "Are you insane? I'm not getting anywhere near whatever that is."

Tom looked at Eleanor.

"Okay, okay," she said, "but I'm making no promises." She positioned herself at the other end of the car and looked at Tom expectantly.

"Here we go," he said. Using the blanket, he was able to corral the critter and put it in the chest, but not without it almost getting away. Actually, it had made a beeline for Kristobal. The young man screamed so loudly it was now likely every citizen of Pennsylvania was fully awake.

"What is it?" said Eleanor, who hadn't gotten a good look at it.

"A boa constrictor, a young one, about four or five feet long. Beautiful markings."

Eleanor said, "I have several friends in LA who have them as pets."

Kristobal just stared at her blankly. "This is a nightmare. All I wanted was my sunglasses and my same salary, and instead I'm almost killed by—by that thing!"

Eleanor smiled. "Kristobal, you love animals. You have a pet too."

"A Jack Russell terrier, Eleanor. Don't you dare compare my little Hemingway to that . . . to that serpent from Hell."

Eleanor said, "That's got to be somebody's pet. It's not like boa constrictors are indigenous to Pennsylvania."

Tom agreed. "Probably got out of its cage and was scared to death."

Regina said, "I guess I'll take charge of it and find out whose it is. Can't be too many people on board with a snake. At least I hope not." She didn't look too happy about taking the boa, thought Tom, and then he had a sudden brainstorm to rival anything Max Powers could come up with.

"I tell you what, Regina, let me hold on to him for a bit while you check to see whose it is."

"What are you going to do with it?"

"There's a special friend on board I'd like to show it to."

"Well, okay, but just don't let him loose."

Tom looked over at Kristobal. "You can come down now." The man gingerly crept off the table. "You said you were looking for your sunglasses," said Tom. Kristobal nodded. "Well, my pen is missing, and so is Father Kelly's cross."

"My silver brush has disappeared too," said Eleanor.

"And Mr. Powers said his gold-plated money clip is gone too," added Kristobal.

"And remember that creep Merryweather is missing some stuff," added Tom. "I think we do have a thief on board."

Regina rubbed her forehead. "Why me, Lord, why me?" She wrapped her robe around her more closely and said, "Okay, I'll file a report with the Amtrak police when we get into Chicago. They'll probably need to talk to you, get your statement too. I'm sorry. This is pretty rare, I have to tell you. Most people leave valuables out all the time with no problem. I'm really sorry."

She wearily trudged off, and Eleanor said, "What are you going to do with the boa?"

Tom smiled. "I told you, show it to a special friend."

"Who?"

"You'll see. Come on, Kristobal, we'll need you."

"Look, I'm not getting in trouble over some snake. I never wanted to take the train in the first place. I mean, Mr. Powers has his own jet, for God's sake."

Tom said, "Just do what I say and it'll be fine."

A few minutes later, outside Gordon Merryweather's compartment, someone peered in and saw that the lawyer was lying in the dark solely in his underwear, his brief of choice being the blue bikini style. The man hadn't bothered to lock his door.

Kristobal and Tom crept forward on their knees and placed the ice chest on its side. Tom had explained all about Merryweather to Kristobal, and he'd reluctantly agreed to help. Tom slowly opened the door and lifted the top off the chest. Both men heaved, and the boa went slithering into the compartment. Tom reached in, hit the switch by the sink, filling the room with bright light, and then slid the door closed.

Kristobal had already fled before Merryweather screamed. Eleanor and Tom raced the other way and hid around the corner. They heard frantic banging on the door, and then it flew open and Gordon Merryweather ran out. He fell, picked himself up, fell again, and then half-rolled and half-crawled down the hall. As soon as he was out of sight, Tom coaxed the snake back into the chest quite easily and passed it off to Kristobal. The poor reptile seemed traumatized by the sight of the paunchy lawyer in his indigo-blue skivvies.

Next, Tom and Eleanor raced off and caught up with the frantic Merryweather. When he turned, Eleanor let out a loud scream and covered her eyes. "That's him."

"There's a thing, a snake, enormous, in my room," yelled Merryweather. He grabbed Tom's sleeve. "I'll show you. It's—it's terrible. It almost killed me."

"A snake, on the train?" said Tom skeptically.

Regina came running up. "Now what's going on?"

Tom said, "This guy claims there's a snake in his room. That it almost attacked him." Out of Merryweather's line of sight, he gave her a wink. Regina caught the meaning immediately.

Eleanor said, "I saw this man running by half-naked. I think he looked in on me. I got this gentleman to come with me to see if we could catch him."

"What?" said Regina. "You mean, like a Peeping Tom?"

"Yes. It was terrifying. I thought he was completely naked."

Eleanor groaned and shuddered with the aplomb of a trained actress.

"So that's what the other passengers have been complaining about," said Regina. She turned to the stricken lawyer. "Just what in God's name do you think you're doing? You think because you're some big-shot you can run around nearly naked and peep in on women and scare them? Do you? Well if you do, let me tell you, you don't want to mess around with Amtrak. And when we get to Chicago, you're going to find out why not."

Merryweather sputtered, "I . . . I . . ."

Tom pulled out a notepad and pen. "Is that *Merryweather* just like it sounds? And can I get the exact name of your law firm?"

"There was a snake in my room," wailed Merryweather. "I'm no streaker. I'm not a pervert."

"*Streaker* and *pervert*, those were exactly the words I was looking for," said Tom as he wrote furiously.

"I'll show you, I'll show you." Merryweather pulled them down the hallway to his compartment—as it turned out, his completely *empty* compartment.

Merryweather yelled, "It was here, I swear. At least I think it was."

"Were you sleeping?" asked Eleanor.

"Well, yes, and then the light woke me up."

"Maybe you left the light on, fell asleep, and you just dreamed about a snake. Did you ever think of that?" said Eleanor.

Merryweather looked at her with an expression that said, no, he hadn't really thought of that.

Regina said, "You've disrupted this whole train. I'm calling the conductor. He'll probably want to turn you over to the police in Pittsburgh."

"No, no!" screamed Merryweather. "That will ruin my reputation, my law practice."

"You should have thought about that before you started running around scaring people with those skinny marshmallow legs," said Tom.

"Please, please, I'll do anything. Anything."

Regina, Eleanor, and Tom looked at each other.

"Well, it is Christmas," said Tom, after a lengthy silence broken only by the whimpering litigation virtuoso.

Regina tapped her foot and, giving Merryweather a look of immense disgust, pointed her finger in his face. "Okay, fine, it's late and I'm tired. But let me tell you one thing, lawyer man, if I ever have one more moment's trouble with you *ever*, your butt is in the fire, you understand me? This all comes out, you got it?"

"Absolutely, absolutely." He looked pitifully at Tom and his notepad.

Tom very slowly put it back in his pocket. "Okay, but just because it is Christmas. But remember, I can write this story at any time, and I've got witnesses. Okay?"

"Yes, yes, I understand. Okay."

Regina snapped, "Now get some clothes on."

Merryweather raced inside his compartment and slid the door shut.

"Okay," said Regina, as she ceremoniously tapped Tom and Eleanor on the shoulders, "you're now officially honorary members of the Capitol Limited Club. I don't know exactly how you brought that man down, but I've been waiting a long time to see it."

"Hey," said Tom, "all you need is a boa constrictor, some accomplices, and a twelve-million-pound train, mix, and bake."

A bit later Regina located the owners of the snake and returned it, with instructions to keep it under wraps for the rest of the trip and to say nothing about its presence on the train.

As Tom and Eleanor walked back to their compartments,

he chuckled. "That felt like old times. Remember all the practical jokes we pulled when we were overseas and things were slow and we were bored?"

"No, I remember all the practical jokes *you* played. And I don't remember being bored very much. Overstimulated was more like it."

He stopped and so did Eleanor. "Come on, you have to admit, it was great, wasn't it?"

"It was different," was as far as Eleanor would go.

He said hesitantly, "You know, I'm taking this trip not just for my dad, but to sort of find out where I'm supposed to be going with my life."

"Let me guess: You're leaning more toward Yemen than Duncan Phyfe."

"I guess it's in some people's blood to roam. I could never be happy looking at the same four walls all the time."

"Or the same person inside those four walls."

"Look, are you telling me you didn't have the time of your life doing what we did?"

"It was fine, for a while. Then it wasn't fine anymore."

"Fine! I can count on one hand the number of people who've gotten to do and see what we did. Look at the stories you have to tell your kids and grandkids."

"I don't have either."

"If it was so damn bad, why'd you stick it out for so long?"

"You know what they say, love makes you do crazy things."

"I still don't know what went wrong. It's not like I suddenly changed."

"No, Tom, you never changed. I guess I did. Goodnight."

"Ellie . . ."

She turned back. "It's Eleanor now, Eleanor. That changed too."

Tom went back to the lounge car and sat miserably watching the country drift by. The Cap picked up water in Pittsburgh, but Tom didn't call Lelia because while he could deal with snakes and pompous lawyers, he wasn't brave enough to deal with the voice of Cuppy the Magic Beaver when she felt wronged. He tried not to think about Eleanor, so of course, that was all he thought about. The Cap had made up some time, but it was still over two hours late. Tom finally fell asleep from exhaustion.

At five-thirty in the morning, the PA came on, and Tyrone's voice greeted him. "Good morning to you, good morning to you, there's so much to do, good morning to you. Thankyou, thankyouverymuch." And then he announced that the train was officially late, but that breakfast was hot and on time and came with a medley of Elvis holiday favorites at no extra charge.

Tom used the larger shower facilities on the lower level, having to wait behind another passenger. The man left his watch in the changing room, but Tom saw it and returned it before the man had gone far. In the dining car he had breakfast with Father Kelly, who was in good spirits despite the loss of his cross. He did lower his voice and asked Tom if he had by chance seen a naked, hysterical man on the train. Tom disclaimed any knowledge of that odd event and gently suggested the priest needed to get more rest.

They watched daylight come as they pulled into Toledo, where the train took on more water. Later, in the vast fields of northern Indiana, Tom watched from the lounge car as a horse and sleigh carried a family through the falling snow. It was as picturesque as any holiday card he'd ever seen, and it reminded him of a very special day he and Eleanor had shared years before.

They'd skied many of the most challenging slopes of Europe. In Austria, though, they'd taken a break from hurtling down mountains and, instead, had hired a sleigh and driver and taken a wonderful, all-day journey over the most pristine snow-covered land either of them had ever seen. They'd eaten lunch by a cheery fire at an honest-to-goodness castle, then ridden back under a full moon. It was a day never to be forgotten, or perhaps equaled. Or repeated. Clearly, he wouldn't be taking any more sleigh rides with the woman.

The Cap finally arrived in Chicago at eleven-thirty in the morning Central time, after serving passengers an extra meal for being late. The train uncoupled its mail and express cars, then slowly backed into the station. Tom came down with his bags, thanked Regina, and gave her a generous tip.

"I believe I should be paying you," she said, and they shared a hug. "I'll introduce you to my mom in the station lounge later, before the Chief heads out."

"I'm looking forward to meeting her if she's anything like you."

Tom saw Herrick Higgins getting off farther down. He pointed him out to Regina. "He's a really interesting guy. Too bad he had to retire. He really loves trains."

Regina said, "Herrick didn't retire, he was laid off. Budget cuts, him and two hundred other managers. It's a shame. That man knows more about trains than anybody. He rides the train at his own expense. If we have room, we let him bunk in the dormitory car with us. It's sad, real sad."

Tom saw Max and Kristobal up ahead, and he joined them.

"Heard you had an interesting evening," said Max.

"Not quite the word I'd use," said Kristobal.

"Where's Eleanor?" asked Tom.

"Already inside." Max looked upset. "I think she's trying to get a flight to LA. I'm not really happy about that. Can't you talk to her, Tom?"

Tom laughed. "If you *really* want her to take a plane, I'll talk to her, sure. Otherwise I think I should just stay out of it."

With the snow coming down ever harder, they headed toward the warmth of bustling Union Station in Chicago, their ride on the legendary Capitol Limited completed. What lay ahead were the Southwest Chief and a journey of almost twenty-three hundred more miles—almost three times the distance they'd just ridden—together with twenty-six train stops. Curiously, though, Tom felt ready for anything. As it would turn out, he'd need to be.

chapter eighteen

Chicago's Union Station symbolized the prodigious dimensions of the city it inhabited: It was big and brawny, with multiple levels, car-rental counters, food and other retail outlets, and long golf carts whizzing passengers around. They headed to the Metropolitan Lounge, found an empty area, and spread out. Tom sat comatose while Kristobal made numerous phone calls, and Max met with Steve and Julie and various other people in the lounge going over last-minute arrangements for the wedding. Eleanor wasn't there, and Max finally sent Kristobal looking for her.

Amtrak police came, led by Regina, and they all filed their theft reports. They were told that many passengers had discovered items missing and that a search for the thief or thieves was ongoing. The police thought it likely that more than one person was involved because of the number of items taken and the passengers targeted. In all probability, they were informed, the gang had gotten off the train before Chicago. Tom held out little hope that he'd ever see his pen again. Much more significantly, he held out little hope of seeing Eleanor again.

He was therefore very surprised to see her walk into the lounge with Kristobal about an hour later. She slumped next to Max.

"When's your flight leave?" he asked.

"It doesn't. Everything's booked solid. Ironically, the fastest way to LA right now is by train."

Max sat back and rested his eyes, although his lips almost twitched into a smile. "Sorry to hear that. Guess you'll just have to slum it with us rail bums." He opened his eyes and winked at Tom.

"Looks that way," said a scowling Eleanor.

"If it makes you feel any better, I've been banned from flying in the United States," said Tom. Kristobal gave him an odd look and drew back some. Tom explained quickly, "It was all a little misunderstanding at the security gate at La Guardia."

"No," said Eleanor, "that really doesn't make me feel any better."

Regina returned a few minutes later. Tom knew the woman she came back with had to be her mother, although the two didn't look a thing alike, except in the eyes. If it was possible, the woman made Agnes Joe look girlishly petite. Tom had visions of Aretha Franklin, only bigger. As it turned out, the wattage of the woman's personality was far greater than even her vast physical dimensions.

"This is my mother, Roxanne," said Regina, before Roxanne took over the show in a booming voice that made heads turn all over the cavernous Metropolitan Lounge.

"I understand you babies are cold, tired, depressed, and ROBBED! Umm-umm. Now, we can't have that. The good Lord won't hold sway for long over that sorry state of affairs." A few minutes later, blankets, pillows, snacks, and other sundry items appeared. It was much appreciated by them all, and even Eleanor appeared to be in better spirits.

Roxanne settled down in their midst as though a queen with her fawning constituency. "Lord, what a day already. I'm waiting on some important passengers coming in from New York. I'm taking charge of them, and taking charge they need." She pointed her finger at Max. "Now, this man I know because I should have been in that last movie you did, that musical thing with that skinny little white girl? Now come on, baby, you need a new casting agent. You got to get tuned to the genuine article. A real pair of lungs with a nice kick to 'em." In an instant she hit a note so high and with such vocal force that Tom gripped his coffee mug hard to block the vibrating sound waves from maybe cracking it wide open.

Max's chin appeared to bounce off his chest. "I'll certainly keep you in mind for the next one," he said.

"Uh-huh, you do that, baby. My people will talk to your people, only I don't have any people, except two teenage grand-kids with size-thirteen feet eating me out of house and home. Bless the Lord for He will sustain me, or at least keep them boys fed." She looked at her daughter. "Now, Regina, don't you have a train to look after? You think the little old Cap is gonna take care of itself without your sweet touch? You think Amtrak is paying you good money to sit around listening to your mama shoot off her big mouth, daughter dear?"

"I'm going, I'm going," Regina said, smiling. It was evident to Tom from the way Roxanne watched her daughter as she walked off that she was a very proud mother.

Roxanne turned back to them. "Regina tells me we also got us a couple getting hitched, and that old fortune-telling lady named Misty riding with us. I hear we missed out on the snake and the naked lawyer, which just distresses me to no end. I'm not talking about the naked lawyer—that sight I could do without. I mean the boa constrictor. Nothing better than a boa on a long train trip to keep your toes warm, you understand. My dearly departed husband, Junior—that man loved me, but he never kept my toes warm, 'cause men never think of that. So I guess from a woman's point of view, you get yourself a loving man and a cute little snake, then you got yourself the whole package. Praise the Lord! Now tell me all about what happened. I've just got to hear it."

Tom did, and they all had a good laugh at Gordon Merryweather's expense. "Consider it an early Christmas present to Amtrak," said Tom.

Roxanne said, "Thought you'd be on the New Orleans train headed home, baby."

They all turned to see who she was talking to, and there was Misty in full prognosticator regalia, her arms lifted to the ceiling. "I just had a premonition that my destiny this holiday season lay west instead of south, isn't that right, sweetie?" She batted her eyelashes at Max.

The director smiled and said, "I've never had my fortune told so well nor so energetically as last night."

"I'm here merely as a humble servant to the mysterious forces of the stars, Max."

Eleanor stared in perplexity at the obviously smitten director and then at Kristobal, who merely shrugged and whispered, "I'm not my mogul's keeper."

"How you doing, Misty?" said Roxanne. "Hey, you know that fortune you told me last time, girl?"

"The number 153 special, about the huge following of young males you'd encounter in your life?"

"That very one. Well, honey, it came true."

"Did you have any doubt?"

"If I did, it just went away. Although, to tell you the truth, sweetie, I was hoping for something a little closer to my own age." She pointed at the door to the lounge, where a stream of young African American boys in uniform was pouring in.

Roxanne rose. "That's the LA Boys' Center Choir. They performed at Carnegie Hall and now they're heading home for Christmas, and it's up to yours truly to make sure they get there with all their little pieces intact. Y'all excuse me for a bit."

As she walked away, Agnes Joe came across her path. "How you doing, Agnes Joe? Got your regular compartment on the Chief all ready. Now, you know, you making me look bad. You lose any more weight, girl, I'm gonna need help finding you."

They all watched as Roxanne went over to the milling group of youngsters, where she met the beleaguered-looking chaperones and then tried to get the attention of the boys, without much success. They looked tired, bored, and ready to do anything except listen to yet another adult.

That abruptly ended when an enormous bellow poured forth from Roxanne. The young men instantly formed two tight columns, their eyes so wide and full of fear that Tom imagined it was only the support of one slender shoulder wedged against its neighbor that kept them all from collapsing to the floor. Roxanne marched them over to one corner of the room and talked to them in a low voice.

A minute later she turned to the full lounge and asked, "Who wants to hear some singing? You folks want to hear some fine singing while you wait for your train?"

The crowd in the lounge was mostly older, and Tom wasn't sure some of them could even hear that well, although it was pretty much impossible *not* to hear Roxanne. They all said that they would love to hear some singing.

Roxanne turned to her young consignees, did some vocal warmups, and then led them in a series of Christmas classics, keeping her own voice at a level that never once interfered with the beautiful falsettos of the choir.

Max said, "They're terrific. She's terrific."

Misty sat down on the arm of the couch he was on. "She leads the choir at one of the biggest Baptist churches in Chicago, and she's also a lay minister there. Roxanne Jordan can sing gospel and the blues like no one I've ever heard, and I live in New Orleans! And any passenger with a pulse who's ridden on a train with that woman comes out of it a better person. You don't have to be a fortune teller to see that."

As the singing wound down, Roxanne led the choir out in a conga line, singing and making train noises while the audience applauded loudly. Senior Amtrak management, who'd come from their offices to watch, just shook their heads, smiled, and clapped right along with everyone else.

Tom trailed Kristobal over to the coffee counter. "Thanks for your help last night with the boa," said Tom.

"Oh, you're so welcome," Kristobal said sarcastically, then softened his tone. "Actually, it was kind of fun. My exgirlfriend's father was just like that, an obnoxious jerk, and she hated him for it."

"Well, I guess you almost missed the whole thing."

Kristobal looked at him. "What do you mean?"

"I understand you all were supposed to be on an earlier train. Ellie didn't really know the reason for the change, only that Max's plans changed."

Kristobal shook his head. "No, I made the arrangements for the earlier train, only the idiot travel agent put down the wrong date. She had us on the later train. When I tried to get it switched to the earlier one, there were no more sleepers available, and Mr. Powers doesn't do coach, believe me. So we flew in a day later. I called Eleanor to tell her of the change. I didn't see a reason to explain why. She'd been in D.C. all week anyway."

Disappointed, Tom said, "I thought it might have been somehow intentional, our being on the same train together, what with our past and all."

"Well, I certainly didn't know you two knew each other. And I make the travel arrangements, not Mr. Powers."

"Sure, that makes sense. Well, thanks again."

Ever the suspicious reporter and not completely convinced, Tom tracked down Regina and asked her to check on the matter, using a pretense. She went into the bowels of the station and came back a while later. "I checked with Reservations, and they had a note that Mr. Powers's party was supposed to be on the earlier train, but the agent got it wrong and there were no more sleepers left. So they took the later train. Is everything okay?"

Tom hid his chagrin. "Hey, you bet. Look, you were great. I'll never take the Cap unless you're on it. And your mother is a trip—I mean, a genuine original."

When Tom got back to the lounge, Steve and Julie were there in a panic. The minister had arrived but the best man and maid of honor, married friends of theirs from college, had just called. They'd been in a traffic accident on a snowy road in Michigan. The best man had a broken leg and was lying in a hospital bed, and his wife, of course, wasn't going to leave him.

"We have no best man and no maid of honor," moaned Julie. "I knew this was not going to work." She shook her head, then stopped and stared at Eleanor. "Would you be my maid of honor? Please? We come from the same sort of place. I know I can count on you. Please?"

Eleanor was taken aback, but then agreed, for what else could she do? Then Steve looked at Tom and said, "Well, if it weren't for what you said to me on the train maybe there wouldn't be a wedding at all. How about being my best man?"

Tom looked at Eleanor and finally agreed as well. On that, Eleanor rose and walked away.

Max piped in, "And I'll give the bride away. I've got all boys, and not one of them has tied the knot yet. Can't understand why."

Probably still bitter from his pay cut, Kristobal said, "Well, sir, maybe they've learned some valuable lessons from their thrice-divorced father."

Misty exclaimed, "Three times! Why, me too. I just knew we had a special connection, Max. It really is all in the numbers."

Tom found the circumstances maddeningly ironic. He was finally going to be in a wedding with Eleanor after all these years. Only it was someone *else's* wedding. He wasn't sure whether to laugh, cry, or go jump in Lake Michigan. He finally just sat back to await the Southwest Chief.

the southwest chief

Chicago to Los Angeles

chapter nineteen

⁓

The Southwest Chief was a very long train with many Super-liner cars and a shining snowplow on the front engine. Tom found, to his surprise, that his deluxe accommodations had shrunk to an economy sleeper through some error that couldn't be corrected because the train was full. This would never have happened to Cary Grant and Eva Marie Saint. He wedged inside his allotted space and contemplated that he'd not only have to use the communal shower but also the communal toilet for the next two thousand-odd miles. Fighting strangers for quality time in the john over eight states—that was truly a comforting thought. He found himself growing jealous of Mark Twain, who could simply jump off the stagecoach and run behind a cactus to do his business. Two doors down and on the other side of the aisle from him was Misty. He could see the beaded doorway going up, and the smell of incense was already tickling his sinuses.

His sleeping-car attendant came by and checked in. His name was Barry, he was in his late thirties, and his impressive physique showed him to be a frequenter of the weight room. He was polite and professional, but after Regina and most certainly Roxanne, Barry seemed sort of a letdown.

Tom decided to call Lelia. There was no answer, however, for which he was very grateful. He checked his watch. It was early afternoon in LA. He left a message, saying he was sorry about Erik and the misunderstanding about the gingivitis and her poor toenails, and then hung up.

To get his mind off his troubles he started thinking about the thefts. Pretty much all the first-class compartments had been hit, which made sense. And yet there was an exception: Agnes Joe. She hadn't come forward when the police had taken their report, so presumably the thief had skipped her. But why— unless Agnes Joe were the thief? Pretty stupid, though, to steal from everyone except yourself.

Then he took another tack. Perhaps not stupid but brilliant? Because most people, including the police, would come to the conclusion he just did. And he'd seen the duffel in her room that was stuffed to the gills. She hadn't unpacked it at all.

As he was thinking this, the Chief pulled away from the station. He looked at his watch: 3:15 P.M., right on time. Of course, so was the Cap initially.

Just then Kristobal came by with a camcorder. "Mr. Powers asked me to take some shots of the train and people and such. He said we can look at it later, and maybe it'll give us some interesting story angles."

"And you can always film the wedding," suggested Tom.

Kristobal sighed. "He actually told me to do that. This is what I went to film school for, to be a wedding videographer? If I were a big star and had my own trailer, this is the point I'd be stalking to it, calling my agent and never coming out." He added, "Oh, Eleanor asked me to ask you what you were wearing to the wedding."

"Asked you to ask me? Okay, great, tell her I'm wearing Armani. I always wear Armani to train weddings. She knows that."

Kristobal brightened. "Cool. I'm wearing Armani too." He swung his camera around and walked off.

The Chief roared along in a leisurely southwest direction, making four quick stops in Illinois before passing over the mighty Mississippi on a long, double-decked swing-span bridge dating from 1927. They were now in Iowa. The only stop in that state was at Fort Madison, which they made at about half past seven. As they headed on toward Missouri, Tom made his way to the dining car, where he shared a meal with Father Kelly and Misty. Steve and Julie were seated at the table behind them, and they talked back and forth about the upcoming wedding.

Eleanor, Max, and Kristobal were missing in action. Tom hadn't seen Agnes Joe at all.

Tom glanced at Misty. "You and Max seem to be hitting it off. Although he seems like a guy who has lots of lady friends."

"Oh, honey, I know it's just temporary. Trains have a way of bringing very different people together, but once the trip is over, so is the attraction. And I'm way past getting my heart broken over a man, if that's what you're thinking."

"It is, and I'm glad to hear it."

Misty said, "The stories I could tell of the faithless male species." She glanced at the priest. "And I *would* tell them if you weren't here." She pinched Father Kelly's cheeks, and he seemed delighted by the attention.

"I have to tell you," the priest confessed to Steve and Julie, "I've never attended a wedding on a train before. I think it must be a first or something."

"Actually, it's not."

They all looked across the aisle, where Herrick Higgins was eating his dinner.

"It's happened before, back in 1987, on the Texas Eagle. That runs from Chicago to LA too, but by way of Texas. They called it the Love Train. Its route is actually longer than the Chief's."

"The Love Train?" said Julie. "Why did they call it that?"

Higgins swung his legs out into the aisle and sipped his coffee as he spoke.

"There was a legendary conductor on the Eagle by the name of Zeb Love. That man was something. He had a heart of gold and the showmanship of a world-class entertainer. Dressed up as Santa Claus for the kids, gave them gifts bought with his own money. He went into schools to promote train travel and was probably one of the best natural spokesmen Amtrak ever had. His specialty, though, was making people happy while they were on the train. He encouraged people to talk to each other, find out what made their fellow humans tick. Charles Kuralt even did a piece on Zeb. Well, on July 4, 1987, on the Texas Eagle, a couple got married and Zeb Love was right there in the middle of it. He even went celebrating with the wedding party when they got to Forth Worth. Zeb was a special one, all right."

"Well," said Julie, "I hope our wedding is half as nice."

"Oh, it will be," said Higgins. "Roxanne Jordan, I understand, is taking charge of the musical entertainment. With that woman involved, good things will happen. Trust me."

Up in the Pacific Northwest a significant meteorological event was taking place. Competing highs and lows, butting cold and warm fronts, soaring moisture content from off the coast, and upper-level winds that were increasing to enormous speeds were all mixing and spinning and beginning to move in an easterly direction. A similar confluence of weather elements had formed in nearly the same place during one of Mark Twain's trips across the Nevada Territory over 140 years before. The result had been a rip-roaring icy flood and then a blizzard the likes of which most folks had never encountered even in those wild frontier climates. If the story was to be believed—and, in that regard, one was always on dangerous ground with Mr. Twain—the episode very nearly cost the esteemed author his life.

Though still largely undetected by the national weather forecasters, the current storm turned in a southern direction when it slammed into the hard wall of the northern Rockies and slid down the spine of that mountain range like a water leak following an electrical line inside a house. Though no one could yet determine where the forming storm would hit with all its ferocious winter power, its destination seemed to lie right along the path of the Southwest Chief, and at a very interesting spot. It was a very remote, foreboding place in southeastern Colorado, called the Raton Pass, the highest elevation on the entire Southwest Chief route and the toughest passenger-rail grade in the country. Not easy for a train to climb on good weather days, it would tax the Southwest Chief almost to its limit when the weather turned really bad.

Later that night the person in black was once more making the rounds of the sleeper cars. Even more cautious this time because of the heightened state of alertness, the person made absolutely sure no one was around. The thief's efforts were aided by the fact that many people were either eating dinner or attending a very special event in the lounge car. Indeed, people were presently being wildly entertained on the Southwest Chief, and such people were in no position to safeguard their valuables. The thief mouthed a silent "thank you" and went about the larcenous business of robbing fellow passengers.

chapter twenty

~

The lounge car was indeed rocking, and the vibrations had nothing to do with the sections of bad track that the Chief had to race over every day. Roxanne was in the middle of the car, with a hand-held microphone—not that the woman needed any such amplifier to be heard—and was belting out song after song, each more powerful, more viscerally emotional than its predecessor. In the packed car each person's gaze was directly on the woman, absorbing every note pouring forth. The LA Boys' Center Choir, too, had stayed up a little late and was listening with rapt attention to a true artiste who sang only for the love of it. These young men could not have received a better lesson in life than watching and hearing Roxanne Jordan perform while rolling over the rails.

Tom was in a far corner of the lounge, humming along to the tunes Roxanne was singing. After the show was over, the passengers gave her a standing ovation, and then people hung around discussing in great, noisy detail all that they'd just seen and heard.

Down in the smoker lounge, Max and Misty were enjoying cigars purchased in Chicago, and Misty was reading the palms of all who wanted their fortunes told. Since it was the Christmas season, she kept her predictions very upbeat, finding in the lines of each extended palm the potential of holiday miracles.

Back in her compartment, Eleanor was making some notes about potential script plots, but she was struggling to concentrate. The process was different this time. She was used to taking other people's work and tinkering with it, not creating her own material from scratch. She kept doodling on her pad, until she realized she was spelling "Tom Langdon" in fat, three-dimensional letters. She ripped up the paper and threw it away, then lay back with her hand over her face.

"Troubles?"

Eleanor looked at the doorway, where Roxanne was standing and staring at her. She was dabbing the sweat from her face with a wet washcloth after her prodigious entertainment efforts.

Eleanor sat up. "Just a little frustrated, I guess."

"Well, you missed a fine show in the lounge car, if I do say so myself."

"Actually I heard it. They piped it in over the PA. You were terrific. The best I've heard." Roxanne glanced at the floor, which was littered with balled-up paper.

"How's the train story coming? We could use a blockbuster Max Powers movie about trains to get the country and the government excited about us again."

Eleanor gave an embarrassed smile. "Well, I have to admit, I don't know all that much about trains. I haven't taken one since I was in college, at least not in this country. And I'm not sure a few days riding the rails will educate me enough to do the thing justice."

Roxanne perched on the edge of the couch bed.

"Well, I've been working these trains longer than most, and I still don't know it all. I guess that's why I like my job so much: something new every day. Sometimes it's good, and sometimes it's not so good, but it keeps me hopping and using my head, and that's a good thing."

"How long have you worked this train?"

"Oh, me and the Chief have been courting now going on twenty-one years. Up, back, up, back. Know every bit of sagebrush in New Mexico, every wheatfield in Kansas, even know some of the farmers by their first name. Wave to 'em when we go by. I could drive the train with my eyes closed, only Amtrak frowns on that sort of thing."

Eleanor pulled out a fresh piece of paper and made some notes. "I bet the farmers wave back."

"Girl, I've gotten three marriage proposals in the last two years. One gent tied a banner to his John Deere and raced the train. It said, 'Will You Marry Me, Roxanne?'"

"That's pretty creative. It's nice to be popular."

"Oh yeah, farmers like their women with some meat on 'em, and I fit that bill." She stood up. "If you're having trouble coming up with ideas, why don't you come with me to make my rounds? I guarantee it'll stimulate *your* creative juices."

After Roxanne's show had ended and the boys' choir had returned to their quarters in coach, Father Kelly came into the lounge and started chatting with Tom. Max and Kristobal joined them. It turned out the priest and the director had much in common.

"I wanted to be a priest," said Max. "Well, more accurately, my mother wanted me to be a priest. Even joined the seminary, but it didn't stick. I wasn't wired for it. And I liked women too

much. Forgive me, Padre, but it's true. It was actually an easy decision. Yet if I'd taken the vows, it would have saved me millions
in alimony."

Tom said, "I briefly considered the priesthood myself." He
looked at Kristobal. "You ever think about being a priest?"

"Oh, sure, doesn't every Jew?"

Tom mouthed a "sorry" to the man and took a swallow of
his drink.

"Well, I'm a confirmed film buff," said Father Kelly. "And I
truly appreciate your talent, Max. I've seen all the classics and I
thought moviemaking would be an exciting way to spend one's
time, but then I received this very strong calling, and my hands
became tied in the matter, so to speak. Though don't believe for
a second that priests don't admire a pretty girl. It just takes a
back seat to a higher power."

Just then Agnes Joe came in and joined them. She was
dressed in holiday colors that actually rode well on her challenging frame. They'd all finished their drinks, and Agnes Joe offered
to take away the empties and bring them new ones. She came
back a few minutes later with fresh refills for everyone. The men
reached in their pockets to reimburse her, but she shook her
head. "My treat. Consider it an early Christmas present."

Father Kelly said, "Bless you for taking such good care of
us."

Tom watched as Herrick Higgins, a couple of chairs over,
stared out into the night. The man seemed deeply preoccupied.

Tom called out, "I'm taking your word, Herrick, that sleep
will come easier tonight."

The older man smiled. "It will. The Chief is the fastest train
to the West Coast, the only one that maintains the level of track
speed you find in the east. Just under forty hours to LA, about
ten less than the other western trains."

Kristobal blanched. "Forty hours! Gee, a virtual bullet. I could almost fly to Australia and back, *twice*, in that time." He finished his comments with a hearty, "Chooo-chooo!"

Higgins smiled good-naturedly. "Well, bullet trains would be nice out here. Flatland is good for it, but you got some tricky grades too. And the government would never fund that. Most other major countries have seen the benefit of high-speed rail corridors. However, one needs vision to see the payoff from such an undertaking, and 'vision' isn't something our leaders associate with train travel." He pointed out the window. "Now, the Chief follows the old Santa Fe for the most part. Takes you through some rugged country. Dodge City. That's where they based the TV series *Gunsmoke*, you know."

"*Gun-what?*" asked Kristobal.

"I guess you're too young to remember that," said Higgins.

"I guess so."

"We go through some high places, 7,600 feet high at Raton Pass, a little less than that at Glorieta Pass, and then we descend into Apache Canyon, but that's after we get through Las Vegas."

"Las Vegas!" exclaimed Father Kelly. "I didn't know this train went to Las Vegas. Does it stop long enough for people to get off?" He looked around. "Well, not that I'm really into gambling or anything, but I do occasionally like to have a go at the slots."

"It's not *that* Las Vegas, Father," explained Higgins. "It's Las Vegas, *New Mexico*. It's the stop right after Raton. And not a neon tube or gaming table in sight."

Father Kelly looked very disappointed. "Ah well, some things are just not meant to be, I suppose."

"Well, Padre," said Max, "I'll do you one better. We're having a wedding on this train tomorrow, and there's a young bachelor on this train who needs a bachelor's party, and I intend to provide it and you're all invited. In fact, attendance is mandatory."

"Well," said Father Kelly, "that sounds very nice. I'm assuming libations will be served?"

Max winked. "Padre, my whole compartment is a libation." He told them the time for the party.

Tom rose. "I'll be there," he said.

Max glanced at him. "You want to start now, feel free. Maybe we can sit and talk for a bit."

"No, I think I'll go for a stroll."

"On a train?" exclaimed Kristobal. "What's there to see?"

"You'd be surprised," replied Tom as he walked out.

Tom moved down the corridor. The lounge car was still full, the dining car was serving its last meal of the day, people were in a festive, friendly mood, and thus many of the sleeper compartments were empty. It was a perfect time for a thief to strike again, and Tom wanted to see if the crook on the Capitol Limited had managed to hook a ride on the Southwest Chief. He also wanted to check out one sleeper in particular.

He knocked, and when he received no answer he poked his head inside Agnes Joe's compartment. Fortunately for him, the door couldn't be locked from the outside. It was empty. The phonograph was set up on the fold-down desk, as it had been on the Cap. The place was neat and tidy, with few personal possessions laid out. There were two pillows fluffed up and leaning against the wall at the head of the couch, and a blanket was neatly folded there. Two suitcases were against one wall. Tom didn't bother with those. He was more interested in the duffel bag that was wedged between the wall and chair, just as it had been on the Cap. And a blanket was also covering it.

He checked the corridor, drew the privacy curtain closed, and unzipped the bag. Instead of loot, he found something inexplicable. It was newspapers balled up, just like the bunch that Regina had been carrying on the Cap. He looked at some of the papers. They were from various editions of newspapers on the East Coast. Unable to make sense of this, he kept looking through the bag until he found a photograph of Agnes Joe and what Tom took to be her daughter. He didn't know for sure, because the two women could not have looked more dissimilar. The younger woman was taller than Agnes Joe and was one of the most beautiful women Tom had ever seen, truly a stunner. And she was dressed in a circus performer's outfit, so at least that much of Agnes Joe's story was true. He looked for a date on the picture, on the front and back, but there was none. Agnes Joe looked about the same, so it couldn't have been taken that long ago. They seemed happy or at least cordial in the photo. He wondered what had gone wrong since the picture had been taken, something that might explain why the mother wasn't spending Christmas with her only child.

Not wanting to risk discovery, he put the photo back in the bag and slipped out of the compartment. He went to the other section of sleepers, stopped dead, ducked inside a vacant unit, and peered out cautiously. Agnes Joe was emerging from one of the units. She looked around, as Tom had, to see that no one was watching. She didn't appear to be carrying anything, but she could have had something in her pockets. She headed off in the opposite direction. Tom slipped out, moved down the corridor, and peered into the compartment she'd been in. He didn't see anything that identified whose unit it was. He was about to go in to determine who was staying there, but he heard people coming and walked away. However, he got the letter of the unit, and he figured it would be fairly easy to find out whose it was.

As he walked off, his thoughts returned to a seemingly lonely woman with a curious background, gregarious nature, and propensity to stuff old papers in her bags and invade other people's dwellings on a moving train. His trip of soul-searching and personal discovery was turning more into an investigative journalism outing, solving the matter of the modern train robber, who was perhaps named Agnes Joe. For many reasons, however, he hoped she was innocent.

As he came through the lounge car he saw Herrick Higgins at the other end peering anxiously out the window.

"What's up?" asked Tom. "You look a little uptight."

Higgins smiled, but Tom noted there wasn't much sincerity behind it.

"Oh, nothing much. Just watching the snow coming down."

"Well, snow can't hurt a train."

Higgins didn't smile or nod in agreement. "We'll be hitching on a third engine at La Junta before we cross the Raton Pass," he said.

"Is that normal practice, or because of the snow?"

"Oh, it's normal. See, it's quite a climb, and a third engine just adds a nice little comfort zone." His gaze returned to the snow falling outside, and his expression grew serious again. Tom walked on, but he glanced nervously back at the old railroad man, trying without success to read his thoughts.

chapter twenty-one

~⁓~

Upon Roxanne and Eleanor entering the coach car housing the boys' choir, Roxanne pulled out a can of Lysol and started spraying everywhere. "Okay," she said, "we got us some serious travel funk going on here. Now, do not try to deceive Ms. Roxanne about this for she has five sons of her own and lots and lots of grandsons, and thus she has a Ph.D. in what she likes to call 'stinky young men syndrome,' and that just won't cut it on Ms. Roxanne's train. Do we all understand this?" All the young men nodded. "Good, now I have two showers reserved for you for the next hour, and we will make good use of that time, won't we?" They all nodded again. She assembled them in two rows. "Three minutes per boy per shower, no more no less, for this train does many wonderful things but it does not make water out of air. And we will shampoo and we will get behind our ears and between our toes, won't we, and we will come out with not one dirty digit because there will be an inspection—oh yes there will. And the good Lord will look down upon all of you squeaky clean young men and He will bless you this Christmas like no other."

For emphasis she sang snatches of tunes Pearl Bailey and Billie Holiday had made famous, and then the chaperones marched the lads out.

"How did you end up being the choir's caretaker?" asked Eleanor. "I understand the singing connection and all, but is there something else?"

"They're good boys, with a lot of potential, but also lots of things in their way too, especially where they're going back to. I won't accept that fifty or twenty or even ten percent of those boys won't make it to adults, I won't! Every one of them, every single one of them, is going to make it. I'm taking a month-long vacation come this summer, been saving up for a while now, and we're going to go on the road, me and those boys, and we're going to play some places, and they're going to see some things that will make their bellies burn to do the right thing in life. They'll find dreams they never thought they even had, and old Roxanne will be right there holding their hands 'til they don't need me being Momma anymore."

"That's quite an ambitious undertaking," said Eleanor.

"But they're worth it, don't you think?"

Eleanor smiled. "I think they're more than worth it."

They went into the next coach, where a dazed-looking man was walking up and down the aisle.

Roxanne said in a low voice to Eleanor, "You'll find that coach on the long-distance trains can be an interesting place. You want some stories, you could do a lot worse than plunking yourself down right here."

She said in a loud voice, "Hello, Ernest, you feeling okay today, baby?"

"Demons, demons everywhere, Roxanne—out the window, in my clothes, the food. I saw some in my Diet Pepsi."

"I know, I know, but I tell you what, I saw you were going

to be on the train so I brought some antidemon dust. This concoction is guaranteed to take care of any demon there is, including supersize." She handed him a bag that she pulled from her pocket. "What I'd do, Ernest, is sprinkle that on you, but no one else. You don't want to waste it, 'cause that's all I got."

"Thank you, Roxanne, thank you. You're the only one who understands."

Ernest went off, sprinkling himself along the way.

Eleanor said, "Sounds like he might need professional help."

"Yeah, I thought so too, but what I think he wants is attention. He's got nobody, so far as I can tell. He's been riding this train for years, never hurt anybody, just walks around, looking crazy, but I don't believe he is at all. He dresses like he's homeless, but this train trip is beyond the purse of any homeless person I've ever met, and I've met quite a few. I found out he's an engineer at a firm in San Diego. He's the sort probably never had a lot of friends, and now that he's around forty-five or so, I don't think he knows how to make them. I've spent time with him, and he's intelligent, articulate, but his brain's not wired the same as you and me. When he first gets on the Chief he always does the demon thing. We get past that, then things are cool."

"Why do you think he takes the train so much?"

"Well, nobody wants to be alone, especially around Christmas. I'm sure you know that most suicides happen around the holidays. Besides, this isn't a train this time of year. It's a social club of strangers looking for a friend."

A frantic-looking older woman ran up to Roxanne waving her ticket. "Oh my God, I don't know where I'm going."

"Well, honey, tell me where it is you want to go, and then we'll work from there."

"Denver," said the woman.

"Denver, okay, you need to be on the Zephyr, not the Chief. The Chief goes to LA and not by way of Denver. I'm surprised they let you on here."

"I think I stepped on the wrong train."

"Well, the Zephyr does leave out of Chicago too."

"I can't believe this is happening. My daughter and her family are expecting me for Christmas. She told me she'd fly out and ride back with me. I don't like to fly and my husband has passed on. She said my faculties weren't sharp enough to travel by myself, and maybe she's right."

"Hey, you had enough 'faculties' to come ask for help, didn't you?"

"Yes, but when I don't show up in Denver, she'll know. Then all Christmas she and her husband will be saying 'We told you so.'"

"Who said you're not getting to Denver in time for Christmas?" asked Roxanne.

"But I'm on the wrong train."

"For now you are, but see, we're going to get you on the right train."

"I don't understand. How can you do that? You said this train is going to Los Angeles."

"At Kansas City, we'll get you on a short connecting service to Omaha. The Zephyr stops in Omaha, and you'll be there in plenty of time to get on and sail right to Denver. Not a problem at all. I'll make all the arrangements and come get you when we get to KC tonight."

The woman couldn't stop thanking Roxanne for all her help. After she had left, Roxanne said, "People come in here all the time, hot, bothered, worried about everything in the world. You got to read their body cues, solve their problems, get them interested in the trip, make 'em part of the process. You got kids and parents traveling together, you talk to the kids, not to the kids through the parents. The little ones appreciate that, makes 'em feel big and important, and then they listen to you. You bite off a little bit at a time, and some passengers you never really get through to, but most you do. It takes time, but either you work the job or the job works you. That's what I tell my daughter all the time, beat that into her head."

"You've done a great job with Regina, she's wonderful."

"Yep, she's special, all right. Momma's proud of her."

"You sound like a psychologist."

"Unofficially I am. And I got no end of patients."

"You sure you're not an angel dropped from Heaven onto the Southwest Chief? You sound almost too good to be true, and I mean that with mountains of respect."

"Well, honey, I'm a sixty-three-year-old fat woman with sore feet, high blood pressure, and the beginnings of diabetes. I know I don't have all that much time left, and I can either spend it moping and complaining about the things I never got to in life, or I can do something I love and help people along the way. I decided to keep plugging 'til I drop."

They stopped at one seat and Roxanne put her hands on her hips. "Excuse me, what we got here, shug?"

The young man, about twenty-five, was reclining in his seat without any clothes on. Luckily, the space next to him was unoccupied, the car was darkened for sleeping, and no one else had noticed, at least not yet.

"Hey, it's cool," said the young man.

"I bet you're cool, you ain't got no pants or a stitch of nothing else on."

"Well, I'm from Arizona, this is how everybody sleeps in Arizona."

Roxanne said, "Is that right?" Eleanor had averted her gaze, but Roxanne sat right next to the man. "Now let me get something straight with you, slick. We're not in Arizona, we're in Missouri, and while I know they call Missouri the Show Me State, you don't have nothing I haven't seen before, so I don't need no showing of it. Now, if you don't get all your clothes on right now, you're getting off this train before we get to Kansas City."

The young man chuckled. "I gotcha there. La Plata was the last stop, and there's not another one until KC."

"That's right, there's not, is there?" Roxanne stared at him pointedly until it started to dawn on the guy.

"You wouldn't put me off in the middle of nowhere? You can't do that," he sputtered.

"I wouldn't call the middle of Missouri the middle of nowhere, would you, Eleanor?"

Eleanor shook her head. "No."

Roxanne continued, "I mean, folks live there. So it has to be *somewhere*. I know that the farms are quite a ways apart, and it's December and cold as I don't know what, but it's not *nowhere*. In fact, the place we'll let you off, all you got to do is walk about thirty miles, southwest I believe—or maybe it's northeast—and there's a motel or something like that if memory serves me correctly, though they might have torn it down, it was very old."

"Thirty miles! I'll freeze."

"Well, not if you have your pants on. And be optimistic about life. I don't tolerate whiners. You're young, strong, you can probably make it."

The man's eyes bulged. "Probably?"

Roxanne pulled out her walkie-talkie. She didn't depress the button, something Eleanor noticed but the young man didn't.

"Service boss to the conductor and engineer. We got us a red alert, situation one-four-two, repeat one-four-two. We'll need to stop and discharge a passenger. Over."

"Wait!" said the panicked man. "What's a one-four-two?"

"Oh, honey, that's just train talk for an uncooperative passenger. On big fancy planes, they just tie you up and sit on you, because they can't open their doors six miles up." She smiled sweetly. "But we don't have that problem on a train, now do we, shug? See, on Amtrak we just kick your little disruptive butt off wherever we want. Now, we do provide a flashlight and a compass to help guide you once you've been discharged. That's official Amtrak policy, and a good one I think." She looked out the window. "Mercy, the snow's picked up again, looks like a regular blizzard." She spoke into her walkie-talkie. "Service boss here again. On that one-four-two, bring a shovel and a first-aid kit with frostbite applications for the discharged passenger. Over."

"I'm dressing, I'm putting my clothes on," yelled the young man, ostensibly loud enough for the person on the other end of the walkie-talkie to hear. "You can cancel the one-four-two thing."

Roxanne looked at him solemnly and slowly shook her head. "I'm afraid once it's been ordered, we really can't take it back. And it's a long trip and for all I know you might try this nonsense again and somebody might see you, like a little kid or an elderly passenger, and get really upset."

"I swear to you," said the young man as he frantically dressed, "I will not take any of my clothes off. I will sleep in my clothes. I promise."

"I don't know. You feel that? The train's already slowing down, and the engineer might get mad if I tell him it's a no-go. You know how much it costs to make an unscheduled stop on a train this big?"

"Please, please. I promise. No more nudity."

Roxanne sighed heavily and then said into her walkie-talkie, "Okay, service boss here again, let's cancel that, repeat, cancel the one-four-two." She stared at the young man, her expression that of a woman in complete control. "Now look here, baby, I see one inch of something of you I shouldn't, then you going off this train. I don't care where we are, middle of the desert or highest mountain. No more reprieves, we understand each other?"

He nodded meekly and then pulled the blanket over his head.

"Night-night, Arizona," said Roxanne as she and Eleanor walked off.

The two women went down to the lower level, where Roxanne inspected the choir's bathing operation. Satisfied with the progress, she and Eleanor headed to the lower lounge area and sat at an empty table.

"Boys' choir, antidemon dust, and a naked man from Arizona. You've had a busy night."

"Oh, honey, this was actually pretty tame. The things I could tell you."

"I wish you would."

"Well, maybe we can spend some time together off the train."

Eleanor was beginning to think that she could get Max to make Roxanne a paid consultant on the film project when the train started to slow down noticeably.

"Is there a problem?" asked Eleanor.

"No, this stretch of track has speed restrictions and a few gate crossings. Come with me. I'll show you a nice little benefit to train travel that you positively can't enjoy on a plane."

Roxanne led Eleanor down to one of the train's vestibules,

where she opened the upper window of the train door, allowing in a burst of refreshingly cold air.

"God, that feels wonderful," said Eleanor.

"I come down here a few times each day, just to clear my head, smell the air, get a close look at this land without an inch of glass or nothing else in the way." They watched the country-side pass by for a bit, and then Roxanne closed the window as the Chief picked up speed. "I got Regina to do this a couple times a trip too. Gives you some peace, recharge your batteries."

"How many kids do you have besides Regina?"

"Nine, all grown of course. And twenty-three grand-children."

She shook her head. "You don't look nearly old enough."

"Well, I started really early, maybe too early."

Roxanne shot Eleanor a glance. "You have any kids?"

Eleanor shook her head. "Never even been married."

"Now, you want to tell me how a beautiful, smart, suc-cessful sort like yourself never landed a good man who loved her?"

"Maybe I'm really not that beautiful, smart or successful."

"Baby, take one look in the mirror. And I doubt you'd be working with a man like Max Powers if you weren't pretty well endowed in the brain and talent department."

"Well, it happens, you know, people do end up alone. All sorts of people."

"Yes, it does, and there's always a reason for it too. Care to tell me yours?"

Eleanor looked away and fiddled with her fingers while Roxanne studied her closely. "Wait a minute, let me see if I can guess. You found you a good man who loved you, only it didn't work out, maybe he never asked that all-important question that a woman desperately wants to answer yes to, and you finally went your separate ways." She added quietly, "Until you saw him again on this train."

Eleanor glanced at her sharply, a suspicious look on her face.

"The way you and Tom Langdon act around each other it's pretty clear. Plus the train gossip grapevine is alive and well on the old Chief."

Eleanor's face flushed. "Well, my goodness, if I'd only known how transparent I was. I can't tell you what a relief it is that so many people I don't even know are aware of my romantic history—or should I say fiasco."

"I'm not looking to pry, Eleanor, but I am a good listener."

Eleanor finally took a deep breath and looked across at Roxanne. "Tom Langdon is a wanderer, always has been, always will be. He craves adventure, he craves change like other people need food. He's the sort who couldn't make a commitment if his life depended on it. And, no, he never asked me to marry him."

"But I understand you haven't seen him in years. Maybe he's changed."

Eleanor shook her head. "Men like him don't change. He's back in the States traveling around and writing fluff instead of covering wars overseas, but that won't last. Six months from now he'll be off doing something else. I lived with him for years. I know how he thinks." She paused and added, "And he has a girlfriend. He's going to see her in LA."

"You think he's made a commitment to her?"

"I doubt it."

"You mean you hope not."

Eleanor just looked away.

Roxanne said, "Let your heart be your guide, girl. If you truly love him, I say give him another chance. It may be your only chance for happiness."

"What if feelings have changed over time? What if you're not the same person you once were?"

"Eleanor, love is like a good piece of wood: It just gets stronger and stronger as the years go by. Take it from someone who had it and only lost it when the Lord decided it was time I shared Junior with Him. It sounds corny, I know, but it's really the only thing that works between two people. The only thing."

chapter twenty-two

Kansas City was a major stop where many people got on and off and the train lingered awhile as it refueled and restocked. Roxanne escorted the woman heading to Denver by way of the California Zephyr to where she needed to go. Tom took the opportunity to step out for some fresh air before the bachelor party started. Recalling what Herrick Higgins had said, Tom watched as more pieces of America climbed aboard the train, no doubt flush with stories to tell, experiences to exchange, perhaps friendships, however short-lived, to form.

The snow was falling hard, and he sought shelter under one of the overhangs.

He glanced over in surprise as Eleanor climbed off the train and headed toward him.

"Little stuffy on the train," she explained.

"Yeah, me too."

They both stood there awkwardly, until she said, "I can't tell you what a shock it's been seeing you."

"I thought a million times about contacting you over the

years. But I never did. Call it pride, stubbornness, stupidity. Take your pick, they're all there."

"Well, I guess with the way things ended I can't blame you."

He drew closer. "Do you believe in second chances?"

She pulled back a bit. "Tom, I can't take that hurt again. I can't."

"You left me, remember?"

"After all those years of being together, it was time to put up or shut up," she said bluntly. "I needed a commitment, and I didn't get it. I assumed your career took priority over everything else."

"People can change, Ellie."

"So I've heard. Do you really think writing about antique furniture will last? And you have a girlfriend you're going to see for Christmas. Are you ready to commit to her?"

"It's not that sort of relationship."

"Of course not, you're not that sort of man." She shook her head and looked away.

Tom gripped her shoulder and turned her toward him. "It's not that sort of relationship because I don't love her. There's only one woman I've ever loved, Ellie, you know that."

"Tom, don't do this to me, please."

"So why did you come out here? It's freezing."

"I . . . I don't know."

"I don't believe that. I think you know exactly why."

"Maybe I do."

"Nothing in my life has been as good as what we had. Nothing! I've been searching all these years for something."

"I've been looking too," she said, "and not finding it."

"It can't be just a coincidence that we're both on this train. It's an omen, don't you see? It was meant to be."

"You sound like Misty. Love doesn't work that way. It's not some magic fairy dust. It's something you work at every day."

As she flicked a strand of hair out of her face and the full force of those emerald eyes fell on him, it might as well have been ten years prior or a decade hence, it didn't really matter to Tom. In the wash of lamplight, the woman's gaze was as hypnotic and intoxicating a thing as Tom had ever experienced. He thought he was taking a step back, but he actually moved closer to her. He watched his hand slide another errant strand of auburn hair out of her face. Then his fingers moved to her cheek and gently rubbed it. She didn't move to stop him.

"Well, maybe it's time I started to work at it."

He took a deep breath, glanced up for a second, and his lips parted and his gaze held on the figure walking his way. He shook his head in disbelief, because this was the second shock that he'd received in a little over twenty-four hours. How many more thunderbolts could he survive?

It was Lelia Gibson striding toward the train, a caravan of redcaps in her wake, tugging along her prodigious baggage. The woman was incapable of traveling light. It was one of her fortes, packing with indefatigable vigor, each outfit planned for a particular segment of the journey, each accessory judged with an eye as critical as the ablest general plotting battle tactics.

Tom took a step back from Eleanor, who'd closed her eyes, her lips searching for Tom's but not finding them.

"Ellie."

She opened her eyes, slid a hand across his cheek as he took another step back.

"What's wrong?"

"Really quick, think of the worst bit of timing you've ever had in your life."

"What?" she asked in a bewildered tone.

He glanced once more at Lelia. She was closing in. He wasn't sure if she'd seen him yet, but it was only a matter of time. She obviously knew he was on this train.

"The worst piece of timing in your life. Think of it right now. Okay? Please?"

"I actually think this is pretty bad timing on your part," she said in a very annoyed tone.

"Just think of it!"

"Okay, okay."

"Have you thought of it?"

She hesitated for a moment. "Yes, so?"

He let out his breath. "So, I just beat it. I just crushed it, in fact. I'm the undisputed king of bad timing." He pointed toward Lelia. "My sort of girlfriend in LA? That's her. Lelia Gibson."

Eleanor swung around and stared at the approaching group.

"Did you know she was boarding the train?"

"No, that one qualifies in the total, heart-stopping, shock-of-a-lifetime category."

Eleanor folded her arms across her chest and moved away from Tom. It was then that Lelia saw Tom and waved frantically. As she barreled down on her target, Eleanor retreated even more, until she was just a shadow in the darkness. As Tom watched her recede, it was as though all the blood in his body was going with her. He turned to face Lelia. He took a little solace in the fact that things certainly couldn't get any worse. Yet indeed they could.

chapter twenty-three

The National Weather Service issued advisories for the far Midwest and Southwest regions, citing the potential of a severe winter storm that was making its way south down the spine of the Rocky Mountains. The full fury of the tempest it would become was considerably masked by adjacent meteorological conditions in the Pacific Northwest, ameliorating safeguards that would fall away as the weather system moved through Wyoming and then into Colorado. About the time the storm suddenly unleashed all its might on the border between Colorado and New Mexico, it would be too late to issue any more warnings. All that would be left would be to read about the land squall of the decade in the newspapers and recount it to future generations in hushed tones.

Herrick Higgins had taken advantage of the long stop in Kansas City to see the engineer. They'd discussed the weather reports coming in from Amtrak Central Dispatch. Though Higgins was no longer employed by the rail service, there was no one who worked passenger trains for a living who wouldn't welcome his wise input and counsel. He and the engineer were friends going back twenty years, and when Higgins told him he didn't like the way things were shaping up, particularly since they were heading into Colorado, the engineer took serious note. Higgins also told the man to pack on as much fuel as possible.

"We'll all keep our eyes open," said the engineer. "As soon as we hear anything new from dispatch, I'll let you know."

Higgins went back and sat in the lounge car as the train finished taking on supplies and passengers. Over the course of his long career, he'd seen just about every possible equipment foible, personnel miscue, and weather mishap. He'd learned to go with his instincts in those circumstances, instincts honed from over thirty years of doing the job. He didn't like the way the sky looked, and the way the wind was blowing. He didn't like the sharp angle of the snowfall. He kept staring out the window at a sky that seemed to promise nothing except trouble.

"What are you doing here, Lelia?"

"Is that all I get after traveling all this way to surprise you?" she said. "Do you know you can't get a direct flight from LA to Kansas City? I mean, what is that about? I had to fly through Denver. It was a nightmare. And all I get is 'What are you doing here, Lelia?'" She gave him a hug and a kiss, and he felt extreme guilt, for they had a relationship after all. They were dating, sort of; they were going to Tahoe for Christmas. Rediscovering Eleanor had caused him to nearly forget all that.

"I'm sorry, it's just a shock seeing you. I thought you might have called it quits after the Erik episode."

"Don't be silly. Why don't we get on the train and talk about it. I'll fill you in on everything."

"Everything, what everything?"

"Later, on the train, after I unpack." She gave her ticket to one of the redcaps and told them to get her bags on board. She tipped them generously with both money and a dazzling smile. She was dressed in classic Hollywood, meaning expensive and eye-catching. The poor Kansas City redcap battalion would never be the same, Tom felt certain. They probably would have paid *her*, just for the privilege of toting her matching Gucci leather bags and being in her company.

As they walked toward the Chief, Lelia slipped her arm around Tom's. "You know, I've never been on a train before. And for the holidays too, it's kind of nice. Do they have massage services on board? And perhaps a beauty parlor, like they do on cruise ships?"

"Uh, that would be a no. They do have a checkerboard in each sleeper unit, but you have to bring your own checkers. Oh, and they do have lots and lots of liquor, and let me tell you right now, that's a wonderful thing."

"Well, maybe you can give me one—a massage, I mean. Oh, I brought the naughty teddy," she added coyly, leaning up against him.

As they were boarding, Tom saw Eleanor out of the corner of his eye. She was watching them both closely, and for one of the few times in his life he felt totally and completely helpless. They stepped on the Chief, said goodbye to Missouri, and the train slid into the flat farmland of Kansas as the darkness deepened.

Lelia set up in her sleeper compartment, but not without some complaints as to its lack of spaciousness and queries as to whether there were any rental units with mahogany paneling and possibly access to a private valet. A hopelessly smitten Barry, the sleeping-car attendant, flexed his neck muscles and puffed out his chest and did a few arm curls with her luggage, while regaling the woman with train factoids. However, Lelia remained unimpressed and suitably aloof. She did intimate that if he could somehow scrounge up a proper tea service and provide all meals in her room, she might favor him with a smile now and then and also perhaps show him some calf and the flash of a well-defined thigh. And so off Barry went, determined to accomplish all that she had asked.

Tom came by her compartment after she'd settled in. "I like what you've done with the place," he said, smiling.

"Where are you staying?"

"In the poor person's sleeper down the road a piece."

"Well, you can sleep in here tonight."

He sat down on the edge of the turned-down bed. "Look, I have something to tell you. I didn't think it would be like this— I mean, on the train and all—but I might as well tell you now."

She put her hand over his. "I think I know what you're going to say. That's the reason I flew all this way."

"It is?" *How could she have known about Eleanor?* "Why *are* you here?" he asked.

"After what happened with Erik I was furious with you, I really was. But it was nice too. I mean, your being jealous and all."

"Thanks, I'm glad I could do that for you."

"Well, I started to think things through. We've been together awhile now, and decisions have to be made."

"I couldn't agree with you more."

"And I've made my decision, and I didn't want to tell you over the phone and I couldn't wait until Christmas, because this might change our plans for the holidays."

Tom sighed in relief. "I really think we're on the same page here."

She leaned forward and put both hands on his shoulders. "Tom, I want to get married."

All he could say was, "To who?"

"To you, silly, and I think it's to *whom*. But you're the writer."

"You want to marry me? You flew all this way to tell me you want to get married? To me?" He rose in his agitation and paced in his anxiety, and the result was that Tom banged his head against the large window like a bird desperately trying to escape confinement.

"Lelia, this is a long way from seeing each other a few times a year for fun and games. This is for a lifetime, and every day, good times and bad."

"Don't you think I know that?"

He pointed at her. "Is this some new class you're taking? Some New Age psychedelic voodoo parapsychology crap?"

She stood up. "No, this is about me. I'm not getting any younger. My biological clock isn't just ticking, its alarm is ringing, and I've hit the snooze button so many times it doesn't work anymore."

"You're saying you want to have children?"

"Yes, don't you?"

"You're asking me if I want children?"

"Are you deaf? Yes!"

"How do I know if I want kids? I didn't know you were going to come and propose tonight. Let a guy catch his breath, will you."

She put her arms around him. "I know it's all of a sudden. But we're good together, Tom, really good. I've got plenty of money and we can do whatever we want. We'll travel, play, enjoy good times, and then settle down and have a huge family."

"Huge? Huge family? How huge?"

"Well, I'm one of eight."

He looked at her petite frame. "You work out six hours a

day. Are you saying you're going to let your body bloat up eight times? Even if we space it out a kid every two years, you'll be sixty by the time the last bundle of joy pops out, Lelia."

"Well, I thought we'd have one the regular way and adopt the rest—you know, all at once. Sort of an instant family."

He put a hand through his hair with an impulse to tear most of it out. "I can't believe this."

"What, did you think we were just going to do our little bi-coastal thing until one of us died? That was not a relationship of permanence, Tom."

"Agreed. It wasn't permanent."

"I know this is a lot to throw at you. Take your time and think about it. It's two days to LA. Just think about it, and then let me know."

"In two days? You want me to let you know if I want to get married and have eight kids, in two days?"

"Well, depending on your answer, we'll have a lot to do, so, yes, promptness would be appreciated."

She kissed him on the cheek and took his hands in hers. "Now, what were you going to tell me?"

He just stared at her open-mouthed, unable to speak, since no words were strong enough to survive the acid eating through his throat. They just melted like snow on a griddle. He turned to leave.

"Where are you going?"

He found his voice. "To the bar."

"When will you be back?"

"Two days."

chapter twenty-four

As Tom staggered to the lounge car to find support at the bottom of as many tequila shots as he could fire into his body, the Chief hurtled on to Lawrence, Kansas, primarily known as the home of the University of Kansas. They'd reach that stop at about one-thirty in the morning, followed by Topeka at two, and thereafter in fairly quick succession Newton, Hutchinson, Dodge City, and Garden City, their last stop in Kansas before entering Colorado. La Junta, the site of the marriage, was the second stop in Colorado, and about two hours before the Chief began its assault on the Raton Pass.

The storm was now fully formed and, driven by fierce upper-level winds, was plowing south, knocking against the immovable frame of the Rocky Mountains. So far the winter in the area had seen above-normal snowfall, and the mountaintops were heavily wreathed in white. The winds kicked some of the fallen snow around, but no serious damage was reported, and while forecasters had their eye on the moving mass of swirling wind and moisture, they had no reason to be-

lieve it was any different from countless storms that had come
before it.

The Chief would have to ascend toward the Raton Pass,
navigate the half-mile-long tunnel that ran under the pass, and
then descend into the station stop at Raton. As soon as the train
exited the tunnel, it would leave Colorado and enter New Mexico. There'd also been considerable snowfall here, and the
mountaintops were caked with many feet of hardened snow that
normally wouldn't leave until summer, and even then some of
the highest peaks would retain their white beard pretty much all
year round. It would take a lot to dislodge all those millions of
tons of snow.

Eleanor wandered through the train, trying to stop from dissolv-
ing into tears. She looked in on Father Kelly, who was sitting in
his compartment, fully dressed and reading his Bible. He invited
her in, and she sat down next to him.

"Can't sleep?" she asked.

"Well, Max is hosting a bachelor's party for Steve, and I'm
resting up for that. You know, when I had my parish, I worked sixteen hours a day and slept hard for eight hours at night, my mind
free from worry because of Him, and because I'd done my best
during the day. And now that I'm 'out of the service,' so to speak,
I don't work nearly as hard and I don't seem to require nearly as
much sleep. And the train is a soothing place to read and reflect. I
spent all my time and consideration on my parishioners' trouble
for all those years, and I guess I didn't reflect enough on my own.
Pretty late in life to arrive at that conclusion, isn't it?"

"Better late than never," she said.

He said diplomatically, "I saw Tom with that lady. They
seemed to know each other very well."

"I guess they should. They're sort of a couple, somehow."

"Oh, I see."

She looked at the Bible in his lap. "Any advice in there for a broken heart?"

"There's help in here for anything that ails you, Eleanor."

"I go to Mass regularly, but I haven't studied the Scriptures as much as I should have. Maybe I should do something about that."

He smiled. "Well, better late than never. I'll be talking to Him later, and I'll be sure to say a blessing for you. I'll even make it a double."

"I really appreciate that, Father."

"They say that during the week of Christmas any miracle is possible. Of course, as a priest I believe that miracles are always possible, but it does seem that around the birthdate of Jesus there's a more positive energy out there."

"That's a nice thought," she said unconvincingly.

"Things might look bad now, but in matters of the heart you'd be surprised how quickly things can change."

"Actually, that's what I'm afraid of."

"Where there's faith, there is no fear."

She smiled weakly. "What part of the Bible is that from?"

He patted her hand. "That one, my dear, is from Father Paul Joseph Kelly. And you can have it at no extra charge."

Roxanne walked through the lounge car, doing a last check on things, and saw Herrick Higgins still sitting there staring out the window. She sat next to him.

"Why don't you get to bed, Herrick? I have a spare bunk in the transition car I fixed up for you."

"Thank you, Roxanne. I'll get to bed shortly."

She followed his gaze out the window at the plunging snow. "I put extra food on at KC, just in case."

"You're a wise woman. One can never be too careful."

"You getting nervous on me after all these years, Mr. Higgins?"

He shrugged and smiled. "Maybe I'm inventing worries just so I can feel useful again."

She put a hand on his shoulder. "They should never have let you go. When we all heard about it, that was the consensus up and down the line. Some folks work these trains, they don't care, just drawing down a paycheck, but you're not like that. People like you put the soul in these big hunks of steel."

"*And* people like you, Roxanne."

As the Chief rolled on, she said, "I've been doing this a lotta years. I wonder when it's time to make the last train stop and call it a show."

"When and if you do, do it on your terms, Roxanne, not anyone else's."

"Well, there might not even be trains ten years from now. What happens then?"

He smiled. "Then we tell our grandchildren how wonderful they were to ride."

Tom was intercepted by Max and Misty before he could reach the lounge car.

"I need a drink," he told Max. "I need a drink so unbelievably bad. If I don't get one I'm not responsible for my actions."

Max said, "I've got every drink you can think of plus a case of chilled wine in my compartment. Let's start the bachelor's party right now. And I decided, why limit it to the guys? So I invited the girls too."

"Actually," said Misty, "I think that was my idea."

"How'd you manage all the booze?"

"He's Max Powers," said Misty.

"I just phoned ahead to Kansas City and said 'Charge it.' This isn't exactly rocket science, kids."

"I love it when he calls me a kid," said Misty. "Makes me feel so young."

"We have a wedding tomorrow, and you and Eleanor and the others are playing pivotal roles. So along with the party we have to rehearse too."

"I don't think that's such a good idea right now, Max," said Tom.

"Don't be silly. Take it from me, I know what I'm talking about. I do this for a living. You have to rehearse or else you'll screw up. We owe it to Steve and Julie to put on a good show. Now come on, kiddies, Uncle Max always gets his way."

The man literally skipped down the corridor, obviously enjoying himself immensely. Misty followed, and that left Tom to trudge miserably after the impish pair.

Max sent Kristobal out to round up Steve, Julie, Eleanor, Roxanne, and the minister who'd be conducting the service. The latter was tall and trim, with short gray hair, a wise look, and kindly eyes, the perfect image of a man of the cloth. Tom actually would have preferred Father Kelly who was also in attendance. The priest tried to chat with his colleague, but the minister was quite standoffish and Father Kelly finally gave up. Max's compartment consisted of two rooms arranged as a suite. Tom looked around at the spaciousness. "How'd he manage this?"

"He's Max Powers," said Misty.

The director took center stage and passed out pieces of paper stapled together. "Okay, here's the script for tomorrow including each scene—I mean, each part of the wedding."

Tom slid over to Kristobal, who was manning the bar that had been set up in one corner. "Got any scotch?" he said.

"I'm afraid all we have is twenty-five-year-old single-malt Macallan's. It's Mr. Powers's personal favorite."

Tom stared at him. "Well, I guess that'll just have to do, won't it?"

"I spent all afternoon typing out those scripts," said Kristobal. "Max, of course, had a million changes, he always does. The man is brilliant, I have to give him that."

Tom sipped his scotch and looked over at Eleanor, who, it seemed to him, was trying mightily not to make eye contact with anyone, particularly him. And who could blame her? She was studiously going over the script while Max barked directions to everyone.

Tom had just worked up the courage to go over to her when Lelia flounced in and sidled up to him.

"I understand there's a bachelor's party going on that *my* Mr. Langdon failed to tell me about." Then Lelia's gaze fell upon Max Powers. Tom noted that as soon as the director saw Lelia, he tried to hide behind Misty.

"Max? Max Powers?" said Lelia. "My God, it *is* you." Lelia fussed at her hair and tugged at her dress though both were immaculate.

Max turned back, acted surprised, and then said, "Lelia, is that really you?"

Tom said, "You know each other?"

"Oh, it was years ago," said Max quietly.

"But it feels like yesterday, Max," said Lelia. "I auditioned for one of his films, a minor role. It was years ago, but he was already a legend," she added in an awestruck tone.

"Now, Lelia," said Max nervously, "my ego is big enough without your adding to it."

She didn't appear to hear him. "I didn't get the role. You remember the film, Max?"

"No, sweetie, I really don't. I've lost so many brain cells since then."

"It was *Fall of Summer*, about a young couple falling in and out of love during a summer holiday."

"Right, right, of course."

"I never really knew why I didn't get the part of the girl's best friend, Bambi Moore."

"Obviously, one of my biggest mistakes, Lelia. I made lots of them early on in my career."

"Well, you had the decency to take me to dinner one night. Do you remember that?"

"Of course, dinner. It was lovely."

"And dinner stretched to breakfast. I trust you remember that part of the audition." Lelia hiked her eyebrows and puckered her lips.

"Let's break out the booze," shouted Max, "and get this rehearsal really rolling."

Max's considerable skill as a director and obsession over the smallest detail were felt by all that night. Again and again he put them through their paces.

Finally Tom called for a break, over Max's protests, which were quickly shouted down by all hands.

Lelia walked over to Eleanor while Tom looked on in horror at this imminent clash.

"I understand you're the maid of honor and Tom is the best man. How fun and convenient for you."

"You really think so?" said Eleanor. "Those weren't the adjectives jumping to my mind."

"Tom and I are going to Tahoe for Christmas."

"You went from LA to Kansas City and got on a train headed back to LA so you can go to Tahoe for Christmas? That's quite a circuitous route to take."

"Well, I had something very important to ask Tom."

"Oh, what was that?"

"To marry me."

Eleanor looked over at Tom furiously, and then Lelia said, "Somebody told me you and Tom once dated. You don't have hepatitis, do you?" she added with an impish grin at Tom.

"Excuse me?" said Eleanor.

"You know, it's funny, Eleanor . . . it *is* Eleanor, isn't it? Well, it's funny Tom never once mentioned your name. I guess it wasn't a very memorable relationship."

"Sure he mentioned my name," said Eleanor. "Probably when you two were in bed together." Lelia's mouth dropped so far Tom could see the woman still had her tonsils.

"So, how's everyone doing on drinks?" was all he could think to say.

With one more fierce glance at him, Eleanor said to Lelia, "Don't worry, honey, you can have him."

As Eleanor stormed out Tom raced over, but Lelia grabbed him. "Did you hear what she said to me?"

Tom stopped and watched as Eleanor disappeared down the hall.

"Tom, did you hear me?"

He finally looked at her. "Lelia."

"What?"

"Shut up."

Lelia seemed poised to erupt at him, but she simply spun around on her heels and left.

As Tom's world was collapsing, Roxanne stood up and said

to Max, "Okay, baby, let's cut to the chase." She held up her script pages. "This stuff is okay, but I'm gonna need some wiggle room to improvise."

"Wiggle room? Improvise?" said Max nervously.

"Yeah, you know, do some things on the fly, play off the energy of the crowd."

"But it's a wedding, Roxanne. And preparation is the key to any successful project like this. I've got all the songs I want you to sing listed and in due sequence."

Steve and Julie just looked anxiously at the pair as they squared off.

"I'll be prepared, but you can't cage the wild bird, Max. You got to let the wild bird fly when it wants to, or else it dies."

"But—"

She put a hand on Max's shoulder. "Look here, baby, you trust me, don't you?"

"Well, sure, but—"

"Then that's all I need to know." She turned to Steve and Julie and patted their hands. "Now you two get a good night's sleep. This train will be rocking tomorrow, in your honor. I promise you one thing, you're never gonna forget Roxanne Jordan and the Southwest Chief."

As people started to trickle away, Tom stood there looking so miserable that Max finally came over to him. "You look like you could use another drink." Max mixed two cocktails and the men sat down.

"So, that Roxanne is great, isn't she?"

"Yeah, great," said Tom distractedly.

Max slapped Tom on the thigh. "Sorry there wasn't a girl popping out of a cake at the bachelor party. I didn't think it would be appropriate with the ladies present, and, to tell you the truth, Amtrak probably would have balked at that one."

Tom finally focused on the director. "So, you—what—
dated Lelia?"

"Well, I wouldn't call it dating, actually. It was just the one
time, as far as I can remember. My memory is not what it was.
Hey, did *I* hear right? Lelia asked you to marry her?"

Tom nodded.

"Man, I guess women do that these days. So does that mean
if you divorce she has to pay *you* alimony?"

"She won't have to pay me anything because we're not getting married."

"Look, Tom, I'm not trying to butt in or anything, but Lelia
is beautiful, and doesn't she do some cartoon thing that brings
her big bucks?"

"Cuppy the Magic Beaver, Freddy the Futon, Petey the
Pickle."

"Right, Cuppy, Petey, that's good stuff. I think one of my
exwife's step-grandkids used to watch it. Anyway, okay, she's
beautiful, she's got bucks, and she asked you to marry her. So
don't rush your decision, you might not get another chance. No
offense, you're a good-looking guy and I like you, but you're not
exactly a spring chicken anymore either."

"You're right, she's rich, she's beautiful—and I don't love
her, Max."

Max sat back against his seat and let out a long sigh. "I've
done the deed four times now. Who knows—maybe there's a
fifth in the works for me."

"And you loved them all?"

The director leaned forward and his expression grew
somber. "Patty was my first wife, married right out of high
school. I joined the army, then moved to California. We had four
kids. We were dirt poor but she never complained, not once. She
could stretch a buck further than anyone I've ever met. I broke

into the movie business. I was just starting to make it when she died." Max grew quiet, looked out the window at the passing countryside. "Yeah, I loved Patty with everything I had. I'll always love Patty. My three exwives?" He shrugged. "I married them, had some good times, divorced them, and that was it. I loved them, in a way. But not like Patty. If she'd lived I'd never have even looked at another woman. I guess there's something special about your first love. Now I just play the field and I have fun, but I'm not all that proud of it. None of it's permanent. You know?"

Tom nodded. "I know."

Max looked at Tom. "You ever been married?" Tom nodded again. "Did you love her?"

"Let's put it this way: She was no Patty."

Max drew closer to Tom and said in a low voice, "Again, I'm not trying to butt in, but can you answer a question for me?"

"I guess."

"Why aren't you and Eleanor together?"

"You saw what happened. She just stormed out of here."

"Well, you can't blame her really. Your girlfriend flies in from LA to propose. Now, God knows I'm no expert in affairs of the heart, but that's not exactly the ideal way to win back the love of your life."

"I've tried, Max, I've really tried."

"Well, you know what?"

Tom looked at him. "What?"

"If she's really *your* Patty, I'd try harder."

chapter twenty-five

Eleanor was back in her compartment about to swallow a sleeping pill of enormous diameter when someone knocked on her door.

"Go away," she yelled.

"Eleanor? It's me."

She looked blank for a moment, trying to identify the voice through the dulled filters of her very overwrought mind.

"Julie?" She went to the door and opened it, and there stood the young bride-to-be, tears in her eyes. She was holding a long garment bag.

"What's the matter? Steve's parents didn't call again, did they?"

Julie shook her head. "And neither did mine."

Eleanor looked confused. "I'm not sure I understand."

"Can I come in for a few minutes?"

"What? Oh, um, sure." Eleanor slipped the knockout pill in her pocket. "But it's late and you have a big day tomorrow. You need to get some rest."

The two women sat on the edge of the bed.

"So your parents didn't call and you're sad because . . ." she coaxed.

"Well, I suppose a girl envisions her parents being at her wedding. I mean, most brides I've known have been control freaks about their wedding, and it's not like I feel helpless or anything. But, still, you imagine your father giving his little girl away and your mom telling you everything's going to be okay. And, well, I don't have any of that."

She suddenly burst into tears and sobbed for some time while Eleanor held her tightly. When she finally stopped, Julie wiped her eyes and looked embarrassed.

"I'm sorry. I'm a grown woman and I should be able to handle this, but I just feel so alone."

Eleanor brought her a damp washcloth to wipe her face.

"You have every right to feel that way, and I guess I've been a pretty lousy maid of honor."

"Well, you were recruited at the last minute. You don't even really know me."

"It shouldn't matter. We're both women. You're going to be a bride tomorrow. That's all I should need to know."

"Have you even been married?"

"No," said Eleanor quietly, "but I've thought about it a lot. Imagined every detail of it, down to the finger foods and flower displays. I don't dream about it as much as I used to, though."

"Why not?"

"It's a simple matter of time. Years go by, the chances of it happening steadily diminish."

"Well, all you need is someone who loves you and you love him back."

Eleanor smiled when she actually felt like bawling harder than Julie just had. "Yep, that's all you need." She touched the garment bag Julie had set on the bed. "What's this?"

Julie looked embarrassed again. "It's my wedding gown. I haven't tried it on since I bought it. I thought maybe, you know."

"What a wonderful idea," said Eleanor.

"You sure you don't mind? Like you said, it's late and I'm sure you're tired."

"Actually, I *was* tired, but now I'm not."

Eleanor helped Julie into her dress, a simple yet elegant outfit of cream white that fit perfectly. As she was about to place the veil on Julie's head, Julie took it and put it on Eleanor. The two women stood side by side in front of the full-length mirror.

"You look beautiful, Julie."

"So do you."

Julie started laughing hysterically and Eleanor finally joined her.

Later, as Eleanor was about to pack up the gown and Julie was in the bathroom, Eleanor put the veil back on and held the gown up to her and looked in the mirror.

"Ellie?"

She looked over where the door to her compartment had slid open with the curves of the track and the acceleration of the Chief. It was Tom, staring at her. Her arms couldn't move. She just stood there mutely covered by another woman's wedding dress.

"Ellie?" he said again as he stepped through the door.

At that moment Julie came out of the bathroom and looked at each of them. "Sorry if I interrupted something," she said.

Eleanor lowered the gown, took the veil, and carefully packed it all away while Tom watched. She handed the garment bag to Julie, gave her a hug, and said with a smile, "Sleep hard, your whole life changes tomorrow morning. For the better."

Julie kissed her on the cheek, turned, and walked past Tom, who still stood there, looking as awkward as he did confused.

"What do you want, Tom?"

"You looked really beautiful in the dress, Ellie."

"It's late, shouldn't you be with Lelia?"

"I don't love Lelia!"

"Well, she seems to love you. I assume you must have shown some affection, or made some comment or promise to her, because I find it hard to believe the woman would have flown all this way to ask you to marry her out of friendship or kindness. Frankly, she doesn't strike me as the type."

"I'm telling you, our relationship was not like that."

"Really, so what was it like to make her come all this way?" She folded her arms across her chest and waited expectantly.

"How do I know why she'd do something like that? She's nuts."

"You've been seeing each other how long?"

Tom sputtered, "About three years. But off and on."

"Off and on? Three years?"

"Yes!"

"And you expected her to be content with that?"

He just looked at her blankly.

Eleanor continued. "So she wanted to make a commitment but you didn't. You were perfectly happy with popping in, popping out, sharing the good times not the bad, and going your solo way when you felt like it?"

"It's not like that, Ellie. I'm not like that anymore."

"Sure you're not. You haven't changed. Not a bit."

"It would be different. With the right woman."

Eleanor rubbed her temples. "Listen, we have a wedding to do tomorrow. Someone *else's* wedding. I need some sleep."

"We can't leave it like this."

"Oh yes we can, and we are."

He moved to take her in his arms but she firmly pushed him away. "We'll do our duty tomorrow, we'll get to LA, and we'll go our separate ways. This time for good."

"Ellie!"

"Goodbye, Tom." She slid the door closed with finality.

chapter twenty-six

⌒

The dawn broke over the high plains of Colorado near the New Mexico border, but the sun was completely hidden by a vast sky of threatening clouds. The snow lay thickly over the ground, covering the ubiquitous sagebrush. Most folks assembled for an early breakfast, because word had spread rapidly about the upcoming nuptials. As the train neared La Junta, the excitement grew and virtually all the passengers and crew crowded into the lounge car such that there was barely enough room for the wedding procession, which consisted of the bride and groom, and a maid of honor and best man who never once looked at each other. Even though they walked in together arm-in-arm it was as though an invisible force separated them.

The wedding went off without any major glitches. A group of musicians Max had hired and who'd gotten on early that morning played the traditional "Wedding March" and other tunes. Kristobal filmed the entire event, and Max directed as best he could, with most people on the train not even knowing this was a Max Powers production of sorts. Tom and Eleanor did their respective parts though Tom, for one awkward moment, couldn't find the ring and then for one even much more awkward moment seemed to be trying to place it on Eleanor's finger instead of handing it to Steve. Then that was all straightened out and Tom was able to step back and quietly ponder various suicide opportunities that might come his way.

The bride and groom kissed right as the train stopped at La Junta, and Julie raised her fist in the air and shouted, "Yes!"

Normally, Pike's Peak would be clearly visible at the stop, but not even that towering chunk of rock could be seen through the cloud cover. All throughout the ceremony Herrick Higgins had sat quietly in his corner and watched the vicious-looking sky.

Everyone on board threw rice, and outside the window a group of mostly train personnel from the station did the same, the white kernels disappearing rapidly in the swirling snow.

At La Junta the Chief also attached the third diesel engine to help it over the pass. As the train pulled out of the station, the crowd lining the track roared in appreciation at the "Just Married" sign that had been hung on the last car of the Chief and the strung tin cans rattling just below the sign. It was an enviable beginning to any marriage.

Then the party on the train really started, highlighted by the enormous feast Max had also paid for. As people stuffed themselves and the official wedding photographer took photos, Roxanne came sweeping out in a flamboyant costume that was definitely not Amtrak standard issue. She was trailed by the LA Boys' Center Choir, also dressed in their finest. The crowd grew quiet, the musicians stood ready, and Roxanne and the choir began to sing. It was all a vast yet delicate thing of beauty. They sang classical songs, then the blues, then some hiphop, and next a string of tunes from Nat King Cole to Sinatra. Roxanne followed that up with a solo by urging Steve and Julie to "Think . . . Think . . ." and then belted out "Chain of Fools," doing her best Aretha Franklin impersonation and next the queen of soul's signature piece, "Respect." The crowd was so into it by this time that people were standing and shouting out each letter with her: "R-E-S-P-E-C-T!" The woman's voice was booming, and she was swirling around the floor in intricate dance steps with a grace and litheness that belied her great size. Sweat was streaming down her face and neck, and she seemed truly possessed by something heavenly as she shouted out a series of "Amen"s.

Max could only sit back and smile. He ceremoniously tore up his script when Roxanne looked over at him, and then she pulled him up with her and they danced together, at which point everyone else joined in. While the Capitol Limited had probably seen such strutting before, this was probably a first for the Southwest Chief.

Lelia pulled Tom over, but he managed to promptly pull himself away, citing nausea, which wasn't altogether a falsehood. It had truly been a rough night for him, much of which had been spent in the communal bathroom giving back most of the alcohol he'd drank. Poor, deserted Lelia looked around and spotted Kristobal, who was packing away the video equipment.

"Care to dance?" she asked the handsome young man. Kristobal looked up and his eyes perceptibly widened at her glamorous figure and attire. "You work for Mr. Powers, don't you?" Kristobal nodded. "I'm Lelia Gibson."

His eyes widened further and he blurted out, "Lelia Gibson, the voice of Cuppy the Magic Beaver?"

She was taken aback. "Why, yes. You know the show?"

"Know the show? It was my favorite when I was a kid. My little brother still watches it. And all my nieces and nephews, it's their number-one program. You're terrific. I saw you at Mr.

Powers's party last night but I never heard your name. And I only knew you, well, by voice."

Lelia looked flustered. "You watched it as a child? My, I have been doing the show a long time, haven't I?"

Kristobal dropped all pretense of self-restraint or professional dignity, so overwhelmed was he. "And Sassy Squirrel and Freddy the Futon and Petey the Orange Pickle, they're all classics. I cried during the episode when Petey was caught in the storm drain and all his color was washed out. The depth of emotion you gave him during that tragic scene. It took me weeks to get over it. Look, I don't mean to gush, but I just can't believe you're on this train. Would it be asking too much for your autograph? My family is just not going to believe this. My little brother is going to freak."

"Why, certainly you can have my autograph, um . . ."

"Oh, where are my manners? I'm Kristobal Goldman." He gave her hand an enthusiastic shake that almost lifted petite Lelia right out of her outrageously expensive, open-toed three-inch heels.

"I tell you what, Kristobal, I'll autograph anything you want if you'll dance with me."

An astonished Kristobal bowed deeply and off they went.

While everyone was preoccupied at the wedding and party afterward, about twenty more compartments were robbed of various items, from watches and rings to bracelets and even Max's pair of Bruno Maglis. Once more the thief made a clean getaway, although there was someone lurking in the corridor who might have seen something suspicious. Yet no alarm was given, and the thief quickly melded back into the partygoers. The bag of loot was bulging more than ever, and they still had a day remaining before their scheduled arrival into LA.

During the night before the wedding the storm had settled over the border between Colorado and New Mexico. Virtually locked in place by a high-pressure system, the clouds were now so heavy with moisture that something had to give; and it did at about three o'clock in the morning, with the Chief still over eight hours away. The gauges used to measure snowfall were filled within an hour; the enormously strong instruments erected to quantify windspeed were toppled in thirty minutes. All commercial flights were instructed to give the area a wide berth and all nearby ski resorts were closed.

The Raton Pass had endured five winter storms already, and the snow packed on the mountains was kept there by freezing temperatures and the weight of the snow itself. When the current storm finally came crashing down, two things happened: The temperatures actually rose a few degrees, and the new snow fell so heavily and so fast that it didn't simply settle on top of the snow below, it hit and then slid, with more snow falling and tumbling right behind it. Thus tremendous momentum was built up in a very short time. By seven o'clock conditions were near whiteout. Then at nine-thirty, there was a sudden lull in the storm and the forecasters predicted the system had exhausted itself and would rapidly dissipate, with a change in the prevailing winds now directing the worst of it north and east.

Someone once said to Mark Twain, upon the occasion of a sudden rain shower, that he hoped the storm would stop, whereupon Twain had replied that the odds were good because it always had. He'd also remarked that weather in general was very accommodating: If one didn't like what it was doing at any given moment, all one had to do was wait a bit and the weather would change. Twain had never put much stock in weather predicting, no doubt sensibly concluding that the science of foretelling what Mother Nature intended was a sorry one at best and a fool's gamble at worst.

Well, some things hadn't changed, because even with satellites and super Doppler radar and other state-of-the-art devices to help them, the meteorologists following the current storm did what meteorologists often do: They got it wrong. The blizzard had been merely resting. Now millions of tons of Pacific moisture and galelike winds were perfectly posed to add one to the history books.

chapter twenty-seven

Most of the wedding partygoers had dispersed by now, but Max and Misty, Kristobal and Lelia, and Herrick Higgins were all sitting in the lounge car. Tom and Eleanor had left separately right after Roxanne had finished singing, and they hadn't been seen since. Roxanne had gone to take care of train business and get the choir settled back down after their hard work. Married now, Steve and Julie had been given an empty double deluxe in which to officially commence their honeymoon with, no doubt, considerable gusto.

The Chief was now well past Trinidad, Colorado, and had its sights set squarely on the Raton Pass. Everyone watched as the train started its ascent. As the grade grew steeper, and the deep whine of the three engines grew louder, there was a creeping uneasiness among the passengers. The vast amounts of snow being pushed off the track by the lead engine's plow could be seen at every curve. It was a wonder that the engineer could see at all with all that white flying around.

Kristobal said, "Uh, what happens if one of the cars comes loose? Do we just go barreling down into the abyss?"

Higgins replied, "No, the automatic braking system comes on and the car stops. Train technology has come a long way over the years." He pointed out the window. "We'll climb to 7,580 feet at the highest point."

"That's pretty high," said Kristobal.

"Well, it's not the highest track elevation in this country. That's on the California Zephyr past Denver at a little over 9,200 feet. In South America—I forget which country—there's a train track at an elevation so high they have to give out oxygen to the passengers. We go through a half-mile-long tunnel that runs under the pass, and once we get out of that we're in New Mexico. We'll descend down the eastern side of the Sangre de Cristo Mountains and into Raton. Raton's at an elevation of 6,666 feet, so while the descent is sharp, it's not really that far."

Misty looked stricken, and she grabbed Max's arm. "Did you say 6,666 feet?"

Higgins looked at her over the rim of his coffee cup. "Yes, ma'am."

"Are you sure that's the elevation? Exactly?"

"Well, yes, ma'am. They measure those things pretty precisely."

"Oh my God!" said Misty.

"What's wrong, honey?" asked Max.

"Don't you see, 6-6-6-6? It's the worst possible combination of numbers, it's even worse than a triple 6."

Max turned pale. "You're right, the mark of the Devil, plus another 6. Totally bad karma."

"Is this really a problem?" asked a nervous-looking Kristobal.

"In my line of business, it doesn't get much worse," said Misty emphatically. "Can we stop the train?"

"Isn't there a brake rope to pull, like in the movies?" asked

Lelia. She was seated next to Kristobal and was anxiously clutching his arm.

"Uh, no, they don't have those anymore," said Higgins. "Now just calm down, it'll be okay. The Chief runs this route twice a day, east and west." He checked his watch. "We'll be entering the tunnel pretty soon."

"Is it dark?" Kristobal wanted to know.

"Well, most tunnels are, son," replied Higgins judiciously. "But we won't be in it long. In and out in a blink and then on to Raton and New Mexico."

Tom eyed the diamond ring in his hand. It had belonged to his mother, and ever since her death he'd carried it with him. In fact, he'd very nearly pulled this ring out and handed it to Steve instead of the one he was supposed to. In turn, that bit of confusion had also led him to start toward Eleanor with the band of gold rather than merely handing it to Steve to place on Julie's finger. He pocketed the ring, examined himself in the mirror, smoothed down a few stray hairs, adjusted the tie that Kristobal had loaned him for the wedding ceremony, took a long breath, and told himself for the hundredth time that this was what he had to do.

A few minutes later he knocked on Eleanor's compartment door. She slid back the curtain, stared at him, then drew the curtain back and he heard the door lock click into place. He rapped on the glass again. "Ellie, I really need to talk to you, right now."

"Go away!"

"I need to ask you something, and I'm going to ask you right now."

She flung the door open so hard, metal plunked hard on metal.

"I thought I'd made myself *more* than perfectly clear!"

Tom reached into his pocket for the ring and started to shakily descend to his knees.

The interior of the train was thrown into darkness as the Chief entered the tunnel. The next events happened with terrifying suddenness. All of the snow covering the southern crest of the mountain closest to the train tracks broke loose from the over-powering strength of relentless wind gusts and the tons of new-fallen snow. Officially, the avalanche started at 11:15 Mountain time, and it raced down the mountainside at tremendous speed; it was enough snow that, if it were melted, it would have formed a decent-sized lake of considerable depth. The avalanche hit the slide fences located between the mountain slope and the train tracks, which had been installed there for the very purpose of detecting track intrusions. The impact occurred with such force that it not only flattened the steel fence but also ripped it off its supports and carried it down the mountain.

This collision sent an automatic red alert to Amtrak Dispatch that, in turn, instantly communicated to the engineer of the Southwest Chief to stop the train dead in its tracks pending further developments.

The Chief had just emerged from the tunnel under the Raton Pass when the signal was given, and the engineer applied the brakes with the swiftness that the gravity of the situation required. Indeed, he didn't need the warning by Amtrak Dispatch because he could see the awesome spectacle clearly through his windshield, though it was a considerable distance up the track. So powerful was the tidal wave of snow and rock that it spread out laterally, and a substantial tributary headed dead at the Chief with enough potential lethality to cause the engineer, who'd been running this route for fourteen years, to whisper a quick goodbye to his wife and kids. He'd seen many things during his railroad career but nothing that came close to what was presently bearing down on him and his train. He closed his eyes, because all he could envision happening in the next few seconds was the utter destruction of the Southwest Chief and all those on board.

As the train lurched to a halt, everyone sensed that this wasn't a normal stop. When the idling train began to shake as though an earthquake were occurring, they became sure of it. Thankfully, they couldn't see what the engineer could, but they all heard a growing rumble that was immediately identifiable to several people on board who'd heard such sounds before.

"It's an avalanche," shouted Tom, as he looked out the window.

Eleanor paled. "My God."

He ripped a mattress off the bed, grabbed Eleanor, threw her on the floor, put the mattress on top of her, and then covered the mattress with his body as the train continued to shake and gyrate and the sounds of the mountain's snowy skin sliding off became deafening.

Back in the lounge car everyone was under the tables. Some scribbled last will and testaments on napkins, others stumbled through long-forgotten prayers. Max and Misty clung to each other, and Lelia and Kristobal did the same, his long arms wrapped protectively around her.

Higgins was under the table too, but he was looking out the window still, his worst fears realized with sudden ferocity.

Miraculously, the enormous sideways thrust of the hurtling snow stopped before it knocked the train off the track. However, when the engineer finally opened his eyes, the only thing he saw was an impenetrable wall of snow.

He managed to report in to Amtrak and was told that, presumably, a second avalanche on the other side of the tunnel had taken another slide fence with it. A minute or two either early or late and the Chief would be at the bottom of a ravine, not a single person on board having to worry further about the upcoming holiday. Yes, lucky indeed, the engineer was told by Amtrak Dispatch, though he'd seen that for himself. On the other hand, the Chief was now sandwiched in, unable to go either forward or back, and the storm apparently was just getting started.

The meteorologists had now weighed in with an updated forecast, an accurate one this time. The region was being blasted by a winter storm the likes of which hadn't been seen in thirty years. The old storm had claimed over six hundred lives, with some people, cut off from every known point of civilization, having died of starvation. They were folks in remote, inaccessible areas, precisely like the one in which the Chief was now idling helplessly.

Higgins looked to the sky as high winds began to sweep off the mountain and buffet the Chief with such power that the enormously heavy train was rocking back and forth at unsettling angles. In all his years working the rails, he'd never been in a position quite like this. Looking out the left-side window, no one could fail to see that it was a long way down. With the snow continuing to fall, another avalanche couldn't be ruled out. And the next one just might take the Southwest Chief with it.

chapter twenty-eight

﹏

An hour later Roxanne issued a formal announcement over the train's PA system, telling people what had happened and what was being done to help the trapped train. The latter was fairly meager, since there wasn't a whole lot that could be done right now. As she explained, with twin mountains of snow blocking both the way to LA and the rails back to Chicago, the Chief squarely in the middle, and a blizzard hammering the region with high winds and snow, the best that could be done right now was for people to remain calm and in their compartments. It wasn't an easy instruction to follow, and the corridors were constantly filled with anxious folks seeking more detailed information.

Herrick Higgins had gone up to speak with the engineer and come back with an even more worried look. Tom and Eleanor had joined Misty and Max in the lounge car, where they alternated between staring out the window at a sheet of white snow, tensing with each slam of wind against the walls of the train, and occasionally peering out at the two-hundred-foot drop off the left side of the train. Lelia had discreetly retired to her compartment with her new compatriot, Kristobal.

"I knew this was going to happen," said Misty. "Four sixes, how could it not happen?"

"Well, I've been doing this a long time," said Higgins, "and it's never happened before. Train travel is the safest way there is to get around, even safer than a plane if you look at the numbers."

"Could there be another avalanche?" asked Misty. "One that hits the train?"

"It's Mother Nature," he replied, "so anything's possible, but I think with two avalanches already, most of the snow that's going to come down already did."

Tom looked at the old railroader. "So what now? How do they get to us? We can't exactly wait for the spring thaw."

"No, we can't. But getting to us is a little difficult. The freight company that owns these tracks is a good one, with lots of resources, but with the track blocked by all that snow and the weather the way it is, there's not much they can do. These are tight quarters here, not a lot of room to maneuver. And there's really no place for a small plane or helicopter to land, even if the weather settled down."

"Well, that's comforting," said Max.

Roxanne came up looking exhausted. She'd been everywhere in the last hour or so, calming passengers, consoling the boys' choir, making sure that all the things that could still be done on the train to make people more comfortable were done. She sat down and caught her breath.

"Well, on top of all this, it seems that the crook that hit the Cap got on board the Chief: A bunch of people have reported items missing."

Max shook his head. "This is truly amazing." He and Misty exchanged glances.

"The good thing," said Higgins, "is that we added the third engine at La Junta, so we have an extra powerplant to help us through." Roxanne nodded at this.

"What do you mean?" asked Max.

"The electrical power that keeps the lights, heat, et cetera going comes from electrical generators in the engines—generators powered by the diesel-fuel engines. Head-end power, it's called."

"So when we run out of fuel, we run out of electricity," said Tom.

"Basically that's right. But with an extra engine, it gives us more time."

"How much more time?" asked Max.

"Hard to say. We took on extra fuel in Kansas, but the Chief refuels at Albuquerque, about two hundred and fifty miles from here."

"And it took a lot of fuel to climb the pass, so the diesel tanks aren't exactly full," said Tom. Higgins nodded. "So we could be talking hours here, couldn't we, before the power goes."

"Well, the engineer is doing all he can to conserve fuel."

"Can't we put all the passengers in a few cars and cut off power to the others?" suggested Max.

"No, the system doesn't work that way. The engines generate true hotel-like power, and whether they're heating three cars or ten, it's the same fuel consumption. Now, when I went up to see the engineer, we did come up with a strategy. He's alternating among the three locomotives, putting one and then another in standby mode, which is the setting for supplying electrical power while standing still. That balances fuel supply among the units and conserves fuel, because the units not in standby mode are placed in slow idle and fuel burn is minimal."

"Why not just turn some of the engines off?" asked Eleanor.

"Burns too much fuel to get them started again," said Roxanne.

Higgins nodded and said, "And the other problem is that trains don't carry antifreeze in their coolant system because it takes too much water. You have to keep the engines idling to prevent the pipes from freezing. In weather this cold, once you turn off the head-end power and the heat fails, you have less than an hour before the pipes start freezing. Then you have no water for food preparation, drinking, sanitary requirements."

"I'm glad we put on extra food in KC," said Roxanne. "We'll start rationing right now, because we have no idea how long we'll be here." She rose to go back to work. "If I need help, I'm sure I can count on all of you, right?"

They all nodded back. She smiled bravely and trudged off.

Four hours later it grew dark. Most people had returned to their compartments and covered themselves with blankets and were now contemplating their possible demise.

Tom stopped in on Father Kelly, who was reading his Bible. "You know, you might want to lead a service on the train, Father, to lift people's spirits."

The priest said, "But not everyone's Catholic."

Tom looked out the window where the snow was still coming down and the wind was still slamming into them. "I'm not sure it really matters right now."

"I'm a little rusty, I'm afraid."

"It's like riding a bike, you never really forget how to do it."

Tom found Max and Misty cuddled together in the double deluxe. Misty was still depressed, but Max had regained his jocularity even with his missing pair of Bruno Maglis. "Figure the person who took them needs them more than me."

"That's generous of you," said Tom.

"I got way too much stuff as it is. But I have to tell you, with everything that's happened, this will make a great movie—if I just live through it to actually film it."

"Max!" scolded Misty.

"Always figured I'd go out in some enormous bang of a thing. Never thought it'd be on a train, though."

"Thanks, Max, that's very encouraging," she said.

"Aw, come on, Misty, it's all written in the stars. Tell me, what's your prediction? What do the cards tell you?"

"Max, not now."

"Are you telling me one little disaster is going to turn you from everything you believe in? That's pretty wimpy faith."

Misty sighed, pulled out her Tarot cards, started shuffling them, and then began laying them out, one at a time. At first she seemed totally uninterested in the process, glancing anxiously out the window with each mighty rumble of wind. But as she kept turning the cards over she started focusing and a deep frown creased her forehead. Finally, she said, "That's funny."

"What is?" asked Tom.

"Well, apparently we're going to be rescued."

"That's good news," said Max. "How?"

"Well, by something with six legs, that's how."

"Six legs?" said an incredulous Tom.

"Six again. That makes five sixes. Isn't that worse than four sixes?" asked Max.

"No, it says six legs here and rescued. I'll take it if I can get it," said Misty.

Max rose and went to the bar in the corner. "Well, until the six legs come, I need another bourbon. You drinking with us, Tom?"

"Maybe later, I've got things to do."

"Like what?"

"Like finding something with six legs, that's what."

The story of the trapped train hit all the national and international news wires and the world awaited further developments. Unfortunately, even with all the manpower and resources of the United States ready to save the train, an uncooperative Mother Nature had different plans. No plane within range could take off in this weather, and even if it could, it had nowhere to land. Choppers were also grounded. Everyone was simply waiting for the weather to clear. And since the train still had fuel, heat, and provisions, the situation, while serious, was not life-threatening and the urgency wasn't what it might be. Sit tight, they were told, and help would eventually get to them.

However, back at Amtrak HQ, rescue preparations were at full throttle. Developments were occurring quickly. Communications had been set up with the freight company that owned the track the Chief was sitting on, and the two organizations were jointly mapping out a strategy that would be executed when the weather abated.

Calls had also gone out around the country for the equipment and the manpower that would undoubtedly be needed to clear the tracks. Folks at Amtrak were dubious that they'd get much of a response, it being so near Christmas. In the all-points message that went out, however, someone had been alert enough to include the fact that Roxanne Jordan and the recently "retired" Herrick Higgins were on board the Chief. Within hours, thousands of calls and e-mails started flowing in from train personnel all over the country volunteering their services and giving up their Christmases to help.

Amtrak now had the manpower, and the equipment would become available shortly. Yet there was little they could do about the weather, which seemed to just keep getting worse.

chapter twenty-nine

The darkness grew deeper outside, the only sounds those of the wind and the snow falling against the roof and tinkling against the windows. Rest wasn't easy for anyone. With every little creak, people did not see images of sugarplum fairies and a fat man and his reindeer but rather envisioned the violent end of their lives.

There was another problem besides fuel and food running low; thankfully no passenger was aware of it, though the train people and Higgins certainly were. It concerned the snow buildup on the tops of the train cars. The weight was tremendous and while the cars were well built, they had their limits, and tons of snow piling on top severely tested those limits. The wind helped them, since it continually blew the accumulated snow off the cars. Yet the falling snow more than kept pace and quickly replaced the amounts blown away by the wind.

Most people chose not to eat dinner in the dining car, preferring to stay in their rooms and either snack or not eat at all but rather stare out the window helplessly. That helped with the food-supply burn rate, but at some point people would have to eat, and the Chief only had food for about another day or so. Roxanne had sent a team of men out to check under the train cars for freezing pipes. There were none as yet, they reported back. The men had been dressed in layers of clothing, yet when they came back in from such a short period outside, they were covered with snow and shivering uncontrollably.

The fuel problem was even worse. Higgins explained the situation to Tom and Eleanor as they quietly ate their dinner in the dining car. "Once the fuel runs out, we have lots of problems that will rapidly get worse. No water, pipes bursting, no heat."

"And if we do run out of fuel, even if they reach us, how can the train move? It's not like the air force where they can refuel a plane in the air," said Tom.

"Well, they'll attach engines with full tanks to the Chief and pull her along. But, like you said, they have to get to us first. I went up into the lead engine, and I saw how much snow is piled across the tracks up ahead, and it's a lot. It'll take a while to clear that."

"So maybe instead of waiting for help to get to us, we need to get to help."

"Where?" asked Eleanor. "Look around, Tom, we're in the middle of nowhere."

"Any ideas on that score, Herrick?" asked Tom. "You probably know the Amtrak route system as well as anyone."

Higgins thought about this for a bit. "Well, there's actually an interstate highway, I-25, that runs parallel to the pass between Raton and Trinidad and then veers north to Denver."

"A highway, that's something," said Tom. "We get to a car, that car gets us to help."

"Only they shut it down because of the storm," said Higgins.

"Okay, what else?"

The veteran railroad man thought a bit more and then finally shook his head. "No, that wouldn't work."

"What, say it."

"It wouldn't work," he insisted.

"Herrick, right now, I'd take the craziest idea you have. Maybe we can make it work."

Higgins shrugged and hunched forward. "There's a resort near here, in the mountains. It's a ski resort in the winter and then a dude ranch in the summer called the Dingo. It's only been in business a few years, but it's a big place, very well equipped and organized with lots of manpower. I went there a few times with my sons and their families and met the owners, a couple of transplanted Aussies who made a fortune on Wall Street and headed west for fun and something different. Problem is, you have to travel over some pretty rough terrain to get there, maybe a four-hour hike. It can be done by people in good physical shape in fair weather, but it would be impossible on foot in this storm."

Tom stared at him. "But not on skis."

"You have skis?" asked Higgins.

"I was going to Tahoe for Christmas. I've also got every conceivable sort of outerwear, boots, gloves, flares, compass, helmet light, you name it."

"It's really rough terrain, Tom."

"I've skied just about everything there is, Herrick, in all sorts of conditions. All I need from you is what direction and anything else you can tell me about the lay of the land."

"Do you really think you can manage it?" asked Higgins.

"I can promise you my best shot, that's all. And what do we have to lose?"

"How about your life?" Eleanor said.

"Well, it's my life, isn't it? It's not like I've got anyone to mourn me."

On that, Eleanor got up and left.

Higgins quickly gathered together the conductor, Roxanne, and the train engineer in the dining car with Tom to discuss it further. Neither the engineer nor the conductor liked the plan at all.

The conductor said, "He's a passenger. And while I appreciate the offer, Tom, I really do, if anything happens to you it'll be my responsibility. I can't let you go. We just need to sit tight and help will come."

"Can you get Amtrak Central on the communications phone? Or maybe we can contact the owners at the Dingo and they can send someone here," Higgins said to the engineer.

The man shook his head. "The storms disrupted the signals. My last call in to Central was hours ago. Haven't been able to get them on the horn since."

Roxanne added, "We've even tried all the cell phones on the train, and nobody's got any signal strength. We can't reach Central, the resort, or anybody else. Might as well be in the Stone Age."

"Look," said Tom, "I'm not going to just sit here and let this storm devour us. I'll sign any waiver you want, absolving you of all liability in case something happens to me. I had to sign one when I was reporting overseas. I'm a big boy, I'm used to taking care of myself."

"It's not just that, Tom," said Roxanne. "We don't want anything to happen to you, honey. It's not exactly a walk in the park outside right now."

"I've been in worse conditions, Roxanne, trust me." He gazed at each of them. "Just let me try. That's all I ask. If I can't get through, I'll come back, simple as that."

They all looked at each other, and finally the conductor and the engineer slowly nodded. "Okay."

Tom went to the baggage car with Roxanne and retrieved his ski equipment. Back at his compartment he was readying things when he felt someone behind him. It was Eleanor.

"I'm just getting ready," he said quietly.

"I see." She just stood there.

"Is there something you want? I'm kind of busy here."

"I don't want you to go."

"Okay, stop right there. I'm going."

"I guess you think you're going to save the train and everybody on it."

He looked up sharply. "Yeah, that's the general plan. No need to thank me for being a hero."

She came forward and perched on the edge of the seat. "Don't you think you might be running away instead?"

"I'm going out in a blizzard and risking my life to get help and you're calling me a coward. Thanks a hell of a lot."

Eleanor didn't shrink from this verbal attack.

"Do you really want to know why I left you in Tel Aviv? Maybe you should hear it, since you might not be coming back."

He looked at her a long moment and then he sat down too. "Well, I have to say your timing is as bad as mine but, sure, lay it on me."

She took a moment to compose herself and then said, "You're a loner, Tom, and that's how you like it. You're responsible for yourself only, no one else."

He started to erupt, but she froze him with a look.

"I've been waiting years to say this, and I'm going to say it and you're going to listen." She paused and continued, "I loved you, Tom, with everything I had. I loved you. You had me totally and completely."

"*Had* you, past tense."

"Don't you realize that just while we were together you were kidnapped once, imprisoned, and almost killed three times? You kept taking those crazy risks for the next story and you never thought about what that was doing to me. Every time you went out the door I didn't know if you were coming back. Didn't you notice I was doing less and less reporting and more and more worrying? I just wanted to go home. I wanted one place where you and I could stay and be together. I didn't want to get on another plane. I didn't want to watch you go on another assignment wondering if I'd ever see you again. After all those years of wandering I wanted a white picket fence, a back-yard garden, and a husband who left at nine and came home at five. Only you never asked. I guess the wandering was more important to you than I was."

"You gave me an ultimatum, Ellie. You gave me a few minutes to make a life-altering decision."

"No, I didn't. I'd been asking you for years, you just didn't want to hear it. When I came back that morning and told you I wanted to leave, it wasn't spontaneous. It took me weeks to work up the nerve. I went out for a walk to finally gather the courage. Well, I got my answer."

She rose to leave. "Now, you can get on your skis and go and try and rescue the train. Off on another adventure, all by yourself. I hope you'll be safe and I hope you write a great story based on it. But don't think that you're doing it for anyone other than yourself."

She left. Tom sat there, staring after her, his hand in his pocket, idly fingering the ring.

chapter thirty

The dining car was full of hungry passengers for breakfast, and Roxanne watched worriedly as the supplies in the kitchen dwindled rapidly. The food in the lounge car had been exhausted the night before and tempers were already starting to flare, keeping her busy as she put out each fire using all the good humor and diplomacy she could muster. There were a number of infants on board, and as diapers and milk started running low too, their cries, which ran the length and breadth of the train, put everyone further on edge.

Father Kelly finally found the courage to hold a prayer service in the lounge car, and it was well attended by all faiths and denominations, even a few agnostics who were looking for solace. The priest was a little rusty and stumbled at times, but his effort was sincere and people came up to him afterward and thanked him for lifting their spirits.

He confided to Agnes Joe, who'd helped him during the service, that it was the best he'd felt in years, and it actually made him reconsider his retirement.

When Higgins wasn't consulting with the train crew on how best to conserve fuel and power, he went out into the storm and personally checked under the cars for evidence of freezing pipes. When he came back in it was lunchtime, and over several cups of coffee he regaled the dining-car patrons with stories of the Wild West starring Jesse and Frank James, Billy the Kid, and other desperadoes. Not only the children but adults listened to these tales with wide-eyed awe. He also told the story of legendary Pullman porter John Blair, who practically single-handedly saved an entire trainload of passengers caught in a forest fire in Minnesota in the late 1800s. "They were in pretty desperate circumstances," said Higgins, "because there's nothing worse than fire. You put fire up against snow"—he motioned out the window—"and I'll take snow every time. May not seem like it, but we're pretty lucky on that score."

Roxanne smiled in appreciation of the point Higgins was making and poured him another cup of coffee.

Agnes Joe had been staring out the window of the dining car for quite some time. When Roxanne asked her what she was looking at, the woman pointed at something that Roxanne had to squint to see through the falling snow.

"It's Christmas Eve, you know," said Agnes Joe.

Roxanne nodded. "You're right, honey, and when you're right, you're right."

A bit later Eleanor came into the car and joined Agnes Joe and Roxanne. They were looking out the window, and Eleanor followed their gaze. Two men, heavily clothed, were struggling to bring something covered in a tarp into the train.

"What's going on?" asked Eleanor.

"You'll see," said Roxanne.

As the first man came back on board, hefting his end of the load, she saw that it was Barry, the sleeping-car attendant. The tarp had fallen off the object he was carrying, and Eleanor saw that it was a stunted pine tree that had been growing on one of the slopes. Most of the snow had been shaken off outside, but hard clumps still clung to its branches and the pine's skinny trunk. As the second man climbed aboard, his hood fell away and she gasped, for it was Tom.

"Christmas deserves a Christmas tree," he explained. "Actually, it was Agnes Joe's idea."

They set it up in the lounge car on a hastily fashioned base, and children came and decorated it with anything they wanted. After an hour's time, the little pine was truly beautiful—or at the very least interesting—having been strung with everything from fake jewelry to bubblegum baseball cards hung with rubber bands to plastic action figures to a long strand of tinsel that a woman had brought with her for a family Christmas in Albuquerque. Several of the children made a big star from paper and glue, colored it a shiny silver, and hoisted it on top of the tree, which was an easy enough thing to do, since the tree was only about four feet high. Yet to the folks trapped on the Chief, it was a thing of breathtaking beauty, bubblegum cards, action figures and all.

Tom had sat with a hot cup of coffee and watched as the fabulous holiday tree overcame its modest origins.

"It's beautiful."

He looked up. Eleanor was gazing at the tree and then glancing at him.

He nervously fingered his coffee. "Well, takes people's minds off things. And it's nice to hear a kid laugh right now."

"Mind if I sit down?"

He motioned to the empty seat.

"I thought you'd be gone by now," she said.

"Yeah, well, sometimes plans, if not people, change."

"How have your plans changed?"

"I decided not to go. I decided to stick it out here. One for all and all for one."

She sat back. "I have to say, I'm surprised. I didn't think anything I could possibly say . . ." Her voice tapered off.

He finished for her: "Could get through my thick head?" He smiled weakly. "Look, Ellie, I just decided that it would be better to stay here and help. By the time I got to the ski resort, *if* I got to it, the storm would probably be over and the cavalry arrived." He paused and then added, "And if not, well, then better to be here too." Their eyes locked for a long moment, and then he abruptly stood up.

"Where are you going?" she asked.

"I've got some things to take care of. Long overdue."

A few minutes later Tom stopped in to tell Lelia his decision on marriage was a no. "I really like you and care about you, but I'm not going to marry you and have eight kids. I hope you understand."

She didn't look like she understood at all. Tears streamed down her face, and she clutched at his arm.

"Isn't there anything I can say or do to change your mind? We seem so right for each other."

He shook his head. "I don't love you, Lelia. And I'm pretty sure if you think about it enough, you're going to see that you don't love me either."

"It's just that we've been together for so long."

"Complacency doesn't equal love."

She sniffed into her handkerchief and said in a trembling voice, "I don't know, maybe you're right."

At that moment Kristobal emerged from her bathroom and looked at them both.

"Kristobal?" Tom said, clearly surprised.

"Am I interrupting something?" the young man asked.

"No," said Tom, as he shot a stern glance at snuffling Lelia, "but apparently I am."

She looked at him innocently. "He's been helping me through these trying times. And he gives a wonderful pedicure and back massage."

"I'm sure he does." He looked at Kristobal. "*Ciao.*"

Tom left and walked down the hall more relieved than he'd been in a long time, now that Cuppy the Magic Beaver was no longer bearing down on him. In a way he felt sorry for Kristobal, but he was a big boy.

One positive if surprising event had occurred. All the items that had been stolen on the Chief—and many of the items that had been taken during the trip on the Capitol Limited—had been returned to their rightful owners. No one had seen anything, and no one could explain why the thief had experienced such a dramatic change of heart. Roxanne and Father Kelly simply put it down as a Christmas miracle.

After dinner, which was served with red and white garnishes in honor of the holiday, everyone was asked to gather in the lounge car. As people arrived, they were surprised to see that a mock stage of sorts had been set up at one end of the car. Max served as the master of ceremonies, whipping the crowd into a mass of expectation before pointing at the stage and calling out, "Do I hear something? Do I hear a special something coming?"

All attention was riveted on the stage when a puppet appeared there and a child screamed out excitedly, "It's Cuppy the Magic Beaver!" And then another little boy called out, "And there's Petey the Pickle!" And then Sassy Squirrel and Freddy the Futon joined their famous friends onstage, and the good times began.

Working the hand puppets from behind the stage were

Lelia and Kristobal. Lelia always carried the puppet characters with her in case she ran into any children; she often gave them as gifts. She did all the voices perfectly, switching from a piece of furniture to a pickle to a woodland creature with the smoothness of a true professional.

During a break in the proceedings, Kristobal whispered to her, "I've never been more honored in my life." They shared a kiss offstage while Sassy and Cuppy were bopping each other in the head onstage as all the children and even the adults roared with laughter.

Santa arrived precisely on schedule, played by burly Barry wearing a proper Santa suit, which was kept on the Chief for just such occasions. The role of Santa was so popular, in fact, that Amtrak employees routinely fought, gambled, bribed, and lobbied during the year to play the lead role each Christmas. Gifts were dutifully handed out by Santa's elves, played by Tom, Eleanor, Max, and Misty. The passengers contributed the gifts from gift-wrapped presents they'd brought with them. Everyone participated with good grace and humor, and the children were happy and laughing, which relieved the adults' tension immensely.

Father Kelly, again with Agnes Joe's aid, led them all in prayer and a Christmas Mass of sorts. The minister who'd married Steve and Julie had been asked to participate, but he had refused and stayed in his compartment. Steve and Julie were not seen much. Apparently they were not allowing even an avalanche to put a damper on their honeymoon, and who could blame them.

The boys' choir sang Christmas carols with Roxanne, and everyone joined them, giving it their best. On this occasion, it seemed that everyone's voice possessed a sweet melody. As the night deepened and little mouths started yawning with increasing frequency, folks said their goodnights and strangers slapped each other on the back, declaring it a very fine Christmas Eve. Then they went off to sleep.

Eleanor and Tom went with Roxanne to settle the choir down. They were about to leave when one of the boys called out to her.

She sat next to the little boy, whose name was Oliver.

"What's up?" asked Roxanne, as Tom and Eleanor stood next to her.

Oliver's eyes seemed as big as his whole body. He had a voice that could charm and delight the meanest soul on the planet, and he was usually a happy-go-lucky sort, but now he looked worried.

"Patrick said there's no God."

Roxanne gasped. "What? Patrick, you get yourself over here, boy."

Patrick came up in his striped pajamas and glasses. He was one of the older boys, tall and lean, with a very confident manner. He read constantly and was gifted academically.

Roxanne towered over him and put her hands on her substantial hips. "Explain yourself. Why'd you tell him that?"

All the other boys poked their heads over their seats to watch and listen. Tom and Eleanor exchanged glances.

"It's a simple process of elimination, an evolutionary cycle, really." He adjusted his glasses, as though a very youthful professor addressing his class.

"Come again?"

"Well, first there was the Tooth Fairy. You lose a tooth, you put it under your pillow, and the next morning the tooth is gone and there's money in its place. Most kids discover that's a myth when they're five or so, although I of course learned it much earlier."

"You're ten now, Patrick," said his brother Tony, "and you still put your teeth under the pillow."

"That's because I want the money, Tony, not because I still believe." Patrick turned back to Roxanne. "And then you had the Easter Bunny, another falsehood that's discovered perhaps around age seven. Next up is Santa Claus. That fellow who played him tonight, for example: Wasn't that one of the train—"

Roxanne eyed the younger children, who looked ready to cry at what Patrick was about to say. "Let's move on, Patrick," she interrupted, "and let's get right to God."

"Very well. If there was a god of good, then why would he let something like this happen? We're supposed to be home right now, spending Christmas with our families. Instead, here we are in the middle of a snowstorm running low on fuel and food. How could a god, if he existed, allow such a thing?"

Despite his confident presentation, Roxanne sensed that Patrick was as scared as the rest of them, and was really hoping she'd explain why there *was* a god rather than agree with him there *wasn't*.

She sat Patrick down next to her and cradled Oliver on her lap. "Now, the problem with your reasoning is that you're assuming our being stuck here is a bad thing."

Patrick adjusted his glasses. "Well, isn't it?"

"Not wholly, no. Let's consider it. Let's look at the facts. What happened tonight?"

"The snow fell harder, and the kitchen ran out of food."

"Besides that."

Oliver spoke up: "We celebrated Christmas Eve and opened presents. That's a good thing."

"We could have done that with our own families," countered Patrick.

"True," said Roxanne, "but would your families be scared

and hungry, and would they be in a strange place with people they don't know?"

The boy thought about this. "Well, no."

"But the passengers on this train are, right? They really don't want to be here because this isn't their home, right, they want to be with loved ones, family?"

"Right," said Oliver enthusiastically.

"But that's my point exactly," said Patrick.

"No, if I remember correctly, your point was how can there be a god if such a bad thing could happen. And I'm questioning whether it's a bad thing at all to have a bunch of people who don't know each other, who're scared and hungry and wanting to be anyplace but here for Christmas, spend the evening together and have so much fun that they're laughing and singing along and giving away presents they'd gotten for their own family to people they don't even know."

She looked at Tom and Eleanor. "You two had a good time tonight, didn't you?"

Eleanor smiled at the children. "It was one of the best Christmas Eves of my life."

"Well, I guess you have a point there," conceded Patrick.

Tom added, "Maybe God made sure you'd be on this train so that you could sing and make scared people forget about their troubles for a while by listening to some beautiful music."

"That's another good point," said Oliver excitedly.

"Yes, it is," agreed Patrick.

"You see," said Roxanne, as she tucked Oliver in and then led Patrick back to his seat, "it's often said that God works in mysterious ways. You have to really think about what He's trying to do. You can't be lazy and believe in God; He doesn't make it that easy. It takes spirit and faith and passion to really believe. Like most things worthwhile in life, you get back what you put into it. Only with faith, you get back a lot more."

She helped Patrick back into bed and covered him up.

"Any other questions?" she asked.

Oliver raised his hand. "Just one, Miss Roxanne."

"All right, what is it?"

"Can you take me to the bathroom?"

Later that night, Tom and Eleanor stood side by side staring out the window at the snow.

"Well," said Tom, "it's almost Christmas, and I don't hear anything stirring, not even a mouse."

"Right now I'll take a FEMA rescue team over old Saint Nick and his reindeer pitter-pattering on the roof."

"Where's your adventurous spirit, your romanticism?"

"I used it all up, with you," she shot back. She touched him on the arm. "Why didn't you go? The truth now."

"I forgot to oil my skis."

"I'm serious, Tom."

He looked at her. "Ellie, I told myself that I came on this trip to fulfill my dad's wishes. But I really did it because there's a huge hole in my life and I had no idea how to fill it. It's been there for a long time actually. And writing for *Ladies' Home Journal* wasn't plugging it." He struggled. "But the reason I didn't go out there," he continued, pointing out the window, "is because of what you said. You know, all these years I believed you'd walked out on me, that you had abandoned me. I never really saw that it was actually the other way around." He paused. "I'm sorry, Ellie, I really am."

She slowly reached out and took his hand in hers.

He looked around puzzled. "You know, I wasn't kidding. It really is quiet. Too quiet."

They couldn't have known, but earlier the last drop of fuel on the last diesel engine had been used up. And while they were standing there the backup battery-powered lights ran out of juice too. The Southwest Chief finally fell silent and dark.

And then the quiet was shattered by a rumbling sound, and the Chief started to shake and screams erupted from the coaches. Tom and Eleanor looked at each other.

"My God," she said, "it's another avalanche!"

chapter thirty-one

If there was such a thing as controlled chaos, it was taking place on the Southwest Chief. The current crisis was the imminent threat of another avalanche that would sweep the Chief into oblivion. The plunging snow had hit the right side of the train and piled so high that one couldn't see out the windows anymore. The crushing weight of the snow against the Chief was actually starting to tilt it. The plan in response was simple: total evacuation of the train, which, under the circumstances, was far easier said than done. Yet 341 passengers made their way from car to car, until they reached the last coach car, while Amtrak personnel counted and recounted heads and searched every nook and cranny on the train so no one would be left behind.

Covered by blankets, umbrellas, and any other device that could be used against the storm, the long line of people, guided by flashlights and battery-operated lanterns, trekked the short distance to the tunnel. Elderly and disabled passengers and the very young were carried or otherwise assisted. The Christmas spirit must have spread its magic, because stranger helped stranger, the physically fit assisted the disabled. No one complained or fretted about his or her place in line or duties assigned.

Flashlights, lanterns, water, blankets, pillows, first-aid kits, whatever food was left, and any article that could conceivably come in handy was carried off the train. The only complaint came from the engineer, who blamed himself for not backing the train into the tunnel while he still had fuel, and now he didn't want to leave his post. After Roxanne and Higgins spoke to him, the latter explaining that they hadn't thought to back up the train either, that the snow buildup in the rear of the train might have prohibited that maneuver anyway, and, last, that he could watch the Chief from the end of the tunnel, the engineer, whose name was Ralph Perkins, finally agreed to leave his chair at the helm. Higgins left unspoken the fact that the engineer might watch his beloved train hurtle down into the ravine at the front of a tsunami of sliding snow.

Tom, Eleanor, Max, Misty, Kristobal, Father Kelly, and Agnes Joe worked as hard as the crew in pushing, pulling, carrying, assisting, cajoling, and hauling until all were safely ensconced in the massive tunnel. Agnes Joe proved herself particularly adept at crowd control and managing people, and she also had considerable strength in her frame, which she exhibited numerous times during the evacuation.

Tom thought to break out his skis and gear, and Eleanor borrowed a pair from a female passenger who also planned to holiday at Tahoe. Together the two ferried a large quantity of supplies over the packed snow with relative speed.

Camp was set up in the tunnel. Tom went around and surveyed the situation. The lighting was very poor, the food levels low, the blankets too few. The worst problem, though, was the cold. With temperatures in the teens, the burden of less oxygen at their elevation, and the tunnel acting as a funnel for the tremendous winds, it was clear that neither the elderly nor the very young passengers could survive here long.

As Tom contemplated all this, the conclusion became inevitable. He went over to the conductor, engineer, and Roxanne and spoke with them quietly but intensely.

Eleanor, who was finishing helping folks settle down, glanced up and saw the meeting taking place. She joined them in time to hear Roxanne say, "You don't have to do this, Tom, but I love you for it."

"I'm going with you."

They all turned and looked at Eleanor.

"No, you're not," said Tom.

Eleanor looked at the others. "I taught him everything he knows about skiing."

"Eleanor, I can't let you go with me."

"I'm not asking for your permission. If you want to travel solo, fine; I'll have some coffee waiting at the resort for you when you finally show up."

Roxanne hiked her eyebrows. "I think you'd be a lot smarter teaming up with this woman than trying to go it alone."

Tom looked at each of them and finally his gaze settled on Eleanor. "One more job together?"

"Let's go."

As Eleanor was getting ready, Max came over to her and sat down. "I hear you're going to ski to the rescue with Langdon."

"Well, we're going to try."

"It's dangerous out there, Eleanor. Are you sure about this?"

"More sure than I've been about anything in a long time."

"Tom's a big strong guy, he can get it done by himself. I mean, he even told me about once carrying somebody up a mountain with mortar fire hitting all around."

Eleanor stopped packing and looked at him. "The person he was carrying was *me*, Max."

Max stared at her for a few moments and then said very quietly, with none of his usual bravado, "I just don't want to lose you, Eleanor."

She sat next to him and they hugged. "I'll be back, if for no other reason than to write this script and win an Oscar."

"You really love this guy, don't you?"

"Do you believe in second chances, Max?"

"I guess I should: I've had more than my share of them."

"Well, I never did, until now. And I'm not going to waste this one. I doubt I'll get another."

After saying their goodbyes, Tom and Eleanor, packed with gear, headed northeast back through the tunnel. From memory, Higgins had put together for them a rough map of the area and directions to the Dingo. Tom carried the map in his pocket wrapped in plastic. They'd go through the tunnel, start up a crevice in the mountain, and from there work their way north and west toward the resort. With any luck, soon they'd be drinking hot coffee in front of a roaring fire. The air was frigid and very thin at this altitude, and soon Tom and Eleanor were both breathing hard. The tunnel was completely dark, so they had snapped on their battery-powered helmet lights. They had to carry their skis because there wasn't any snow to use them on inside the tunnel.

"At least we don't have to worry about a train coming through," said Tom.

"And here I was thinking our luck was all bad."

As they walked the half-mile to the other end of the tunnel, their hands reached out and gripped firmly. At the end of the tunnel they strapped on their skis.

"You ready?" Tom asked. Eleanor nodded.

They stepped out into the blizzard, managed to find the crevice in the near whiteout conditions, and headed up, each thrust of the ski poles arduous with the ascent. In a very few minutes, they'd completely disappeared into the storm's dangerous embrace.

They pushed through the wind and walls of snow. Their bodies were caked with ice, their limbs growing increasingly numb. They constantly changed direction as Tom recalculated where they were. He had a compass, but he wasn't entirely confident that the instrument was telling him the truth. And trying to find a resort, albeit a large one, in the middle of a snowstorm on top of a mountain was a little more difficult than he'd thought. Yet they plunged on.

Tom and Eleanor navigated numerous steep ascents, often having to wedge their limbs and ski poles against the rocky sides to lever themselves on. In some cases they had to take off their skis and, roped together, simply climb. After clearing all these obstacles, they reached a straightaway of flatland and made good time on their skis, despite heading directly into a wind that seemed to increase with each push of their poles.

The first disaster occurred when Tom broke through a thin patch of ice and fell about ten feet into a hole. With Eleanor tugging on a rope she tossed down to him, he was able to climb out. But he'd lost his cell phone, and, even more devastating, the compass was damaged.

They contemplated going back, assuming they could find the way back, but then decided to keep going. Tom had a good idea, he thought, of the direction, and had picked out some land-marks to help him maintain the correct course. Of course, with the snow blowing from every angle, and things being covered and then uncovered because of the shifting powder, landmarks weren't all that reliable.

Every step, every slope, every climb was made a hundred times more difficult because of the inclemency, and they kept having to stop, turn away from the wind, or find a crevice in the rock to catch their breath. Both their chests burned, and their state-of-the-art clothing was barely holding its own against the numbing conditions.

They found a decently protected area and ate a simple meal, although the water they'd brought was mostly ice. They rested for a while and then hit the trails again.

When it started to grow dark, Eleanor said, "I'm not sure I want to be stumbling around at night on skis. Maybe we should make camp around here."

"Good idea. We can't be that far from the resort." At least he hoped they weren't. For all he really knew, they were ten feet from the train.

They pitched their tent, and Tom got a small fire going us-ing canned sterno. They used it to cook a quick dinner and also to thaw their water. They ate and then settled back close to-gether under blankets to conserve heat and watched the snow pile up around them outside the tent.

The storm seemed to weaken and it grew quiet. They could now talk without having to shout.

"Just so you know, I told Lelia no. She took it very well."

"I'm surprised."

"So was I, until I learned why. Lelia has a new beau."

"What? Who?"

"Kristobal."

"Kristobal! You've got to be joking."

"I'm sure they'll be very happy together. Lelia can come up with another cartoon character based on a boa and call it Kris the Stick."

They grew quiet and snuggled closer.

"Have to conserve body heat," explained Tom.

"Absolutely." She sighed and then said, "Look, if we don't make it back—"

He put a hand to her mouth. "Let's try to think positively. Misty would probably call it a purple aura of power or something."

She gripped his hand with hers. "If we don't make it back, I want you to know something."

His expression grew serious. "What?"

"I never stopped loving you. Not after all these years."

He put his arm around her. "We'll make it back."

As Eleanor shivered, Tom wrapped his arms around her, trying to transfer his body heat.

"Who would have thought we'd find each other after all this time and end up on a mountain in the middle of a blizzard?" she said.

"Hey, if it was easy, anybody could do it." He tried to laugh, but his mouth couldn't quite make the effort.

He remembered what day it was.

"Eleanor?"

She looked up at him. "What happened to Ellie?"

"Eleanor," he said, "Merry Christmas."

She managed to smile. "Merry Christmas."

He dug something out of a zippered pocket in his tunic. "I know this is the lousiest timing in the world, but like I said before, I am the king of bad timing." He rose, then went down on one knee and carefully put the ring on her finger.

She looked at him, her lips parted, her eyes wide in amaze-
ment at what was happening.

"I realize it's been a long time in coming—way too long, in
fact. But you're the only woman I've ever loved and I'll do all I
can to make you happy. Will you take me with all my faults,
weaknesses, idiosyncrasies, pigheadedness, and outright stupidity?" He paused, drew a long, even breath, and said, "Will you
marry me, Eleanor?"

She began to cry, right after she said yes.

As soon as they had finished sharing an official engagement kiss,
the tent blew away and a load of snow fell directly on them,
nearly burying them alive. Tom fought through the layers of
snow and pulled Eleanor out.

"We have to find shelter," he shouted over the wind.

Now that they were officially engaged, Tom was going to do
everything he could to make sure the ceremony actually took
place.

They struggled on, Eleanor growing weaker by the minute, so
weak in fact that she could no longer walk unaided. Tom half-
carried her along for another quarter-mile or so until his strength
finally gave out too. He laid her down, took off his outer jacket, and
covered her with it. Then he surveyed his dismal surroundings.
They were in a flat plain, as far as he could tell, with the silhouettes
of high peaks all around. That was all he could judge, since the
snowfall made it impossible to see anything more. He said one final
prayer, and then lay down on top of Eleanor, using his big body to
block the snow. He sought out her gloved hand and held it tightly.
The memory of his waiting in vain for his mother to pick up the
photograph in the hospital came back to him, and he marshaled all
his mental acuity and sense of touch to detect the slightest weaken-

ing of Eleanor's grip on his fingers. He didn't know what he would do if she started to fail. Maybe he'd simply say goodbye. Something he hadn't done all those years ago.

They seemed to be lying there for hours, the wind howling, the snow hitting his back, each smack like a tiny dagger into him. In Tom's mind he could see the little boy reaching out to him. It was Tom as a small child, reaching out to his adult self, pulling him back to the relative safety of childhood. One's mind played tricks at times like this. He'd been in desperate situations before, but none, he had to concede, quite so perilous. This was, he concluded, after numerous near misses in his checkered career, probably his time to go. He looked at Eleanor and kissed her lips. She didn't respond, and the tears finally started to trickle down Tom's frozen cheeks.

The little boy's image grew more and more vivid. Tom could now actually feel the fingers on his cheek, rubbing his hair. The little boy was speaking to him, asking if he was okay. The vision was more real, more potent than any dream he'd ever had. He kept his grip on Eleanor's hand, even as he reached out to the young Tom, talked back to him.

The child poked him again, and Tom's eyes fluttered open, closed, and then opened again, and the glare of sunlight was painful, so long had it been since he'd actually experienced it.

"Are you okay, mister?" asked the little boy who was squatting next to him.

Tom managed to sit up, look around. The storm was gone, the sky a vast, azure blue, the sun warming, the air a chilly, pure freshness that only mountain heights could inspire. He stared at the boy, unsure if this was what Heaven looked like or not, and finally managed to ask, "What are you doing all the way out here?"

"I live here," replied the little boy.

"Here, where is here?"

The little boy pointed behind Tom. "The Dingo."

Tom looked over his shoulder. The mighty Dingo resort, in all its splendid beauty and enormous redwood buildings, stared back at him. Eleanor and he had almost perished five feet from warm fires, hot chocolate, and hot tubs.

Tom stood on shaky legs, gently woke Eleanor.

"Are we dead?" she asked, her eyes still closed.

"No," said Tom, "but just so you know, you're engaged to an idiot."

He carried her toward the main lodge as a number of adults finally spotted them and came running to help.

Both ends of the tunnel were filled with sunlight but not with any smells of cooking food, since there was none left. Still, at least the storm had passed, and Higgins, Roxanne, the conductor, Max, Misty, Lelia, Kristobal, Father Kelly, and Agnes Joe sat on the ground and discussed what to do next.

"I think," said Father Kelly with great sadness, "that a memorial service might be in order. For Tom and Eleanor, I mean."

Max said testily, "It's a little early for that, Padre."

"If they'd made it to the Dingo, we would have heard by now—the weather has cleared," said the conductor. "Nobody could have survived all that time out there. I never should have let them go. It's my fault."

Roxanne said, "They were just trying to help, two of the bravest people I ever met." She pulled out a handkerchief and wiped at her eyes.

Barry, the sleeping-car attendant, burst into their circle and shouted, "Quick, you've got to see this! I was out checking the other end of the tunnel," he sputtered. "You just have to come and see this."

They followed him through the tunnel until they reached the other end.

"Look!" he said.

They stared at the horses and riders coming their way in a long, impressive procession. There was even a number of large sleighs pulled by teams of horses and loaded down with what looked to be supplies of all kinds. It was as though they'd all been transported back in time and this was a wagon train of pioneers on their way to new lives in the unblemished west.

One of the riders in front lifted his hat to them and called out.

"That's Tom," said Roxanne.

The rider next to him waved.

"And that's Eleanor," said Max.

He raced forward to meet them, slipping and sliding in the snow but not slowing down.

Misty said to herself: "Six legs."

"What?" said Kristobal.

"We were saved by six legs. Four from the horse and two from the rider. Six legs." She whooped and ran after Max, her long scarf dazzling in the beautiful and welcome sunlight.

The timely arrival of food and other items from the good folks at the Dingo lifted everyone's spirits. As the passengers ate and drank, people crowded around Tom and Eleanor and heard their amazing story of survival.

"The guys from the resort knew of this route to the train tracks that the horses and wagons could navigate. A lot easier than the path we took there, but you couldn't even see it with the storm going on." Tom shook his head. "Five feet from the front door and didn't even know it. It's the luckiest I've ever been."

"It wasn't luck, Tom," said Father Kelly. "It was a miracle. I ordered up one special for you."

The conductor's walkie-talkie barked and he held it up and pressed the button. "Go ahead," he said.

"Amtrak Central to Southwest Chief, come in."

The conductor nearly screamed. "This is the Southwest Chief, Central."

"Where is everybody?" asked the voice.

"We evacuated the train. We're in the tunnel. What's the status of the rescue crew?"

"Just look out the tunnel, Homer," said the voice.

They all raced to the end of the tunnel, where there came a deafening roar as twin helicopters appeared over the ridge and hovered by the train.

"We've got a replacement train on the western side of the landslide with three fully fueled engines," said the voice.

"But how do we get to you?" said Homer, the conductor. "There's a mountain of snow between us. And there's snow piled high against the right side of the train."

"Not for long. We've been working on this for a while now. Just stand by."

"Roger that," said Homer.

Ten minutes went by, and then they heard a series of loud pops, and watched as the twenty-foot-high wall of snow in front of the Chief collapsed and slid harmlessly down the mountain. The small explosive charges that had been very carefully laid out at key load-bearing points had worked their magic. Revealed behind the now missing wall was the replacement train, its powerful engines running; the sound was particularly sweet and glorious to all on the long-silent Chief. Next, they were ordered back in the tunnel while the choppers, nose down, hovered along the right side of the train and blew the very dry snow away, allowing the Chief to resettle firmly on the tracks.

Hundreds of volunteers swarmed off the replacement train

and began clearing the rest of the track. Then another team came behind them and repaired the damage done by the slide, while the other volunteers cleared the snow from the sides and off the top of the Chief. During all this activity the passengers slowly reboarded the train.

It took most of the day to accomplish all of this, and the passengers on the Chief took the time to pose for pictures, call their friends and families, and convey suitably embellished accounts of their adventures, tales that grew taller and wilder with every retelling. Reporters reached some of the passengers on their cell phones, and soon stories were ringing the world about the dramatic rescue and Tom and Eleanor's heroics, with more sure to follow as soon as the train pulled into LA. The children played in the snow and made angels, causing Roxanne to remark that the Chief surely had been watched over by more than its share of those fine beings.

Early the next morning the track was ready, the fresh engines attached, and for the first time in a long time the wheels of the Southwest Chief began to turn. Special arrangements had been made permitting the Chief to make only a few of its scheduled stops, including a long layover in Albuquerque. As the train made its way down the mountain on its way through New Mexico and then into Arizona and finally California, the people on board did something they hadn't in a while: They rested peacefully.

chapter thirty-two

As the train rolled through areas of New Mexico where the snow hadn't fallen, the earth turned reddish brown and everywhere were tall, craggy rocks that looked more orange than any other color. Sagebrush dotted this beautiful if haunting landscape, and the passengers stared out the windows, hoping to catch sight of an occasional homestead.

They stopped in Albuquerque for about three hours to refuel and take on more supplies and to let passengers stranded for so long take a walk and enjoy the sunshine after the weary battle they had endured at Raton Pass.

Tom and Eleanor told the others of their engagement and all were pleased by it, Max especially. Lelia even gave Tom a hug and wished him the best. From the way she was clinging to Kristobal and the young man's smitten expression, Tom figured it would only be a matter of time before their own nuptials were formally announced. Tom and Eleanor told their friends they might copy Steve and Julie and take their vows on the train. But only during the summer, said Eleanor. Avalanches weren't going to interrupt her wedding.

There was a marketplace near the train station, where Native American women were selling jewelry and other wares, and there was an old bus that had been set up as a retail outlet as well. Tom and Eleanor strolled in the sunshine and talked about their future together.

"By the way, you never told me who you were seeing in Washington before you left on the train," Tom said. "Do you have a Lelia in your life?"

"Not exactly. It was my grandmother."

They stopped at a little café and had a drink and something to eat. Agnes Joe joined them, extended her congratulations on their engagement, and sipped a cool lemonade with them in the sunshine as she surveyed the surroundings.

"I sometimes think about retiring here and selling jewelry to the train passengers when they stop," she said.

Tom glanced sharply at her. "Retiring here? I thought you were retired."

"Soon enough," she answered cryptically.

"What is it that you do?" he inquired.

"Oh, a little bit of this, and a little bit of that."

"It's a funny thief that returns stolen items as gifts on Christmas Eve," he said.

"Craziest thing I've ever heard of," agreed Agnes Joe.

"Pretty generous of the crook," commented Eleanor.

"Not too generous, since he was only giving people back their own property," countered Agnes Joe.

"Or she," said Tom under his breath.

An Indian guide boarded the train before it left the station, and for the next hour or so he regaled them with tales of the land, Indian reservations, and the history of his people. He got off at the stop in Gallup, known as the Indian Capital of the World, because various tribes, including Hopi, Zuni, and Acoma, gathered for meetings there.

After dinner, many people went to the lounge car and watched a video of the wedding ceremony that Kristobal and Max had prepared. Steve and Julie watched, laughing and occasionally crying as the special moment was replayed for all. To Tom, Steve looked particularly exhausted, and he noted with a smile that as soon as the film was over, Julie grabbed his hand and pulled him back to their honeymoon suite.

It was late at night when they entered Arizona, and Tom found he couldn't sleep. He dressed and walked the halls. He looked in on Eleanor but she was sleeping soundly and he didn't want to awaken her.

As he passed Max's compartment, he swore he could smell incense, and didn't that make perfect sense. He was afraid to go by Lelia's sleeper for the sounds he might hear coming from there. From personal experience he knew that the woman who gave life to the innocent darlings Cuppy, Sassy, and Petey was a lot more racy in her personal life. Poor Kristobal would never know what hit him.

While he was rambling around the train slowed and then stopped. He peered out the window. There was a station here, but he'd thought there'd be no more stops until Los Angeles. He shrugged and kept walking until he arrived outside Agnes Joe's compartment. The woman's phonograph was still playing its Christmas tunes. Her unit was dark, and he assumed she must have fallen asleep while the music played. Then the phonograph started skipping, repeating the same lyrics over and over and then degenerating into a nerve-rattling screeching sound. Apparently the woman was sleeping heavily and couldn't hear it. He tapped on the glass of the door. "Agnes

Joe? Agnes Joe, your record player is going crazy." There was no response and he knocked again, louder. The screeching sound was only getting worse. He looked around and slid open the door. "Agnes Joe?" His eyes adjusted to the darkness, and he saw that the compartment was empty. There was no light on in the bathroom, but he tapped lightly on that door, receiving no answer. He eyed the duffel bag in the corner and was tempted to look inside again. He unzipped the bag and put his hand in. The newspaper was gone, but out came several items, including a watch, a pair of earrings, and what looked to be a very expensive pair of sunglasses. Maybe they were Kristobal's. Here was proof positive. He stood there trying to decide what to do, when he heard footsteps heading his way. He put the items back and zipped the bag closed, shut the compartment door, and then slipped inside the bathroom. He prayed it wasn't Agnes Joe, but his prayer apparently went unanswered, because the compartment door slid open and then was closed. The light came on and he could hear footsteps. He'd left the bathroom door open a crack, and he peered out through this sliver.

It was Agnes Joe, fully dressed in blue slacks and sweater; she held a piece of paper in her hand, and her expression was very serious. He just hoped she wouldn't need to use the john, but then how was he to escape? Wait until she was asleep? The woman didn't look ready for bed anytime soon, and yet what choice did he have? He looked around and was about to back up slightly to sit on the toilet when the train started up again. The rocking motion was just enough to cause him to lose his balance. He knocked against the wall and his hand shot out to steady himself, closing around the shower control and accidentally turning it on. The water hit him with a chilly blast, causing him to scream out a few choice words that, if he'd been Catholic, would have required a trip to Father Kelly for confession and a load of Hail Marys as penance.

He managed to turn the water off in time to stare out at Agnes Joe, who'd opened the door and was studying him, as though he were a curious breed of animal at the zoo.

"Hi, honeypie," said Tom with a sheepish grin.

"Would you care to come out here and tell me what you're doing in my shower?"

He emerged, wiped himself down with a towel, and explained about the phonograph, his coming in, and getting rattled when he heard footsteps.

The story might have worked, if he'd zippered the duffel bag up all the way. But in the darkness he hadn't quite managed it. Agnes Joe looked over at the bag and then back at him.

He decided on a full-frontal assault. He opened the bag and pulled out the items. "You care to explain what you're doing with these things? I'm willing to listen."

She reached in her pocket. What she pulled out and pointed at him made Tom take a step back, his expression one of total shock.

A few minutes later, an ashen-faced Tom rapped on Max's door. It took a few moments for the director to answer, and another minute or two before he opened the door.

"I need your help," said Tom. "We'll need Kristobal too."

Max glanced behind Tom and saw Agnes Joe.

"It's important," said Tom.

They collected Kristobal from Lelia's suite, not without some resistance from the little lady who voiced her displeasure in a decidedly non–Cuppy the Magic Beaver tone. They also woke up Roxanne and brought along Father Kelly too. Converging in the lounge car, they sat at a table, where Tom faced them. He pulled out Kristobal's designer sunglasses, Max's Bruno Maglis, and Father Kelly's cross and placed each in front of its respective owner.

One man looked totally bewildered at what was in front of him, so confused that he never noticed Agnes Joe leaning toward him.

Father Kelly gave out a yell as the handcuffs closed around his wrists. He tried to get up but was wedged in by Max and Kristobal.

Agnes Joe flipped out her credentials, the same action that had stunned Tom earlier in her compartment. "I'm Amtrak police. Undercover Division. And you're our thief, John."

Tom looked at her. "John?"

She nodded. "I got his fingerprints on a beer glass before we were stuck at the Raton Pass. At one of the station stops I sent in an ID request. At the station we just left I got a notice back. His real name is John Conroy, and he's no priest." She sat across from the man, who looked so crushed Tom's heart went out to him, despite the man's criminality.

Agnes Joe continued her explanation. "I used my phonograph trick to make people think I was in my compartment when I really wasn't. I was afraid he'd spotted me lurking around and might decide to lay low for a while. When he performed the Mass while we were stuck at the pass, I assisted him. I was already suspicious of him for other reasons, and that's why I lifted his prints. I did that for some others on board too. He's obviously Catholic and could fake his way through the Mass, but he made enough mistakes to make me even more wary."

"And all the stuff I found in your bag?" asked Tom.

"Roxanne had gotten those items for me from some of the passengers as evidence we might need later. I got you, Max, and Kristobal involved so we could take Conroy without anyone getting hurt or him suspicious. I swiped his cross out of his compartment. When I laid it down in front of him, I thought it would confuse him enough for me to get the handcuffs on with no scuffle. You're not a spring chicken, Conroy, but it's been my experience that you never know. Always better to take 'em by surprise."

"I hate to admit this, but I looked through your duffel before and just found newspapers," said Tom.

"I know, I could tell someone had searched it and thought it was probably you. The newspapers that Regina found in the trash were from Conroy's duffel. He had stuffed it full of old papers to make it look like it was packed as far as it could go. But once he got on the train, he ditched the papers and had a relatively empty duffel bag to fill up with his loot."

They all turned to the old man, who looked even smaller and clearly beaten as he sat handcuffed.

Agnes Joe said, "Care to make a clean breast of it, John? I know you have a criminal record. But you could fill in some details."

He shook his head and said, "What will be, will be."

They called big Barry to stand guard and they trooped to the imposter priest's compartment, where a number of the stolen items were in his duffel. There was nothing of great value in any of it, but it was stolen goods nonetheless.

"I'll call this in," said Agnes Joe.

"What I don't get is why he returned so many of the items. What crook does that?" asked Tom.

"Something is funny about that," said Roxanne, "but at least we have our thief. Now let's all get some sleep."

Tom did just that until about six in the morning, when there was a tap on his door, and he woke and answered it.

Agnes Joe was standing there with two hot cups of coffee. "I thought I'd better bring this as a peace offering for waking you up so early." She was dressed in blue slacks and a sweater, and she had a crisp and efficient air about her.

"You'd make a great actress," said Tom. "I had no clue that you were anything other than, well, I mean . . ."

"An eccentric old woman with nowhere to go during the holidays? Yeah, it's a good cover. People say things around a character like that they otherwise never would. I've busted drug dealers, swindlers, theft rings, and lots of other bad people with my bewildered look, my stupid dresses, and—"

"And your honeypies."

"Exactly."

"Well, I suppose your cover is sort of blown now."

"That's okay, I wasn't joking about retiring. It's time to move on."

"So was any of the rest of your back story true?"

"I worked for Ringling Brothers, not as a trapeze artist but as a horsewoman. I've been married twice, and I do have a grown daughter." She paused and added, "And we are estranged."

"Sorry to hear that."

"Well, she read about the Chief being trapped, and she called last night, to make sure I was okay. First time I'd heard from her in a while. We're going to see each other when I get into LA. She does work for the circus, and she's on the West Coast. We're going to take another shot at it."

"I'm happy for you, a late Christmas present. So what did you want to see me about?"

"Well, I've got a bit of a dilemma, and I wanted your advice. I obtained more info on our fake priest. He was busted years ago for petty thefts—I mean, almost thirty-four years ago. He's been straight since, real job and everything."

"Why the return to crime after all that time?"

"His wife of over thirty-three years just died. I talked to Conroy, got him to open up some. With her gone, he didn't know what to do. He was lonely, just wanted attention. They had two kids, but one died in an accident and another from cancer."

"Boy, that's tough. And it seems like his life of crime stopped when he married her."

"Exactly. Now, I've dealt with lots of criminal types and I've heard all the sob stories and I'm not swayed by that stuff. But the other thing he told me, that's why I have the dilemma."

"What is it?"

"He returned the stolen items on Christmas Eve as presents. The only ones he didn't return, the ones we found in his bags, were nothing much, and he left cash, more than enough to pay for them. I've confirmed that with the passengers they belonged to. He didn't mean to hurt anyone. All he talked about was his wife. And he really helped when the train was stuck."

Tom let out a long breath. "I see your dilemma."

"What would you do?"

He thought about it. "Well, I got a second chance on this trip, and maybe John Conroy deserves one too. Have you called the police yet?"

"Yes, but I gave them no particulars."

"Is the train making any more stops?"

"It can, at Fullerton, a couple of hours before we get into LA."

"Well, maybe the Chief should stop at Fullerton."

"Maybe it should. I don't think Conroy is going to jump into a life of crime. In fact, I know some people near Fullerton who can help him." She rose. "Thanks, Tom. I think we made the right decision."

He smiled at her. "So what's your real name?"

Agnes Joe let her frame droop and her face bloat out, and her hair seemed to whiten right before Tom's eyes. "Well, if I told you that, it wouldn't be a secret, now would it, honeypie?"

chapter thirty-three

At Fullerton the train stopped, and an elderly, tired-looking gentleman got off, no longer wearing priest's clothes. Some friends of Agnes Joe were waiting for him, and they drove off, hopefully taking John Conroy to a better life than felony by rail could ever provide.

Tom went to the communal showers to get washed up before they arrived in LA. As he was going in, Steve the honeymooner was coming out. The young man still looked very weary, yet Tom could hardly feel sorry for him, knowing full well the source of his fatigue.

"I thought you had a shower in your room," Tom said.

"My bride is hogging it," said Steve.

"Better get used to it, buddy," he jested, "and enjoy this part while you can."

As Steve left, Tom went inside the dressing area and started to disrobe. That's when he saw the wallet on the floor under the counter. He stooped to pick it up, thinking it must be Steve's. As he snagged it, some of the contents fell out and he got down on his knees to retrieve them. He glanced at one of the cards he picked up, and the shock was as great as he'd ever had, perhaps even more than discovering Eleanor was on the train.

He held the card up to the light and studied it. It was a SAG card, a Screen Actors Guild membership card, with the name Steve Samuels on it. Tom quickly looked through the rest of the wallet. He found Steve's driver's license—his *California* driver's license—and the picture confirmed that it was Steve, of Steve and Julie, only he wasn't a student at George Washington; he was twenty-eight years old and a dues-paying member of the Actors Guild.

Ironically, the Southwest Chief pulled into the beautiful Art Deco Los Angeles Union Passenger Train Terminal a few minutes ahead of its revised schedule.

Herrick Higgins was met by several senior Amtrak executives, who congratulated him and thanked him for his heroics. Then he was offered his old position back, riding the rails troubleshooting, an offer he accepted on the spot.

Max Powers got off and answered lots of reporters' questions. He looked over to where Roxanne and the boys' choir were doing the same.

"Hey," he called to Roxanne. "I'll be in touch, count on it."

She smiled. "I am, baby, I am."

Then he and a group of passengers, including Kristobal, Lelia, and Misty, left the station and got into a stretch limousine waiting for them outside.

As the driver went to get their luggage, inside the limo Max took out three envelopes and handed them one by one to Steve, Julie, and the minister. Then he popped a bottle of champagne and poured out glasses of the bubbly for all.

"Good job, guys," said Max. "You'll all be in my next picture. Who knows, maybe it'll be about the train."

Misty said, "Max, when you told me what you'd done I couldn't believe it."

"Well, sweetie, though I'd known you only a short time, I knew you could keep a secret, for the right reasons."

"True love," she said wistfully.

"*You* couldn't believe it," said Lelia. "How do you think I felt? Max Powers calls me after all these years and asks for a favor. Some favor, to fly out to Kansas City and pretend to propose. I don't know what I would have done if he'd accepted."

"I knew my man, Lelia. I was pretty sure he wouldn't."

"Pretty sure!"

"I had to make certain he really didn't love you and you didn't love him."

"Of course not, especially after the Erik incident."

Kristobal gave a sympathetic nod. "A lady needs to be pampered. And from now on, that's my job, kitten."

She patted him on the arm.

Max beamed. "You're a fine actress. And see what you gained from my little plan."

"You never told me you had contacted Lelia and included her in the plan," said Kristobal. "I had no idea who she was until she told me her name."

"I'm a man who has this insatiable need to surprise people," replied Max.

"What part were you playing, Max?" Lelia asked.

Misty said, "Why, Max Powers, of course."

Max smiled. "Like Olivier and Hamlet, it's my greatest role."

"You were right, by the way, sir: He asked me about the booking dates and then, as you predicted, he went to Regina."

"He's a world-class reporter, Kristobal; he wouldn't take your word for it. That's why I had Regina in on it."

"And you did all this for Eleanor?" asked Misty. "And she doesn't know about any of it?"

Max nodded. "Not a thing. Eleanor is the daughter I never had. I'd do anything for her. As long as I've known her, she hasn't been truly happy. I knew there was something in her past. Now, she never told me his name, but I did some snooping and found out that Tom Langdon was the big loose end in her life. She couldn't go forward until she knew it was either over or they were finally going to get married. So I've been tracking the guy for about six months. When he booked this trip it was a perfect opportunity for me, because I really wanted to do a train film."

"And the wedding?" asked Misty.

"What better way to make people who should have gotten married rethink what might have been than to put them in a wedding together? So Julie is from the same sort of place Eleanor is from, and Tom reads Steve the riot act after he starts to waver on his decision. That was a good twist, because it may as well have been Tom saying all the things he was feeling. Of course, that was all planned. Every time Tom and Eleanor had a blowup, we had a plan ready."

Kristobal said wearily, "And they had lots of blowups. It was draining, keeping up with them the whole trip."

"You did good, Kristobal. And I'm *not* cutting your pay. Happy Holidays."

"That's a lot of details you covered, Max," said Misty.

"I'm a director, sweetie. My whole life is details."

"Uh, sir, you didn't somehow order up the avalanche, did you?" Kristobal wanted to know.

"Hey, even I'm not that good."

There was a rap on the window.

"Must be the luggage," said Max. He rolled the window down. Tom leaned in and looked at them all.

Max said nervously, "Hey there, Tom. Just giving the new-lyweds a ride to their honeymoon palace."

"I'm sure," said Tom. He handed Steve his wallet. "You dropped it in the shower. Your driver's license and SAG card are in there. Figured you'd need them."

"Tom," said Max, "I can explain."

Tom held up a hand. "I only have one thing to say to you."

Max drew back. "What's that?"

"Thank you." Tom shook hands with Max and then looked around at everyone. "Merry Christmas and Happy Holidays," he said.

He walked away from the limo and found Eleanor, who was with their bags and watching him curiously.

"Who was in the limo?" she asked when he reached her.

Tom turned and glanced back at the car pulling off. He looked back at Eleanor.

"Santa Claus," he answered.

"Santa Claus? Right. We're a little old to believe in Santa Claus."

He put his arm around her as they walked off. "Well, around Christmas, it can be a good thing to believe in magic. You never know, your wish just might come true."

acknowledgments

To Michelle, for always telling me what is wrong and right with the words.

To Larry, Maureen, and Jamie, for taking the time to read the pages and giving me your thoughts. Your support and excitement for all my projects is very important to me.

To Rick Horgan, the new member of the team, for doing a very thoughtful editing job. Your comments made the book much better. Thanks, Rick. Here's to many more!

To the Warner Books staff, who continue to put so much energy and dedication into each of my books.

To Tina Andreadis, for being the world's best publicist, and also a great friend.

To Aaron Priest; as always, your counsel was wise.

To Maria Reft at Pan Macmillan for all your insights and comments on the manuscript.

To Lisa Erbach Vance and Lucy Childs, for keeping all the ducks in a row.

To Deborah Hocutt and Lynette Collin, for keeping the

"enterprise" sailing smoothly. And to Daniel Hocutt, for your website wizardry.

To the staff of Amtrak's Capitol Limited and the Southwest Chief, for all their help. And a special thanks to Lee Jones, Beverly Steward, Monique Bailey, and Keith Williams of the Capitol Limited. I'll never forget riding the rails with you late at night and listening to some great stories.

To the Amtrak staff who helped me understand the intricacies of trains, including Danny Stewart, Jimma Aboye, Christopher Streeter, David Villenuve, Brian Perry, Vincent Teel, Judith Martin, Edward Kidwell, Deborjha Blackwell, Brian Rosenwald, and Douglas W. Adams. You all were great!

A very special thanks to Clifford Black, Amtrak's director of public programs, for answering mountains of questions and giving me a behind-the-scenes peek. Cliff, you're a gentleman and a scholar.

And to David Lesser of Amtrak's *ARRIVE* magazine, for his support and enthusiasm for this project.

From one of the world's master storytellers
comes an enchanting holiday short story...
Please turn this page for

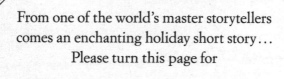

"Waiting for Santa"

by David Baldacci

How do you learn how to live again after holding a warm child in your arms, wanting nothing more than to love and protect her from all harm, and then having to give her up forever less than twenty-four hours later? I've pondered that for the last eight years, ever since my wife died during childbirth on a Monday and our day-old daughter Sara followed her on Tuesday. I had gone to the hospital expecting to leave with the two people I loved most in the world. Instead I went home alone to arrange for twin funerals.

The hardest time of the year for me is Christmas because Sara was born on December twenty-fourth. For the last eight years I've come to the mall to watch the long line of children waiting their turn with Saint Nick. And each year I go home afterward and cry myself to sleep for never being able to hold Sara's hand as she anxiously waits to whisper in Santa's ear.

My family and friends keep asking me when I'm going to get on with my life. I've stopped trying to answer because I don't know what the answer is. In many important ways my life ended with the deaths of my wife and child. I'm not certain that I'm entitled to another one.

This year, as I stood watching the long line of kids and parents, a little girl of about nine appeared near me. She was small with curly brown hair clustered around a perfect oval face that framed enormous green eyes. She looked familiar, but I was sure I didn't know her.

"Hey, mister, can you stand in line with me? My granny's knees aren't so good." She pointed to an old woman who sat nearby. Before I could answer, she took my hand and led me to the end of the line.

She said, "I've seen you here before."

"Yes," I replied, "you probably have."

"Only you just watch."

"That's right," I said. "I just watch."

"Your kids don't like Santa?"

"I had a child, but she died." I don't know why I told her this, but I suppose I was unable to lie to a child.

She patted my hand. "I had a mom and dad, but they died too. Granny says it was in an accident."

"I'm sure you miss them."

"I didn't really know them. But you have to miss your parents. It's a rule."

A good rule, I thought. "What are you going to ask Santa for?"

"Same thing I ask for every year: a mom and dad."

I looked at her grandmother. "I'm sure your granny loves having you with her."

"I'm a lot of work." She added, "And she's not as young as she used to be."

"You want to be adopted?"

"It's the right thing to do," she said confidently.

The firmness of her words startled me. "I'm not sure I understand."

"I can make someone another family, someone who doesn't have kids."

"I guess that's one way to look at it, making a family that way."

"Lots of people can do it."

"I suppose," I said absently. I was growing a little uncomfortable holding the strange girl's hand. But every time I tried to pull away she gripped my fingers tighter.

"Yeah, even people like you. But you have it easy. It's harder for me," she said.

I stared at her. "What do you mean?"

"I have to wait for a grown-up to want me."

"It's not that easy for me either," I said. "Grown-ups have their own limitations."

"But it happens, every day. You'll make a new family and then you won't have to come here and just watch."

"I can't replace the family I lost."

"No, you'll actually have *two* families—two families of memories. That's pretty lucky when you think about it, most people only have one. Right now I don't really have any. So when I get a new family I'll only have one set of real memories. But I've already made up memories of my real mom and dad. I'll never forget them. That's a rule too."

I smiled. "I've never known a child who liked rules so much."

"It's easy when you love someone. Like your kid. I bet you loved her a lot."

"More than anything." I felt myself tearing up and I swiped at my eyes.

"Well, once you love someone, that's it. That love will always be there."

"But what about her? She died when she was very young, she didn't even know me. Like you said, you don't remember your parents. You had to make up memories."

"But that's different. I don't remember them in one way, but

I remember them in another. It's from their love. I know my mom and dad held me close before they died. I know they wanted me. I know they loved me. And once they love you, you never forget it. You can't take it back. It's inside of you forever. I know that, and so did your little girl."

"Another rule," I said weakly as an overpowering sensation of hope flooded me.

"Actually, the most important one of all."

She went and sat on Santa's lap. When she was finished she waved to me. "Thanks, mister."

As she walked off I asked, "What's your name?"

"Sara," she said before disappearing with her grandmother.

I was married a year later, and a year after that we had a son named Timothy. I took Timothy to see Santa when he was two years old. As I was standing there I noticed the old grandmother sitting nearby. I looked around for Sara but didn't see her. Leaving my son with his mother, I went over to the old woman, introduced myself, and asked if her granddaughter Sara had been adopted.

The old woman looked at me curiously for a moment. "I don't have a granddaughter."

I was less shocked by this than I probably should have been. I walked back to my son, took his hand, and led him to Santa Claus. My wife and I hugged while our son jabbered his wishes into Saint Nick's ear. As we left to go home I said a silent prayer of gratitude for *both* my families.

From one of the world's master storytellers
comes a riveting short story
available in print for the first time...
Please see the next page for

"Bullseye"

by David Baldacci

CHAPTER

1

IT WAS FIVE MINUTES TO NOON ON A SATURDAY.

The streets of Georgetown were filled with shoppers. The sun overhead was warming and the breeze brisk and refreshing. The waters of the nearby Potomac had some light froth from the wind. Many boaters were out enjoying the weather.

It was all in all a delightful day to be alive.

Yet there were a few people clustered in the vicinity who were not thinking about the pleasant weather or fun things to do. They had other things on their minds.

Oliver Stone walked down the crowded sidewalk. In his pocket was his paycheck from the Mt. Zion Cemetery where he was the caretaker. His destination was a bank in the luxury mall located on M Street. He would just be able to deposit the check before the bank closed. He did not make much money and had to take care with what he did earn. Yet his needs were few, and his salary also included a cottage in which to live. And he liked being around the dead. They were a quiet bunch. He'd had enough excitement to last him the rest of his life.

Behind him walked another man, partially hidden by a group of giddy teenage girls overburdened with shopping bags filled with purchases from upscale stores. Texts were flying from their collective phones—youthful gossip was now delivered almost exclusively electronically. Indeed, one girl was energetically texting the friend walking beside her, as though actually turning and speaking to her would be somehow uncool or an unimaginable burden.

As he walked along, Will Robie looked up and watched the seagulls drift across the clear sky. It was a beautiful day to do many things, but dying was not one of them. It was never a good day to die, he thought. Yet oftentimes one didn't have a choice on the actual timing. Sometimes your death was caused by someone else's agenda.

Robie had nearly been killed by such agendas several times, quite recently in fact. He couldn't say that he cared for it.

He looked at Oliver Stone, who was about fifteen feet ahead of him. The man had close-cropped white hair. He was lean and wiry and about six-two, nearly two inches taller than Robie. It was a sad testament to the state of general health in America when a lean older man made one immediately think he was suffering from a serious illness. Robie knew who Oliver Stone was, and he also knew that he was not someone to take lightly. And despite his not exactly being a spring chicken, Robie knew the man could hold his own against just about anyone or anything.

Stone turned into the mall entrance. Robie broke off from the giddy girls and turned in there as well, about ten paces back now. Stone hurried up the steps and onto the main level of the multistory mall that had a clear glass elevator leading to the upper floors. Stone didn't bother with the elevator. He just walked briskly up the steps to the next level, turned left, and continued on.

Robie mimicked these movements, rotating his line of sight to take in what he needed to. The mall was crowded but the section where Stone was headed was not. The bank was down here, as were some other businesses that were either not open on Saturday or were, like the bank, about to close.

Next to the bank entrance was a long corridor leading to a service area and restrooms. This was the cheaper section of the mall and none of the popular stores were located here. But banks were notoriously frugal on everything except executive pay, and thus it was the perfect location for one. That was why banks had all the money. They didn't spend any more than they absolutely had to.

Stone passed the service corridor and walked through the large opening into the bank. He nodded at the security guard posted near the entrance. The guard was older, with white hair and a paunch that stretched his rental cop shirt to its fullest extent. The guard checked his watch.

Stone smiled. "Don't worry, I've got two minutes, Charlie."

"You know you can use the ATM outside to deposit your funds, Oliver."

"I like dealing with real people. If the machine chews up my check, where's the proof?"

Charlie smiled. "I bet you don't have an online account either."

"I've heard of the Internet. I've just never used it."

"I only do because of the grandkids. Never in all my life thought I'd be on something called Facebook. Or Google. Have a good weekend."

"You too."

Charlie put his security key into the lock and turned it to the left. A solid wall with the bank's name and logo on it came partially down over the bank entrance. Charlie turned the key back to its original position and the wall stopped descending. He would wait patiently for the customers to finish their business and then he would close up shop fully. He was itching to get home to watch Virginia Tech play Alabama. Kickoff was at one.

Stone went up to stand in line for the next available teller. There were four customers ahead of him and three tellers behind the polycarbonate shield, which would stop most bullets. He looked to his right and saw a youngish dark-haired man in an ill-fitting suit sitting in a small glass-enclosed cubicle. The name-plate on the glass said this was the bank manager. To Stone the man looked like he was half asleep.

While two of the tellers served customers the third was counting cash. To the left of the tellers' enclosure, but outside the bulletproof glass area, was the vault, its thick steel door standing open.

Stone did not turn around when Will Robie entered the bank, ducking under the partially lowered door at one minute to noon. He didn't have to. As he waited in line, he watched Robie in a security mirror bolted to the corner of the ceiling. Stone had never seen Robie before today, but his experienced eyes told him that the man was not here to fulfill a banking transaction. Stone had seen Robie behind him on the street. And so he wondered why he was here.

Is it me? thought Stone. *And if so, how should I handle it?*

Charlie frowned at Robie's popping in at the last minute. He had evidently been hoping that no more customers would show up. The college football game was calling his name. He desperately wanted to see the Hokies knock off the heavily favored Crimson Tide.

Robie did not go to stand in line. He went over to the information table and started looking through some form documents kept there in small cubbies.

Fifty-eight seconds later the clock on the wall clicked to noon.

Charlie turned to tell another group of people attempting

to enter the bank that it was closed. There would be no more customers today.

A moment later Charlie tasted his own blood, arterial spray that reached his mouth. He was already dead, but didn't know it.

His attacker held the older man up while he expired. His colleague turned the key in the lock all the way to the left and the wall rapidly descended. In a few seconds what was going on inside the bank was sealed off from the rest of the mall.

Robie had turned at the moment the knife blade severed Charlie's neck arteries. He would have pulled his weapon but there were two guns pointed at him.

There were four people in total standing at the entrance. They were dressed in blue jumpsuits with hoodies. They slipped their hoodies off and revealed black ski masks underneath covering their faces.

One of them pushed a rolling laundry cart that had a sheet over it. Robie noted the gunmen had heavy weaponry—both machine pistols and subguns. It was a lot of firepower for a bank branch robbery.

One teller saw Charlie drop dead to the floor when his killer let him go, and screamed. Everyone else turned. Everyone else except Stone. He was watching all of this in the surveillance mirror. His gaze methodically panned over each of the gunmen, taking in as much information as he could. It was certainly true that the situation was bad, but that didn't necessarily mean it was impossible to rectify.

The customers and tellers froze when the guns were pointed at them. One gunman held his finger to his lips and walked forward into the bank lobby.

His name was Adam Chase, he was the leader of this group, and he had very little time to accomplish something exceedingly momentous.

"Listen up, everyone. I'm a simple man and the rules are straightforward. You do what we say, you get to go home. You don't, then Sunday does not come for you."

He pointed at dead Charlie.

"That does."

2

CHASE POINTED AT THE TELLERS BEHIND THE GLASS.

"First, you keep your hands in plain view. If you hit any alarm button, silent or otherwise, everyone out here is dead."

The two women and the man looked at each other and slowly lifted their hands.

"Good, now, the three of you come out here and join us."

They didn't move.

A second gunman strode forward and put his pistol against Stone's head. "Now, or the geezer gets his brains blown out," he said.

One of the female tellers unlocked the door and the three of them filed out.

"Thank you," said Chase politely. He stepped inside the tellers' cage and examined the set of alarm switches hidden under the counter. None of them had been activated. He looked at the tellers. "Very smart of you."

The second gunman slapped Stone on the side of the head. "Congratulations, Grandpa, you get to live."

"*He* was a grandfather," replied Stone, glancing over at dead Charlie. "I'm not."

"Then this is your lucky day," said the man, slapping Stone's head again.

Stone's jaw tightened ever so slightly when the man struck

him a second time. Robie noticed this. And he knew Stone would kill the man given the chance.

"Okay," said Chase. "Everybody line up against that wall." He pointed to his right.

Everyone did as he said and they were methodically searched. Out came all phones, electronic tablets, and other communication devices. They were collected in a basket. When Robie's gun was found, Chase held it in his gloved hand.

"Why do you have this? You a cop? A Fed?" He nodded to one of his men, who searched Robie for a badge or creds but found none. He did hold up Robie's gun permit.

"Just a law-abiding citizen," said Robie.

Chase glanced at the permit and then wheeled around and clocked Robie in the jaw, nearly dropping him to the floor.

"I don't like law-abiding citizens. Now get back in line," said Chase, shoving Robie away. "You give me trouble I will shoot you with your own weapon."

Robie staggered over and stood next to Stone, rubbing his jaw.

One of the gunmen produced zip ties. Each hostage's hand was bound to another hostage's. By virtue of their proximity, Robie and Stone ended up cuffed together.

"Now sit," said Chase, waving his machine pistol at them.

They all sat on the floor, leaning against a wall.

While one gunman watched over them, the other three set to work. From the laundry cart several duffels were pulled. They had taken the key from the door lock and also confiscated the spare security door key from behind the tellers' stand. There was no way out now.

Chase looked first at the open vault and then at the bank manager. "The vault has to be closed by twelve-fifteen or the central office will know something is wrong." He waved his gun. "So do it."

Stone glanced at Robie and then back at Chase.

The manager was tethered to one of the bank customers. When he rose, so did she. They were hurried over to an electronic pad next to the vault door. With a gun pressed to his temple the manager punched in the requisite numbers and the massive door slowly swung closed and then locked into place.

"Thank you," said Chase.

"Just please don't hurt us," mumbled the manager, who was breathing heavily.

Chase slapped him. "You don't speak unless you're spoken to. Now we have to go through the bank closing protocols so the central office will believe everything is just fine and dandy here. Let's go."

Chase led the manager and the tethered customer over to the manager's cubicle. "Give us the protocols and the passwords," ordered Chase, "and my colleague here will input them. You slip up on any one of them, you die." He put his gun against the manager's head once more.

Stone and Robie watched as another of the gunmen sat at the desk behind the glass cubicle and started clicking keys on the computer keyboard, following the instructions of the frightened manager. He was sending out preauthorized emails with special passwords that would confirm that nothing was amiss at the bank branch.

Stone's gaze swiveled to the third gunman. Slighter in build than the others and shorter, the person was affixing some devices to the wall entry door. When the ski mask rode up a bit on the person's neck, Stone saw the eagle tattoo there. When he glanced at Robie, he was staring at the exposed neck too. That had been a mistake, both men thought simultaneously. A big mistake. As good as a fingerprint, actually.

Chase escorted the two hostages back to the others.

"Okay, on your bellies and face the wall," he ordered. "Do it now."

Stone shot a glance at Robie, who returned it. The two men seemed to be silently sizing the other up and then communicating a message: offers and acceptances of an alliance that might allow them to survive this somehow.

The hostages scooted around and lay on their bellies. Though on their stomachs, Stone and Robie made sure to lie face-to-face.

"They closed the vault," mouthed Stone.

Robie nodded and mouthed, "So what's the target?"

Stone gave a brief shake of the head, which stopped when the muzzle of a machine pistol sliced between them.

"I don't believe I said communicating was permitted," said the voice.

Stone and Robie looked up to see Chase staring back down at them.

"If you're going to be a problem," said Chase, "we can deal with that right now." He drew his knife with Charlie's blood still on it and placed the serrated blade against Stone's neck. He let the edge bite into the skin and a dribble of blood leaked onto the floor.

Chase withdrew the knife and stood. He stared down at the two for a few moments and then turned and left.

Ten minutes later Chase reappeared next to the hostages.

"Okay, everyone up and into the back room."

The hostages managed to stand with difficulty and then were herded into the back room, which was outfitted as a small conference room. The door was locked behind them.

Stone and Robie looked around.

"Why in here?" Robie asked.

Stone said, "Because they're doing something out there they don't want us to see."

He went over to the bank manager, who was obviously petrified and muttering to himself, while the female customer tethered to him stood awkwardly looking at the floor.

Stone said, "What's worth stealing that's not in the vault?"

The man looked up at him fearfully. "We're not supposed to talk. They'll kill us. They already killed Charlie."

"I'm aware of that. But they can't hear us in here if we keep our voices down. And it doesn't appear that they care if we talk or not. Or else they would have fully bound and gagged us."

Robie added, "Simple enough to do. They obviously brought a lot of equipment with them."

"Are you a cop or something?" asked one of the tellers, a woman who looked to be in her late twenties. "You had a gun."

"I'm not a cop," replied Robie. "And even if I were they've got all the weapons."

"But can't you do something?" implored the teller.

"No," snapped the manager. "We have to do what they say. If we try to screw around with this, they will kill us."

"They've already killed one person," said Stone. "They may not want to leave any witnesses behind."

"We haven't seen their faces," countered the bank manager as the customer tied to him nodded in agreement. "So we can't identify them."

"Seeing someone's face is not the only way to ID them," Robie pointed out.

"We're not doing anything," barked the manager. "Nothing."

He sat down in a corner, forcing the woman tied to him to do the same. He studied his hands and avoided their gazes.

Stone and Robie moved away and looked around the room. There had been a phone in here but it had been removed, as had a fax. There were a few pieces of furniture, and two cheap prints on the wall, and a pitcher of water and some glasses on a credenza. On the wall were some outlets and USB ports and a phone line and port for the fax.

Robie said, "They were thorough."

"They obviously had plans of the bank layout beforehand."

Robie nodded. "And they knew the bank protocols. With the closing of the vault and all."

"Good prep all around. But they didn't have to kill Charlie. That's going to cost them." Stone turned to one of the female bank tellers. "What could they want that's not in the vault?" he asked in a low voice out of earshot of the bank manager.

She looked nervously over at her boss.

Stone said, "He's entitled to his opinion, but it doesn't mean he's correct. I have some experience in these matters and I find it highly unlikely that they will leave here with us still alive."

She said in a low, quavering voice, "We received a shipment of blank credit cards, about ten thousand of them."

"Aren't they in the vault?" asked Robie.

"Not yet. They just arrived today. We were going to load them into the vault after we closed. They're in the storage room in cardboard boxes."

"Blank credit cards," said Stone.

The teller nodded. "You can steal them and then sell them. Criminals can input stolen IDs on them and they can be used as legit cards."

"But if the bank knows they've been stolen won't they simply put a stop on all of them?" asked Stone.

"If they can get the cards operational before the bank finds out, they can run up a lot of charges. They can also reencode the magnetic strip on the back with stolen account data. The bank has had problems with that in the past. They lose millions of dollars that way."

Stone did not look convinced by this. "What else?"

"Well, we have customer account data on our computers. They could download that and sell it or use it to encode either homemade credit or debit cards or reencode stolen ones."

"That might be it," said Stone.

Now Robie did not look convinced. "But can't they hack into the bank's computer systems and do the same thing? Why come here and kill somebody? Now they've got a murder charge against them."

"I have no idea," said the woman, who started to shake and looked like she might be sick.

"Here, have some water," said Stone. He crossed the room with Robie and filled up a glass with water and brought it back to the woman.

She thanked him and drank it down.

Stone and Robie walked off and stood in a corner.

"Do you hear that?" Stone asked.

Robie nodded.

Stone said, "Sounds like someone sawing."

"And I don't think they're cutting into the vault. Not with a hand saw."

"And if they were going to rob the vault they wouldn't have closed it."

Robie added, "And the blank credit cards are in cardboard boxes. You don't need a saw to open cardboard."

"Which means they are trying to go from here to somewhere else," reasoned Stone. "And I wonder where that 'somewhere else' could be."

STONE LOOKED AT ROBIE. "Know the configuration of this mall well?"

"Not really, no."

"I do. I've been coming to this bank for years. And while I don't really have the financial means to shop at the stores here, I have walked around this mall many times."

"So what's in the vicinity?" asked Robie. "What's the possible target?"

"There's a jewelry store on the floor above. A fur shop next to it."

"Jewels are easier to get away with than furs. But aren't the stores open now?"

"The fur shop is closed on Saturdays. The jewelry shop closes at two today."

"So it could be either one," said Robie. He looked over at the door. "You think they plan to kill us?"

"I don't want to wait to find out," replied Stone. He peered closely at Robie. "You like your job?"

Robie stared back at him. "My job?"

"When were you assigned it?"

"I don't know what you're talking about."

"Really? I thought it was obvious."

"What do you mean?"

"You just picked today to do some banking?"

"Saturday is errand day."

"But you claimed you'd never been here before."

"No, I said I didn't know the configuration of the mall."

Stone smiled. "My mistake."

But in that look it seemed that Robie could sense that he was the one who had made the mistake.

Stone looked away when the door to the room opened. It was Chase.

He said, "Just to reiterate, if you cause no trouble, you will not be harmed. The reverse of that is also true." He glanced over at Robie and Stone when he said this. Then he looked at the bank manager. "You, come with me."

The color drained from the manager's face. "But I haven't done anything wrong. I've just been sitting here."

"Now." Chase pointed his pistol and the manager hastily rose to his feet. "And just remember, I don't need a reason to kill you," added Chase. He cut him loose from the woman he was tethered to, put his arm around the man's shoulders, and propelled him out of the room. The door shut and locked behind them.

Robie said, "What do you think that was about?"

Stone shrugged. "Possibly he's recruiting an informant. Or else the man has some more security codes that they need."

"If they want him to be an informant I think he'll finger us pretty quickly. The head guy is suspicious of us already."

"Which means we probably should act with some urgency."

Stone looked over at the fax and communications port.

"Got a way to turn that into a working phone?" asked Robie.

"Actually, I might," replied Stone cryptically.

He took the pitcher of water and poured it into the slots of the electrical outlet. There was a loud pop, a flash of electrical current, the smell of smoke, and the lights went out.

There were screams and a few seconds later the door burst open.

Stone had by then set down the pitcher of water and stepped far away from the outlet.

A flashlight beam cut across them.

"What the hell is going on?" barked a voice. It was Chase.

Stone called out. "We don't know. The lights just went out."

Robie added, "And we smell smoke. There might be a fire. Did you guys hit something out there?"

They heard Chase mutter, "Shit." Then he said, "Out this way, now. Follow the beam of my light."

They did so and were soon back in the main bank area. It was dark out here as well. Stone couldn't tell if the lights were still on outside in the mall or not.

One of the other men sidled up to Chase and whispered, "This is not good. We tried the circuit breaker but something got fried. Maybe we cut a line with the saw."

"The plan goes on. We have portable work lights. Have somebody check out the other room. The last thing we need is the fire department showing up. Then I want them back in there as fast as possible."

"But it's going to take longer now."

"We have a time reserve built in. Just do it."

The other man said something else and Chase turned back to him.

While the pair had been speaking Stone and Robie had drawn close enough to hear enough of this to understand that the gunmen were on a tight timetable.

And Stone had been able to see enough of the room through the sweeps of the flashlight to become reoriented to the outline of the space. Now that he was out of the other room, he had to execute the plan that had started with him pouring water into the electrical outlet.

While Chase and the other man were still talking, he and Robie felt their way along the edge of the wall. Stone found what he was looking for, did a quick search entirely by feel until his hand closed around something, and then placed that object in his pocket. Then he edged back along the wall to where he had been originally. A second later the flashlight beam hit him in the face.

Chase drew closer to Stone and said, "I really hope you're not trying something."

"All I'm trying to do is stay alive, along with everyone else here."

"Get back in the room, all of you," Chase snapped.

They filed back into the room and the door was shut and locked behind them once more.

They sat in the darkness. Stone had turned away from the others and was working away on something he held in his hand.

"Calling the cops?" whispered Robie. He had seen that the thing Stone had taken was his phone from the basket in the other room.

Stone shook his head. He was doing his best to block the small amount of light coming from the phone screen so that the other hostages would not see it.

"A friend," he said in a bare whisper.

"And this friend is better than the cops?"

"We'll find out," replied Stone. "But I have great confidence in my friends."

Stone punched in the number and spoke quietly into the phone when it was answered. When he was done the person on the other end said simply, "On it."

Stone put the phone away in his pocket.

Robie asked, "How could you tell which was your phone in there?"

"By feel. It was the smallest. Everyone else, including you, has one of those large-screen smartphones. I'm a little more old-fashioned. My phone is simply, well, a phone."

"Who did you call?"

"A friend, like I said."

"And what will this friend do?"

"Call my other friends."

"You have a lot of friends?" asked Robie.

"Not a lot. But the ones I do have are quite capable. We've actually done some pretty extraordinary things together, my little club and I."

"Club?"

"Yes. Didn't I say? We're known as the Camel Club."

He took a moment to study Robie in the bare light of his phone.

"I'm surprised your briefing didn't include that," said Stone.

4

ANNABELLE CONROY, TALL, LEAN, and auburn-haired, was the newest, youngest, and only female member of the Camel Club. She was also a first-class con artist, though she had mostly retired from the field.

Mostly.

She had already reached all the other members, except for one.

Secret Service Agent Alex Ford had not answered his phone.

Reuben Rhodes, Caleb Shaw, and Harry Finn were already on their way to the mall in Georgetown.

Ten minutes later Annabelle was standing outside of the mall entrance waiting for them to arrive.

Reuben's battered pickup truck screeched to a halt and he called out the window to her, "Any developments?"

She shook her head. Reuben eyed a car pulling out of a parking space on the street while a late-model Porsche convertible waited to pull in. Available parking spaces on the streets in Georgetown were unheard of and tended to be fiercely fought over.

Reuben timed it just right and slid into the parking spot before the Porsche could beat him there. The young man and his friend in the sports car immediately began yelling and cursing at him. The passenger jumped out and approached the truck. He was lean and buff and his hair was impressively tousled. He was dressed like a movie star trying to look hip. Everything he wore was expensive but tried desperately not to seem so.

With one look at him all Reuben wanted to do was knock him right into the waters of the nearby Potomac.

The guy stuck his face through the truck's open window. "You took our space, asshole. Now move this pile of shit, old man."

Reuben turned off his truck and stepped from the cab. At nearly six foot five and two hundred and seventy pounds he had the enormous size and breadth of shoulder of an NFL lineman. If he had had money he would have bought his clothes at the Big and Tall Men's Shop, with the emphasis on big and tall.

He looked down at the far smaller young man, who had taken several steps backward when Reuben stepped from his truck. With a thick beard shot with gray and wild, tangled hair, Reuben looked more than a little unstable. And he could act crazy with the best of them.

Sometimes it wasn't an act.

He grabbed the front of the man's shirt and jerked him off his feet. "Do you think I'm too old to kick your ass?" he growled, his eyes boring into the younger man's. "Because if you do, then I suggest you and your punk friend give it a try. I haven't had the chance to shit-kick some pricks since Vietnam and I'm getting damn tired of waiting."

The young guy was shaking hard as he took in the old army jacket that Reuben wore and then stared back at the wild eyes and the huge frame.

"We can find another space, dude."

"Damn good idea. Because I'm busy right now."

Reuben hurled him away and hurried down the block toward Annabelle.

When he reached her, Caleb Shaw was just getting out of a cab.

Caleb was in his fifties, paunchy, with gray hair and a trim beard. He wore wire-rimmed spectacles and looked like a librarian, which he was. He worked in the Library of Congress's Rare Book Reading Room. Although he was the most sedate and overtly timid member of the group, he had proved his mettle in action many times in the past.

Caleb said, "A bank robbery? In Georgetown?"

Annabelle said, "Oliver doesn't think the target is in the bank. He thinks they're going after something else using the bank as a launch point."

"Well, that's a bit odd."

"Yeah, that's what I thought," replied Annabelle. "But then odd is usually the only thing we get."

A moment later Harry Finn came rushing up to them. In his thirties, lean and fit, Finn had first run into Oliver Stone because he'd wanted to kill him. Now Harry was one of Stone's closest allies. He had a duffel bag over his shoulder.

"Nothing on the news," he said. "No one must know yet."

Reuben said, "So if not the bank what's the target?"

Annabelle said, "There's a jewelry store and fur place that the robbers might be able to access from the bank. At least that's what Oliver said."

Harry said, "Then we need to cover them both. But what about Oliver? Did he give you the lay of the land in there?"

"He's one of ten hostages. Four bank employees and six customers. There are four robbers, heavily armed, and they put booby traps at the bank entrance in case someone tries to get to them that way."

"Pretty well prepared," said Reuben. "Doesn't bode well."

Annabelle nodded. "And he said they knew the bank's protocols. The closing of the vault by a certain time and emails that had to go out to ensure the central office would believe nothing was wrong."

Caleb said, "What can we do other than monitor the possible targets?"

"I tried to get a hold of Alex but he's not answering."

"Probably on an assignment," said Reuben. "Otherwise he always answers."

"But we don't know for sure that the target is either the jewelers or the fur place," said Harry. "That's just speculation."

Annabelle said, "And there's something else. The robbers killed the security guard."

"Which means they'll have no compunction about killing anyone else," said Caleb ominously.

Reuben said, "Well, we just have to make sure that doesn't happen. But first things first. We need to cover the two potential targets. I'll take the jewelers. Harry can take the fur place."

"Are you armed?" asked Annabelle.

Reuben smiled. "You're asking me that kind of a question?"

Harry said, "I have a pocket and there's something in it. But what about the cops? The FBI? Shouldn't we call them in?"

Annabelle shook her head. "Oliver said not to. The robbers may have a spotter out here. If a SWAT team comes barging in they'll know it. And the robbers might start popping off hostages. We have to use stealth." She looked at Caleb. "While Harry and Reuben cover the two possible targets, you and I have to figure out if there might be another place in the mall we're missing."

The four of them split up. Reuben and Harry entered the mall while Annabelle and Caleb went back to her car, where she snagged her laptop. They entered the mall and went to a coffee shop on the ground floor. Annabelle started clicking keys while Caleb accessed the Internet on his phone.

She said, "Search for anything having to do with this mall. See if you can get the building layout, what all is here, that sort of thing. I'm surfing the Web to see if anything pops."

After thirty minutes Caleb looked up. "I'm not finding much. But there is a place in the garage that is blocked off. I can't find anything on the Web to tell me what it is."

"The garage?"

Caleb nodded.

"Forget the Web, let's go see for ourselves."

Robie studied Stone's face.

"My briefing?" he said.

"You look surprised."

"That's because I am."

Now Stone studied him, his gaze moving up and down Robie.

"What do you do for a living?"

"Is that any of your business?"

"I'm just asking. I work in a graveyard. And you?"

"I'm a lobbyist."

Stone shook his head and pointed at Robie's right hand. "Not with those calluses on your thumb and forefinger. I can't think of anything that gives those marks other than firing thousands of rounds of ammo."

"I'm a weekend skeet shooter, "said Robie.

"Of course you are. And I'm trying out for *American Idol.*"

"You must have me confused with someone else."

"I am rarely confused on points such as this."

Muffled sounds from outside the room interrupted them. Both men jerked when they heard them. More hand tools operating. A saw again. And what sounded like a hammer. And then a crowbar.

"Can't people hear that from outside?" asked Robie.

"Doubtful," said Stone. "Since we can barely hear it."

Robie looked around at the other hostages. "You'd think folks would start missing some of the customers in here. Or the workers. They probably have families and homes to go to."

"Which means whatever these men are doing can be done relatively quickly."

"A jewelry store and fur shop will have vaults that have to be broken into."

"A good point. An obstacle that would take far more time to get through."

"I don't think that's it," said Robie.

"I really don't think so either. My friends will probably arrive at the same conclusion. But there is something else that is located here."

"What's that?" asked Robie.

"Private residences. On the upper floors. Very exclusive private residences inhabited by very rich, exclusive people."

"You think that's the ultimate target?"

"I don't know. But we can't discount it." In the dark he looked closely at Robie. "How is Shane Connors doing?"

Robie said nothing.

Stone continued, "He was a protégé of mine. I haven't seen him in years, of course, but once he did mention an up-and-comer in our profession, and his description pretty well matches you."

"Never heard of him."

"Well, it's not a priority right now," said Stone. "We have other things to concern ourselves with, don't we? But tell him I said hello."

The two men stared at each other for a few brief if telling moments.

"How many floors hold residences?" asked Robie, finally breaking the silence.

"Several, up to the penthouse."

"Who lives there?"

"I don't know exactly. They're rich, like I said. They would have to be to afford a place like that. Probably some VIPs thrown into the mix."

"But I wonder why today? Why strike a target like that today?"

Stone looked thoughtful. "You're thinking that some sort of an event might be taking place today and that's what triggered all this?"

Robie nodded.

"Interesting thought for a lobbyist skeet shooter," noted Stone. He turned his back and slid out his phone. He called Annabelle and told her this information.

He clicked off the phone and was putting it away when they heard footsteps approaching. A few seconds later the door to the room burst open.

In the dim glow of his flashlight they could see that it was Adam Chase. He shone his light around, checking them over one by one.

A moment later emergency lighting kicked in, allowing them to see him more clearly. He clicked off his flashlight.

"It appears that someone has been making a phone call from in here." He held up his machine pistol, to which he had attached a suppressor. "Now, which of you was it?"

None of them said anything. Chase came forward.

"Which one of you was it?"

He put the muzzle of his gun against a female teller's head. "Was it you?"

She whimpered, "No, I swear to God it wasn't me. I don't have my phone. You took it. You can search me. I don't have a phone. Please, please." She jerked back away from him.

Stone stepped forward.

Chase pointed his gun at him. "The manager said you were trouble. Said you were stoking the fires back here."

Stone ignored this. "None of us have phones," he said. "You can have your men search us all. Your information must be wrong."

Chase pointed his gun at Stone's head. "How about I start with you?"

Stone said, "Feel free."

Chase spoke into a walkie-talkie and a few moments later another man came in and thoroughly searched everyone in the room. No phone was found.

Chase looked at Stone and Stone looked back at Chase.

"What exactly are you?" asked Chase.

"I work in a cemetery in Georgetown. I have for years. That's what I am. I just came here to deposit my paycheck, just like I do every Saturday. That's how I knew the guard, Charlie. The man you killed," Stone added.

Chase said, "We get a hint that any one of you is trying anything, I will personally come back here and shoot each of you in the head. Do I make myself clear?"

"Very," said Robie.

The door closed and Chase was gone.

Robie and Stone moved over against one wall. In a low voice Robie said, "What did you do with it?"

"When I heard the door opening I slipped it behind the outlet cover that got fried. They'd pulled it out earlier to see what had happened to it."

"So our communication lines are gone."

"For the time being."

"So I hope your friends are really good."

"Oh, they really are."

CHAPTER

6

BEFORE STONE HAD TO HIDE HIS PHONE, Annabelle and Caleb were walking around the garage area under the building. She spotted it first—a fenced-in area that housed a parking lot only accessible by key card.

Caleb stared through the chain-link fence and then read the sign hanging on the access gate. "They're for the private residences, Annabelle."

She nodded. "This must be the blank on the plans you found online."

"I guess they didn't want to publicize this aspect of the place. I'm sure the folks who own these apartments want their privacy. People with money usually do, unless you're the Kardashians."

Annabelle's phone buzzed.

"It's Oliver."

She listened and said, "Understood and on it. Oliver, how is it going in there?"

She listened again, nodded, and said, "Watch your back." She clicked off and stared at the concrete looking anxious.

Caleb edged closer to her and asked nervously, "Is he okay?"

"You know Oliver. He could be in front of a firing squad and he'd say he was just fine."

"But what *did* he say?"

She glanced up. "Ironically, he wants us to check out the private residences. He thinks the target might lie there."

Caleb gazed through the fence again. "So these people might be going through the bank to get to the residences? Why?"

"Residence," she corrected. "I doubt it's more than one. There wouldn't be enough time."

"Okay, but which one? There are a lot of parking spaces. And they're all filled with Mercedeses and Jags and BMWs. And there's a Bentley over there. These people definitely have money."

"Well, whichever one it is we need to narrow down quickly. I doubt these guys will take too long to get to wherever they're going."

She punched in a number.

"Harry, I just got a call from Oliver. He thinks the private residences on the top floors of the building might be the target, we just don't know which one. Can you check around up there and see if anything hits you? We're on our way too."

She clicked off and said, "Let's go, Caleb."

Before Annabelle called, Harry and Reuben had together been scoping out the jewelry store and furrier. The jewelry store was closed but they could see employees inside, no doubt going through their closing procedure before leaving. As both men watched, the jewelry cases sank down into the floor, and then the top of the floor, which they could see was lined with steel, closed on top of them.

Harry said, "I don't see anyone breaking into that too quickly. Plus, the entrance doors are glass. No cover."

Reuben nodded. "And I don't think you can steal enough furs to make killing a security guard worth it."

Then Harry's phone buzzed and he spoke with Annabelle. When he clicked off he conveyed to Reuben what she had told him.

"So private residences, huh?" said the big man.

"Appears so. At least Oliver seems to think it's a possibility."

"So a robbery of the rich or something else?"

"No clue," said Harry. "But let's see if we can find one."

They hurried through the interior of the mall until they reached the entrance to a private bank of elevators that led up to the residences. A sign on the entry wall said that only residents and their confirmed guests were allowed past this point.

"Looks like something is going on," observed Reuben.

There was a table set up near the entrance to the elevator bank. People in business attire were lined up in front of a reception table being checked in. Then they passed through a security checkpoint where men in suits were standing. The men looked in the women's purses and then allowed them through to the waiting elevator.

"There's a magnetometer everyone has to pass through," observed Reuben.

Harry nodded. "And guys in suits, shades, with earwigs and shoulder holsters."

"Must be the Secret Service. I'd say that whoever they're guarding might be a target. They don't get called up for the small-fry."

"But who?" asked Harry. "The Secret Service protects lots of different types, including foreign dignitaries. I don't remember reading about any kings or queens visiting here."

"Might be one of ours," replied Reuben. "Politicians all over this town. President. Supreme Court justices. Agency heads. Military types. List goes on and on."

"Well, they're definitely Secret Service. I see their lapel pins. So that narrows it down a bit."

"But not enough. And then there's the problem of letting them know there might be a threat without causing some kind of panic."

Annabelle and Caleb joined them a minute later and Harry filled her in on what they had found.

Annabelle gazed over at the people waiting to be cleared into the event.

"But what kind of event is it?" asked Caleb. "That might tell us more about who the target might be."

Annabelle said, "I'll find out." She walked over to one of the men standing in line and gave him a warm, coy smile.

"Okay, this is going to sound really stupid, but aren't you on *Breaking Bad*? The brother-in-law of the meth dealer, Walter White? Right? The DEA guy? Oh, what was his name again?"

"I wish," said the man. He was about fifty, portly and balding. He was dressed in a suit and tie.

She looked over his shoulder. "Oh come on, you have to be. Are you attending some sort of entertainment function? Is Bryan Cranston here? I'm a huge fan. Please tell me I'm right."

"I'm afraid it's just a very dull but necessary political fundraiser for a friend of mine. Congressional race."

Annabelle tried not to look disappointed.

"Oh," she said. "Politicians."

He smiled and handed her a card. "I know. Not as much juice as Bryan Cranston. But it's a necessary evil. Maybe more evil than necessary in these days of paralyzed, do-nothing government. Anyway, here's my card. Give me a call if you ever want to run for office." He appreciatively eyed her long, slender figure. "Or if you just want to have a drink, for that matter."

She looked down at the card. When she looked up, Annabelle caught a breath. Heading into the elevator from what appeared to be a private entryway was Alex Ford. He was there along with the rest of the protection detail. She tried to catch his eye, but he was gone before he could see her.

And when Annabelle saw the person they were guarding, she knew who the target was.

She looked down at the card again and read off the name. When she looked up she had put on her most enticing, flirty smile.

"Okay, I feel really bad, I mean really stupid, Bob." She eyed him shyly. "I've never been to a political fund-raiser. I bet it's not as boring as you say it is."

Bob looked amused. "I could lie and say you're right, but I'm too nice to do that to a beautiful lady like yourself. What's your name?"

"Annabelle."

"Annabelle? Wow, don't hear that name much anymore. Don't get me wrong, I like it," he added when her face formed a pouty look.

He eyed the reception desk. "Well, I was supposed to come with a guest and she couldn't make it, which leaves me one body short. You want to sub in? My treat."

The pout turned to a smile. "That would be so cool."

He looked at her tight black slacks. "Not packing heat, are you? The Secret Service frowns on that."

She slowly slid her hand along her thigh. "I doubt I have room. What do you think, Bob?"

Bob gave a little shiver and laughed. "Sold! Let's go. Now, I'll need to talk you into this thing. Everybody had to be vetted beforehand, Social Security numbers and everything. But I wrote a big fat check for this guy and he owes me, so let's go pull a Salahi."

They walked over to the reception desk.

Annabelle glanced back at the others. She caught Harry's eye. He confirmed with a nod that they all had seen what she had.

The target had just gone up in the elevator.

It was the vice president of the United States.

And apparently somebody wanted to do him harm.

Today.

THE SOUNDS OF THE TOOLS BEING USED STOPPED.

Robie looked at Stone. "Think they're done?"

"Possibly, but we need some more information to make sure of what's really going on here."

They walked over to the two female tellers who sat on the floor tethered together. Stone and Robie knelt down beside them.

Stone said, "Have you worked for the bank long?"

One of the tellers, the younger woman, said, "About three years."

The other woman, in her forties, said, "I've been here ten. And I'm scared to death. We've never had even a hint of a robbery before."

Stone put a calming hand on her shoulder. "It'll be okay."

The woman looked up into Stone's steady, calm eyes and relaxed noticeably. Stone looked like a rock-hard pilot steadying a passenger's nerves while they flew through a storm.

"Thank you for saying that," she replied.

Stone looked at the door leading into the room and then at the room itself. "Every time I've come here I've noticed that the configuration of the lobby is very irregular. And there's a large pop-out on the wall over there where you lost more space. And it goes all the way into the lobby."

Robie glanced at him and then at the pop-out. "There's a corner of dead space in both places," he said. "On the left side next to the teller stand and then in here, which is a continuation of that dead space from the lobby."

The older teller nodded. "When I first came here I asked about that. Like you said, it just seemed like a huge waste of space. I wouldn't have noticed it except my husband is in construction and I guess I'm more attuned to things like that."

"So what was the reason?" Stone asked.

"The way it was explained to me was that when the building was first being constructed an elevator bank was going in there. But at the last minute they changed the location for it. But they'd already built out the shaft and all, and they didn't want to go back and redo that—an expense issue, I'm sure. So they just did the next best thing."

Robie said, "They covered it up."

"That's right. The bank didn't mind. They got a deal on the rent because of it. Not only were they not charged for the dead space, but they also got a reduced square footage rate. Most stores didn't want this space for that reason and also because it was off the beaten path in the mall. Not enough foot traffic. But banks don't care about that. They don't want people to come to the bank. That means they have to hire people like me to serve them. They'd much prefer you use the ATMs or bank online. Saves them a ton of money."

"Does it affect all units on this vertical?" asked Stone. "I mean, do they all have dead space on all the floors?"

"No, I don't think so. At least not as severe as ours. Where the bank is now there was going to be an anchor store, but the deal fell through. Where the pop-out is located was going to be the location of two elevators. They'd already built some of the support structure for it, which made the space basically unusable. It also had something to do with load-bearing components, which nobody wants to mess with. When the bank leased here they just walled in the shaft. But I remember someone telling me that the shaft had not been fully built out, so they didn't have to reconfigure the other units, or at least not as much."

"But does the shaft go all the way up to the top of the building?" asked Stone. "I mean, if they were going to have an elevator here that would make sense. Why build an elevator that doesn't reach all the floors?"

"I think that it must," answered the woman after giving it some thought. "I know the elevator bank was going to start in our space, so there's a solid floor inside the pop-out."

"What about the private residences on the top floors?" he asked.

"Oh, I know they have their own elevator bank."

"So maybe this shaft doesn't go up there?"

"No, my husband put a bid in to do some work here, and that included preliminary site plans and the like. The original plans did not have private elevators. But once it was clear how much the residences were going to cost, the idea of a private set of elevators became sort of a priority. You know, the rich don't like mixing with the rest of us if they can afford it," she added huffily.

"Was there something special about the bank's location?" asked Robie while Stone looked at him intently.

"Like what?"

"Something that made it different from the units above and below it, as related to the elevator shaft?"

"I don't think so. When my husband was shown the plans I remembered him telling me about the pop-out and what was behind it. He said they'd just drywalled around the shaft at our location. I suppose they did that all the way up."

Stone said, "But there must be some reason the robbers chose this space over the others on the vertical. Most other stores don't have armed guards. They had to take that into consideration."

Robie glanced toward the door to the room. "It's the entrance," he said quickly.

"What?" asked Stone.

"Most stores have walls that come down and doors that lock that you can see through. Either glass entry doors or metal link roll-down doors. The bank doesn't. If they had to work on something in the lobby of the other stores they'd be seen, even with the store closed. But not here. It's opaque. Complete privacy."

The older woman nodded. "That's right. Not sure why they designed it that way. I guess they assumed that even if someone broke in they'd have to punch through the roll-down wall and it would be noticed."

Stone added, "And the fact is most stores here don't close at noon on Saturdays."

"Almost none of them," said the teller. "I used to be in retail. Weekends are where the money is made and rent gets paid."

The other teller said testily, "But what does that matter? They *broke* into the bank. They're robbing *us*! Why are we wasting time talking about pop-outs and construction crap?"

"You're right," said Stone. "I was just curious. Just try to remain calm. I believe this will all be over soon."

The young teller glared at him. "Right, with us dead or not?"

"Hopefully not," replied Stone.

He and Robie moved away from the two women and sat together in a far corner.

Robie said, "So that's where the tools come in. They cut into the shaft and they have a direct way up and into another floor without anyone being able to see them work."

Stone nodded. "Perhaps all the way to the penthouse."

"Quite the security flaw if that's true."

Stone said, "Well, I don't suppose anyone thought someone would break into a bank in order to do so. But now we know why it was the bank. They could work unseen, as you said." He glanced at Robie. "Very observant of you. Shane would be proud."

"I wonder what your friends are doing?" asked Robie, ignoring this comment.

"Exactly what they need to be doing. I don't think I can risk calling them again."

"I wonder why they haven't brought the bank manager back."

"I doubt we will see him back."

"Hostage for their escape?"

Stone said, "Possibly. Or some other type of insurance."

"And when they go up the shaft?"

"They'll have to leave someone here to guard us."

"But the odds will be more in our favor, then. Fewer guns to deal with. There are only four of them total. Divide and conquer, right?"

"Yes." He looked at Robie. "Are you up to it?"

"What do you mean?"

"I mean switching assignments midstream like that."

"I'm up for it," Robie said quietly. "Though I have no idea what assignment you're referring to."

"Good to hear. It will be soon, I think. Very soon." Stone glanced at his watch.

"And their escape plan?"

"If they have one."

"They don't look like jihadists to me."

"I never thought they were."

"So they have to have an escape plan."

"Yes, but it just might not look like one."

"I'm not following."

"And I'm not sure what I mean exactly," admitted Stone. "Only I doubt they're exiting the way they came in."

"How do you want to work this, then?" asked Robie.

"I think we'll know when the time is right. The question will be, do they leave one or two men behind?"

"Depending on how they're going to attack the target they might need three, which just leaves one with us."

"But they also might simply need one to attack the target."

"I would assume the target would have some type of security. You can't just go in solo on that."

Stone looked at him, amused. "Surely that hasn't been your experience? I would imagine you go in solo on every job you do. Just as I did."

To this Robie said nothing.

"No," continued Stone. "They might just send one. But if they do, the means of the attack will have to be overwhelming."

"With one guy you're not simply talking about a gun."

"No."

"You're talking an explosive or something along those lines."

"Yes, I absolutely am. You don't do something as elaborate as this and execute with a whimper. Whatever or whoever their target is, it's important enough to justify everything they're doing."

"So they'll be willing to die for it," said Robie.

"And we'll have to be willing to match them on that," replied Stone. "Otherwise, they probably win."

CHAPTER

8

HARRY AND REUBEN PASSED THE BANK, each giving it just a brief glance, and continued, turning down the corridor to the restrooms and service area adjacent to the bank.

They found an orange pylon with a CLOSED sign attached to it in a janitorial closet in the restroom and set it out by the door to the men's room.

Harry knelt down next to the wall on the bank side of the restroom. He opened his duffel and took out a listening device. He attached it to the wall, inserting the other end in his right ear.

He listened for a few seconds and then glanced up at Reuben. "Sawing. And hammers. Hand tools it sounds like."

"Don't use those sorts of tools on a bank vault," said Reuben.

"No, you don't. I think Oliver's theory is right. They're using the bank to get to somewhere else in the building. Maybe the residences. You saw who's there. The VP has to be the target."

"I think so too. But we don't know which residence it is. And until Annabelle checks back in we're running blind. We need more information if we're going to have a real shot at stopping this."

"Maybe we should call in the FBI, Reuben. I mean, it is the VP after all. If this gets beyond us and we haven't told anyone? They might throw us all in prison and forget we're there."

"They might. But though we're few in number I'll take the Camel Club over all the suits at Hoover. What about you?"

Harry slowly nodded. "Agreed."

"Good. Now let's beef up our intel so we can kick these suckers' asses."

Reuben called Caleb and told him where to meet. He clicked off. "Let's go, Harry," he said.

"Where?"

"You'll see."

They met Caleb in front of the mall's administrative office, which was now closed. It was also located down a service corridor. Admin offices generated no revenue and were thus relegated to the cheap, retail-unusable space in the mall.

Reuben eyed the door and the lock. "Looks to be alarmed," he said.

Harry nodded and started searching in his bag while Caleb said, "Annabelle hasn't called yet from the event."

"She will, once she gets the lay of the land," replied Reuben. "She's the real deal. We all know that. Con the pope, that girl could."

"Actually, she probably has," added Caleb drily. "I've yet to meet the man who is impervious to her charms."

Reuben eyed him critically. "Really? Would that include you, Caleb? If memory serves correctly, you spent quite a bit of time in a large van with our gal in a very isolated area where innumerable opportunities might exist to test your theory."

Caleb sputtered, "Don't be ridiculous. I'm not that sort."

"What sort?"

"I'm a gentleman. I would never take advantage of a female professional colleague like that."

Reuben chuckled. "As if you could. She'd kick your butt all the way to Jefferson's library at Monticello."

Caleb's features swelled with indignation. "What do you need me up here for?" he asked. "I presume you have some plan that requires my participation."

Reuben said, "You presume right. You have to cover our six. I need you to go to the end of the corridor. Anybody starts to come down this way you have to distract them and give us a heads-up. And then keep that up until we can make a clean getaway. Improvise when you have to."

Caleb looked incredulous. "Really? Is that all? Do you want me to kung fu them too?"

"Do you know kung fu?" asked Reuben pointedly.

"Right now I wish I did!" Caleb spun on his heel and marched back down the hall.

Reuben's amused gaze followed Caleb down the hall. But when he looked at Harry his features turned serious. "We don't have much time."

"I know," said Harry.

"You can break in there, right?"

"If I can break into the Pentagon, Reuben, I think I can manage an office in the mall."

Annabelle sipped a glass of wine and surveyed the room. There were about fifty people that she could see in the luxurious penthouse apartment. They were clearly all well-to-do and connected and many seemed to know one another. She followed Bob around a bit and listened in on some conversations, but then used a potty break excuse to go off on her own.

She was looking everywhere for Alex Ford but didn't see him. The vice president must be in another room of the apartment. Maybe one had to pay for the privilege of being in such august company in addition to what they'd ponied up already.

Plus, a photo op would probably set one back another five grand. Politics for the people, she thought.

She grabbed another glass of wine and continued her stroll. She nodded and smiled at people as she went, but her gaze kept roaming. The views out the windows were spectacular, but that was not the way they would be coming. The bank was down below. How they would get from there to here she didn't know. But she assumed they had found a way. Otherwise why would they have invaded the bank at all?

She took out her cell phone and tried calling Alex, but he didn't pick up. He wouldn't, she assumed, while he was on duty. But if she could just find him and tell him what was going on...

"Hey, Annabelle!"

She turned to see Bob standing there with some people for her to meet. She smiled politely and turned to the group. But even her rock-hard nerves were starting to crumble a bit. She had to find Alex and warn him. And she could sense time was running out.

CHAPTER

9

Caleb paced nervously in front of the intersection of the main hallway and the corridor leading to the mall offices. He was hoping with all his might that no one would happen along this way. He figured his odds were good. There were no stores around here. It was just dead space in the mall on a Saturday afternoon.

He pulled his phone and texted Reuben. The message was brief.

Hurry up!

Just as he put the phone away, he looked up. His mouth became dry and he gave an involuntarily shudder.

It was a mall cop headed directly his way.

As the beefy man in the dark blue uniform with squeaky belt and shoes approached, Caleb attempted a smile.

"Hello," he said as the man drew closer.

The man looked at him suspiciously. "Can I help you, sir?"

"Help?" said Caleb in a shaky voice. "No, I'm fine. Just... just waiting on some friends."

"Up here?" The guard made a show of looking around at the empty space.

"Y-yes," said Caleb, stammering slightly. "We, I mean they, don't really know the area. I suggested meeting here, you know, just for—it gets crowded downstairs." He paused and swallowed hard. "I don't like crowds."

The guard looked even more suspicious. It didn't help when Caleb gave a nervous glance down the corridor leading to the mall offices.

"Can I see some ID?" asked the guard.

"ID?" asked Caleb shrilly.

"Yes, ID," said the guard, drawing closer. His hand went up and rested on the butt of his holstered gun.

"Cer-certainly, Officer. Do I call you Officer?"

"Sir, the ID, please."

"But I'm not doing anything wrong."

"Then you should have no problem showing me some ID. If it checks out we can all go on our way. How's that sound?"

"But the Fourth Amendment guarantees protection against unreasonable searches and seizures," said Caleb desperately.

"I'm neither searching nor seizing, sir, and you're making this a lot harder than it has to be."

"I'm sorry, I truly am." Caleb could see the cop was definitely suspicious now. He suddenly brightened. "I saw *Paul Blart: Mall Cop* with Kevin James," Caleb said conversationally as he reached inside his jacket for his wallet. "Delightful movie. Very funny. Not an Oscar-caliber film, of course, but quite crowd-pleasing."

The guard did not look pleased by this at all. "Blart was a moron. I'm not a moron. I served twenty-five years with the metro police."

Caleb looked horrified. "No, of course not. I didn't mean to suggest—"

His phone vibrated. As he drew out his wallet and handed his ID to the cop he glanced at the screen.

We're done, coming out. Coast clear?

Caleb looked up at the cop, who was studying his ID, then quickly thumbed his response. *One minute and then hit it.*

"Sir," said the cop. "I'd like you to come—"

Before he could finish, Caleb started holding his chest and gasping for breath.

"I-I-I think I'm having a pa-pa-panic attack. Ca-can't ca—catch my breath."

He started to collapse. The cop caught him and supported him. "Just hold on, sir. I've got you. You're going to be okay."

Caleb pointed to the elevator bank. "Fr-fresh air. Need—outside . . . quick."

"Okay. Okay. I'm going to call an ambulance too."

Caleb drew a painful, shuddering breath. "Out-out . . . side. Hurry."

The guard helped Caleb to the elevator and inside. The doors closed behind them and the car started down.

Five seconds later Harry and Reuben appeared in the main hall. Under Harry's arm was a set of building plans.

"Where's Caleb?" asked Harry.

"Probably gone off to a bookstore," grumbled Reuben. "If there're any left in this place. Come on, we're running out of time."

The door to the interior room opened and Adam Chase stood there, gun in hand. "We are just about done here," he said. "And then all of you get to go on with your lives. Unless you give us problems." He looked at Stone and Robie when he said this.

"No problems," said Stone.

Another man appeared next to Chase. He held a machine pistol in his right hand. His face was, like Chase's, covered with a ski mask.

Chase looked at him and then indicated Stone and Robie.

"Watch them closely," said Chase, and the other man nodded. "Any problems at all, just take them out."

Chase left and the other man put his back against the door, his gaze scanning the room.

In the bank lobby there was a hole in the drywall at the location of the pop-out. The studs had been sawn apart and some concrete blocks broken through, creating an opening large enough for a man to get past.

Chase and his three associates had clambered through the hole and were now staring up the exposed shaft that was framed in by steel beams for the once-proposed elevator bank.

It was dark, of course, which was why they had night optics. They slipped the lenses down over their faces and powered them up.

Chase hefted a backpack over his shoulders. His colleagues did the same. They strung sturdy nylon climbing ropes around their waists and then coupled them using D-links. Then they each picked a section of wall, gripped one of the steel beams, and started to climb. The beams were close enough together that they made good progress. On the lower floors the shaft was formed by concrete blocks, but on the upper floors it was only drywall and studs. Each of them moved expertly, gaining a firm purchase with hands and feet on the beams before hoisting themselves higher. At this pace they would be at their destination very soon.

Harry and Reuben were back in the men's room, the blueprints for the mall and the bank branch laid out on the floor. Harry had quickly studied them and then pointed out the optimal egress.

He made his living breaking into places far more secure than even a bank. He pointed to a section of wall next to the row of sinks.

"I think there is the best spot. We have to assume they'll have the hostages in the interior room there." He pointed to that area on the blueprints. "Right behind this wall is the bathroom in the bank. They did it that way so they could use the same plumbing from this restroom. Saves time and money."

"Right," said Reuben, studying the plans. "But there'll be sentries, Harry. We have to account for that."

"I know. That's why I brought this." He pulled from his knapsack what looked like a handheld wand that TSA personnel would use at airport security, except that it had a small screen on the handle. "Thermal imager," he explained.

He moved it up and down in front of the wall and then checked the readout screen.

"It's clear right now."

"Well, let's hope nobody with a gun has to take a pee in the next few minutes," said Reuben.

Harry drew out a saw from his duffel and began, as quietly as possible, to cut through the drywall.

10

STONE STUDIED THE GUARD IN THE SKI MASK, and the man looked back at Stone.

Finally, the man said, "You got a problem?"

Stone said, "How did you draw the short straw? Are you the junior guy on the team?"

"Don't know what you're talking about. Short straw?"

The other hostages looked on nervously as Stone leaned back against the wall with Robie tethered to him.

"Short straw. Surely you understand the concept. They left you here. They left you *behind*."

"Important job," countered the man. "Guarding all of you."

"Not really. Better to have killed us, drugged us, or tied us up so well we couldn't escape. Why waste someone? You're a small team. Why divide your manpower that way?"

"Why don't you shut up, old man?"

"You should have at least asked for backup," said Robie.

The man snorted. "Backup? I've got an auto pistol. All of you are tied together. You take a step toward me, you're dead. Why do I need backup?"

"For unforeseen things," said Stone. "But apparently your mission leader didn't care about that. About you, I mean. Expendable."

"You don't know what the hell you're talking about."

"Actually, I do," countered Stone. "The rear-flank guy almost always goes down. That's the nature of the beast. And your friends aren't coming back through here to make their escape. But I bet they told you they were."

The other man's shoulders tensed. He snorted and said, "So now you know all about our plan?"

Stone kept staring directly at him. "The motorized outer wall to the bank is key-operated. Charlie had one key. You don't have it because I saw your leader take it. He also took the other key behind the tellers' stand. So you can't open the door to get out."

"Yeah, but he can."

"Do you know what those things were he was having positioned on the overhead door to the bank?" asked Robie.

The man glanced at him but said nothing.

Stone said, "They're either Semtex or C-4 hardwired to a detonator. They're armed and I bet they're configured so they can't be disarmed except remotely. A handful of Semtex can take down a jumbo jet. What do you think those packs will do to this bank and everyone in it? Including you."

Robie added, "And why put those up if they were planning to exit that way?"

Before the man could say anything Stone said, "Because they're not coming back this way. Why would they? Cops will be waiting. It's been long enough that people will know something is up." He glanced at the bank employees and customers. "All these folks have people who will be missing them. Won't take long to realize something is off."

"Shut up," said the man, but his gun hand was trembling slightly.

Stone said, "A vertical shaft up a building allows for lots of possibilities for escape. Lots of floors. That's what I'd do. And I'm sure that's what your friends are planning to do. While you stay behind here. For the cops to arrest. Or kill."

The man's gaze darted in the direction of the shaft, confirming for Stone that his speculation had been correct.

He continued, "They have the plans for the building. That will tell them the best place to branch off the shaft after they've completed their mission. Different floor, masks and jumpsuits come off. They walk away and out of the mall. Gone. Just like that." He snapped his fingers.

"But not you," said Robie. "You're stuck here with us. And when someone tries to open the door to the bank, we'll be vaporized. All of us. You included."

One of the female tellers started to moan. A customer choked back a sob and began whimpering.

The gunman started nervously licking his lips.

Stone said, "So that's what I meant when I said the short straw. You're the sacrificial lamb. Maybe the cops will think you were acting alone. I mean, there won't be anyone alive to say otherwise. That way your buddies get away free and clear. While your ass gets sacrificed. For the cause. Whatever that might be."

The gunman pointed his weapon at Stone's head. "I said, shut up. Or the next person to be dead will be you."

The next moment the man was falling forward, the door having struck him from behind.

Robie and Stone surged forward together. Robie ripped the gun free from the man's fingers. Stone slammed an elbow into the man's neck, sending him down to the floor, where he stayed.

The door opened all the way and there stood Harry and Reuben.

Reuben eyed the fallen man. "Now I'd say that was pretty damn good timing."

"Perfect timing," corrected Stone.

Harry quickly cut all the hostages loose.

Reuben said, "There are C-4 packs strung across the entrance to the bank. No one's leaving that way until the bomb squad comes in and clears them out."

"I take it no one was in the front part of the bank," said Stone.

Reuben nodded. "That's right."

Harry nodded. "But there's a hole in the wall."

"We knew they were trying to get from here to somewhere else. Do you know where they're going?" asked Robie.

"A fund-raiser on the top floor," replied Reuben. "Lots of elite types attending. Annabelle managed to get in."

"And the target?" asked Stone.

"The vice president of the United States," answered Harry.

Stone and Robie glanced worriedly at each other.

Robie said quickly, "Does the Secret Service know?"

Harry said, "Alex is on the protection detail, but Annabelle hasn't been able to make contact with him yet."

Reuben hiked his eyebrows and smiled. "VP. Just your run-of-the-mill stuff. Keeps us from getting rusty in our old age."

THE CLIMB UP THE VERTICAL DID NOT TAKE LONG. The ascent had been practiced many times on a mockup at a facility in rural Maryland. And now, for real, the trip was measured and swift.

They made only one stop.

At the fourth floor.

It took a few minutes to cut the opening in the wall there, and then they were on their way again. Better to have cut the hole now. When they were fleeing from here they would not want to waste time doing it.

As the four of them climbed, Chase gave final instructions. They would not have long after it was done to make their escape.

The shaft was well insulated from the outside as the building had been constructed around it. Still, Chase did not want to make any unnecessary sounds. The timing would be tight. They had lost precious minutes when the power had gone out in the bank. But he had built in a contingency because things never went exactly according to plan.

He checked his watch as they climbed. It would be okay, he thought. They would make it. *They had better make it.*

They reached the top floor and Chase motioned to the person directly below him. Everyone stopped. Chase eyed the drywall in front of him and checked the construction plans for this part of the building that he'd downloaded onto his phone, confirming the location. He pointed to the wall and the person directly below him rose up beside him while holding on to one of the girders. Both men withdrew cutting blades from their belt holders and began to carefully slice away.

It would not take long now.

Robie, Stone, and Harry peered inside the hole revealing the shaft.

"Pretty dark in there," said Harry. "And stale air."

Robie said, "And the higher we go the darker and staler."

Harry opened his duffel bag. "I only have two pairs of night optics."

Robie held out his hand. "I'll take one."

Harry glanced at Stone and said, "I'll take the other."

Stone considered this. It was obvious from his face that he too wanted to go up the shaft. Finally, he deferred to their youth. "Keep me posted." Then he whispered to Harry, "And watch my lobbyist friend."

Harry nodded and said, "If they get by us, don't let them get by you."

Stone gripped the pistol Harry had given him. "They won't. But keep in mind that what goes up doesn't necessarily come down. Or at least *all* the way down."

As the two men prepared to go inside the shaft, Stone took out his phone and punched in the number. He spoke for one minute. When he clicked off he said, "Good luck."

Annabelle looked desperately around the room after her call from Stone. He had filled her in on recent developments, which had only heightened her anxiety in having still not located Alex Ford.

She felt a hand on her arm and almost screamed.

It was Bob, the man she had come with.

"Been looking for you. Have someone I want to introduce you to."

Annabelle caught her breath and said, "I really hope it's the VP. Been dying to meet him."

Bob smiled. "Then it's your lucky day, Annabelle. Just don't use the 'dying' word around him. Gets the Secret Service in a tizzy."

She looked at him. "This is so exciting." But she was thinking, *You really have no idea how exciting.*

"Hey, stick with me, I'll take you places." He gripped her by the elbow and propelled her forward.

They turned the corner and there was the VP.

And on his right-hand side was Alex Ford.

When Alex's gaze caught on her, his lips parted and his eyes widened. Her panicked look immediately drew his suspicion.

But Bob stepped forward. "Mr. Vice President, I would like you to meet my new best friend, Annabelle Conroy."

The nation's second in command held out his hand, his smile wide and inviting. "Ms. Conroy, let me just warn you about this guy. Watch yourself around him."

Bob laughed. Annabelle managed a titter. She glanced at Alex. He was staring directly at her.

She said, "I know this is silly, sir, but can I take a picture? I have my phone. I can take it myself. I know this is a fund-raiser and I'm probably supposed to be charged for a photo, but it really would mean the world to me."

The vice president smiled more broadly. "I think we can make an exception."

Annabelle slid out her phone, stood next to the vice president, held up the phone, and took a shot.

She stepped back and quickly hit some keys. "I'm just sending it to my mom. She'll never believe this." But she was actually typing a text. She hit send.

A few moments later Alex's phone buzzed. Annabelle stared directly at him and then her gaze dropped to his pocket where his phone was buzzing. He slid it out. On the screen he saw multiple missed calls from Annabelle. But the text was what drew his immediate attention.

Assassination attempt coming. Up abandoned shaft from bank. Oliver there. Go!

12

A<small>DAM</small> C<small>HASE</small> C<small>UT</small> O<small>UT</small> T<small>HE</small> L<small>AST</small> P<small>IECE</small> of drywall and insulation, and revealed to him was the back of an ordinary wall outlet with electrical lines running to it. He unscrewed the back of the box and handed it to the person next to him. He looked down at the other two people just below him and held a finger to his mouth. He leaned in close and peered between the slits of the outlet plate on the other side of the wall.

He saw people's ankles and legs at first. When he peered up he saw torsos, and then heads.

He registered on one torso and one head and he couldn't help but smile. His inside source had been worth every penny. It was fortunate for him that political events like this were so heavily scripted while trying mightily to seem impromptu. But they were organized down to the second and, most importantly, location. It was photo op time and the photo ops, according to the event schedule, were to take place in this very room for the next thirty minutes.

He used duct tape to attach the canister to the back of the wall and pointed one end of it inside the outlet slot. The person beside him cut the duct tape with scissors so as to make no noise and handed the strips to Chase.

They worked away until the canister was solidly supported.

The other person checked a small electronic box attached to the canister and then hit a switch on the box. It instantly powered up and he gave Chase a thumbs-up.

Chase placed one last bit of duct tape near the nozzle of the canister, ensuring that it remained directly pointed through the outlet slot. He gave it a pat and smiled.

Then he looked at the other three people with him and pointed down.

They started to descend.

They wanted to be nowhere near this place when it happened. No sane person would.

Many feet below, Robie put a hand on Harry's arm and pointed up. Harry looked up and saw a rope dangling barely five feet above his head. He looked at Robie. Both men drew their weapons and continued their climb up the exposed steel girders.

The two groups met just above the fourth floor, one ascending and the other descending. It was a memorable collision.

Adam Chase and his team had superior numbers. But they had been surprised.

Harry and Robie had not.

The few extra seconds this allowed Harry and Robie cost Chase's team dearly.

Chase cried out and slipped the remote from his pocket. He pointed it upward and was a sliver from pressing the button when it happened.

Two rounds fired by Robie hit him in the head and heart.

Chase's team had been using ropes and pulleys to more efficiently descend after stringing the block and tackle across two girders higher up. The dead Chase hung from one of the ropes for a moment before his grip failed as he died. His body and the remote sailed past Robie and Harry, bouncing off the walls twice before he hit the floor inside the bank with a thud.

A shot blew past Robie's head and smacked into the wall, where it stayed.

Harry drilled the shooter right through his optics lens.

Another body fell.

However, this time was different. The falling body hit Harry, causing him to lose his grip. He fell off the girder and would have also plummeted to his death, if an iron grip had not encircled his wrist.

He looked up to see Robie holding on to him, his other hand gripping one of the ropes that dangled down.

Suspended in midair, Harry started to swing back and forth using Robie as his fulcrum until his feet once more touched a metal girder. He regained his balance and breathed a sigh of relief.

Both men looked up, their guns pointed in the same direction.

"Shit," muttered Robie.

There was no one there.

Stone had seen the two bodies hit the floor of the shaft in the bank. He kept his gun pointed at them and, praying it was neither Harry nor the "lobbyist," he ducked inside the shaft. He was vastly relieved to see that it was not either of them. He took the masks off, revealing two men. Though he didn't know his name, one was Adam Chase. The other was a young man in his twenties. Stone checked the neck of the younger man but did not find what he was looking for.

He was alone in the bank right now. Reuben had led all the hostages out through the hole in the wall that connected to the public restroom in the outside corridor. The police and FBI had been summoned. Stone expected them on the scene at any moment.

Stone's phone buzzed.

It was Harry.

He said, "We got two and missed two, Oliver."

"So there were four total?"

"Yes. I saw them. Did you expect there to be?"

"Actually, yes."

"I think the pair went out through the fourth floor. And whatever they were doing up there, I don't think it happened. I'm going up there to make sure. The other guy you sent with me is following them out from up here."

Stone clicked off and pushed aside the bodies until he saw it.

The remote.

He gingerly picked it up. It was battery-operated. He slipped the back off and took the batteries out.

Then Stone was on the move. He couldn't leave through the bank entrance. He didn't have the key and it was booby-trapped with C-4. So he left the same way Harry and Reuben had entered and the hostages had escaped—through the hole in the wall to the adjoining men's room.

As soon as Alex Ford had gotten Annabelle's text he had launched into full-scale protection mode. Alerting the other agents to the threat, they lifted the vice president off his feet and literally carried him out of the apartment, leaving the other guests stunned.

Annabelle said, "Everyone, please exit the apartment. Don't run, don't panic, just leave now."

But of course everyone did panic. And everyone did run.

Annabelle noted that her escort, Bob, trampled over two older women on his way out.

Annabelle helped the ladies to the door and ushered them out. She made sure the place was empty and then closed the door behind her.

The canister duct-taped to the back of the wall outlet remained silent, the remote meant to engage it safely neutralized. Two minutes later Harry Finn reached it. When he saw the label on the side, his eyes went wide. They had been lucky. Very lucky.

13

STONE RACED UP THE STAIRS TO THE FOURTH FLOOR. When he reached it he slowed down and started watching. The people he was after had seen him back at the bank. He had not seen them. Well, actually he now knew he had seen one of them.

The bank manager had not been in the bank when the other hostages had been led out. That meant he had gone up the shaft with the other three gunmen, leaving the last man on the team down below.

That meant the bank manager was in on it, of course.

That's why he had been taken out of the room. Not as a hostage, but as part of the assassination attempt.

Stone dropped back a bit when he saw Robie emerge from down one hallway. Robie looked quickly around, seemed to spot something, and darted off to the right.

Stone kept his gaze moving until it settled on some people nearing an exit door. The two men were dressed in suits. One was slightly larger than the other. They passed a woman pushing a stroller, startling her a bit in their haste.

Stone headed in that direction. His hand was on the butt of the pistol in his pocket. The two men were past the woman and nearly at the exit door. Stone picked up his speed.

The men were through the door.

Stone raced up behind the woman and said, "Please keep your hands in view. If you don't I will shoot you."

He pushed the muzzle of the gun into her back. "Do you understand?"

She nodded.

He stepped forward and looked down into the stroller. He drew the blanket back. Revealed inside it were climbing equipment, the clothes she had been wearing, and a machine pistol. The collapsible stroller must have been in the laundry cart they had pushed into the bank, along with the rest of their equipment.

Stone looked up at her and then glanced at her neck. "In your line of work, it's not advisable to have such a distinctive tattoo. It sort of gives you away."

Robie had come out on the fourth floor through a hole cut into a storage closet.

Despite what he had said to Stone earlier, Robie was very familiar with the mall. He had been reconnoitering the location for nearly a week. He couldn't be sure his target wasn't lying at the bottom of the shaft back at the bank. But now he had to make sure.

He slowed when he finally spotted the man hurrying down one of the mall walkways, no doubt seeking the nearest exit. He reached for the gun in his pocket.

Suddenly, the man looked back and saw Robie.

And then he started to run.

It was the bank manager.

The man raced down the stairs and into the underground parking garage.

Robie followed.

The men worked their way into the bowels of the place,

which was perfectly fine with Robie. He had no need for witnesses.

They ended up in the equipment area on the very lowest level, well away from any cars and cameras.

From behind a support column the man yelled, "Who are you?"

Robie said nothing. He moved a bit closer, angling his approach to give him a sight line on the man.

The man fired a wild shot that clanged off an overhead pipe and embedded itself in the concrete wall.

"I have money. I can give you money," the man called out.

Robie kept moving forward. He didn't waste time or concentration on responding. He was in full predator mode.

"I have powerful friends," cried the man. "They will kill you if you harm me."

Robie moved to his left and then took a few paces forward. The man was doing him a favor by talking. It was allowing Robie to zero in on his position. The man was also not moving. Staying still in a situation like this pretty much ensured one's death.

The man fired another shot. And then another. They both were wild and they both ended up stuck in concrete.

Robie kept moving forward and to the right. He had his position locked down now. It was just a matter of getting there.

"I will kill you!" screamed the man. "You are just a customer of the bank. I will kill you. Leave now and you will survive. This is your last warning. I am not to be intimidated."

As he said this last part he looked up and saw Robie's muzzle pointed at his head.

His eyes widened and a scream started up his throat.

It would never finish the journey.

One tap to the head, one to the heart.

The man fell forward onto the concrete, dead before he ever got there.

Robie straightened from his shooting stance, turned, and left.

Mission accomplished.

SARIN GAS," SAID ALEX FORD AS STONE, Annabelle, Caleb, Reuben, and Harry listened.

They were all seated around Stone's fireplace in his cottage at Mt. Zion Cemetery.

Harry nodded. "I saw the canister in the shaft. Luckily they didn't get a chance to turn it on."

"They almost did," said Annabelle. "According to what you said, Harry. It was close. He actually dropped the detonator."

"He dropped it when the other guy shot him. He also saved my life. I got knocked off balance and lost my grip on the steel beam. I would've fallen except he grabbed my wrist."

Harry looked over at Stone. "You two were in the bank together as hostages. Who was he?"

Stone shrugged. "I never got his name. He did have a gun that they confiscated."

"So was he a cop?" asked Annabelle.

"He said he was a lobbyist," replied Stone, but he tacked on a smile at the end of this statement.

Reuben said, "Whatever he was, what happened to him?"

Stone shrugged. "He apparently vanished into thin air."

Reuben said, "You got the girl before she got away. But they found the bank manager's body way down in the parking garage. Two shots. One to the head, one to the heart."

"A professional kill," opined Alex.

"How is the vice president?" Stone asked him, changing the subject.

"Shaken but okay."

"And who were the assassins?" inquired Caleb.

"A mixed bag we're still sorting out. One of the guys we found dead in the shaft is Adam Chase. Gun for hire. Do anything for money, including setting off nerve gas in a residential building. And those C-4 packs might have taken down the whole building if they had detonated."

"Was that a backup in case the gas didn't work?" asked Annabelle.

Alex nodded. "We think so. We're still interrogating the sole survivor, the woman. We still haven't identified her yet. She's not in any database. We don't know if it's international terrorism or homegrown. Or it might be a combo because of what we've found out. And that's a terrifying thought."

"The bank manager?" said Reuben and Alex nodded. "Who was he?"

"Bashir Tufail. Pakistani. Came over here eight years ago. No criminal record. Honest, law-abiding citizen. At least as far as we can tell. I've heard some grumblings that our 'friends' at the CIA might know a lot more about him than we do, but they're not sharing."

"A cell? Planted here until he was activated?" said Harry. "To kill the VP?"

"We think so now. He'd been working at the bank for four years but at another location. He's been volunteering to work Saturdays at that branch."

"Because they knew the VP was going to that fund-raiser," said Annabelle. "He was prepping for that."

"That's right."

"And the CIA may know he was not so law-abiding," mused Stone. "That's interesting."

Reuben eyed him keenly. "I recognize that look. What's gotten in your bonnet?"

"Nothing," said Stone. "I'm just relieved we all got out of there alive."

"And a terrorist is no more," said Caleb.

"No more," repeated Stone.

After they all left, Stone was seated at his desk reading when he heard something at his door. He inserted his hand inside a secret crevice in his kneehole and pulled out his pistol. He crouched down, waiting.

And he could wait with the best of them. However, after thirty minutes passed and he heard nothing more he moved to the window and peered out. There was no one on his porch. But he did see a piece of paper tacked to the door.

He opened the door and ripped off the paper and unfolded it.

The message was terse and to the point. He would have expected nothing less.

You were not the target. Tufail was. Didn't know what their plan was. Got lucky it happened while we were both there. You certainly lived up to your rep. And, by the way, I told Shane you said hello. He told me he'd like to see you and talk about old times. You up for it?

Stone looked up and gazed around the cemetery. Without

seeing anything to tell him so, he instinctively knew he was being watched.

He slowly held up his thumb and mouthed the words, "I'm game."

From a thousand yards away, Will Robie, himself a very patient man, lowered his long-range optics. He smiled and set off to deliver the message.